Five Liars

ALSO BY D.L. FISHER

The Perfect Nanny
My Missing Boy
The Stepson
The Widower
Five Liars

FIVE LIARS

D.L. FISHER

JOFFE BOOKS

Joffe Books, London
www.joffebooks.com

First published in Great Britain in 2026

Cover art by Nebojša Zorić

ISBN: 978-1-80573-469-7

From: lisamreynard@reynardaccounting.com
To: lisamreynard@reynardaccounting.com
BCC: joseph.briggs@briggsfinancial.com, brit.jones@brighthorizons.com, brenda.peterson@brighthorizons.com, darrenljost@hotmail.com
Subject: Brit & Joe's White Lie Party

Save the date!

You are cordially invited to a White Lie Party celebrating Joe Briggs and Brit Jones's upcoming nuptials. White attire is requested.

Details to follow.

xx
Lisa (Maid of Honor)

There are three of us lined up in a row.
Two of us will stay.
One of us will go.

PROLOGUE

I can't stop staring at her. At what's left of her face.

Blood seeps from the gaping hole on her forehead. Her eyes are vacant but owlish, frozen in the shock she felt when I pulled the trigger.

Oh God, I've killed her.

I'm a *murderer*.

Sometimes, you don't realize what you're capable of until you're pushed to the edge. That's one thing I know to be painfully, poignantly true. Another truth: it was either her or me.

My eyes sweep down her body, marveling at the angle it's settled on the floor. In life, she was a monster. In death, a contortionist. Her arms are twisted around her head, having flown up to protect her face when she saw the gun.

She barely had a chance to scream for help or to beg me to reconsider. Not that I would have reconsidered.

Her or me.

Besides, I've dreamt of this day. Every act of cruelty has fanned the flames that burned fiercely inside my soul. If I didn't do *something*, I feared they would completely consume me — devour me from the inside out like a forest fire. But I never imagined I'd follow through. It's one thing to think about murder; it's quite another to commit it. In my fantasies, I hadn't considered the possibility, the *consequences*, of getting caught.

I should go, my mind screams as I continue to take in her limp body splayed across the bitter floor. *Someone will come and find me with her.*

But there's nowhere to go. A fierce storm is raging outside, tossing around furniture like litter and severing limbs from trees like a guillotine. It's nearly pitch black out; I can't see a blessed thing.

I should have thought this through. The others will find me with her; they'll know what has happened. They'll make sure I pay.

Unless I get to them first.

CHAPTER 1

Brit

The big day is finally here.

Well, not *the* day, per se, but close enough. The countdown has begun in earnest. This weekend, I'll kick back, relax, and enjoy my final days of singledom before I tie the knot. A week from now, I will officially be the good old proverbial ball and chain.

I wish the wedding were today, but alas, you can't get married without a proper sendoff. Joe and I couldn't bear the thought of spending a single night away from one another, let alone an entire weekend apart. That's why we've decided to forgo the traditional bachelor and bachelorette parties for a joint celebration. This way, we can celebrate together, and I can't help but think, we don't have to worry about any unfortunate *oops* that might derail the wedding.

Not that either of us would dream of doing anything foolish to destroy our storybook romance. It's not every day that you find a match made in heaven.

In a few short hours, Joe and I, and three of our closest friends, will giddily hop aboard flights to Punta Cana, where we'll wine, dine, and frolic in the sunshine to celebrate our upcoming nuptials. Joe booked us a gorgeous villa, for which he is footing the bill. Traditionally, friends treat you to your last hurrah, but I'm not about to argue with my soon-to-be husband.

Not about *that*.

"Brit, have you seen my passport?" Joe stands in our bedroom doorway, his handsome face clouded with confusion. His eyebrows bend toward one another as he stares blankly at his empty hands.

"Of course, darling. It's right there in my purse, next to mine."

Joe's shoulders relax, and a smile forms on his lips, highlighting the straightest, whitest set of teeth I've ever seen. No doubt it is the result of phenomenal genetics or some serious dental work. I've never asked.

"What did I do to deserve a woman like you, Brittany Jones?"

I giggle. "You're a very lucky man, Joseph Briggs."

"That I am."

Joe walks over to the bed where I'm stuffing a neon string bikini into an overflowing weekend bag. He pulls the scrap of a bathing suit from the suitcase and twirls it around a finger, the motion hypnotic. Joe has that talent, the ability to make you forget about what you were doing — *thinking* — only a moment before.

One of his many talents.

"A very lucky man, indeed."

"We're both lucky," I say, meaning it. "But our lucky streak will run out if we don't finish packing and get to the airport. I'd hate to miss our flight." I playfully slap Joe on the chest, and he dutifully returns my bathing suit to the suitcase.

I've got everything I need for the weekend of my dreams. I close the flap of my oversized, overstuffed luggage and force the zipper shut.

Punta Cana, here we come.

* * *

An hour later, I'm snuggled in close to Joe, stretching my bare legs and resting my head on his chest. The view from thirty thousand feet in the air is absolutely breathtaking. There is nothing but billowing clouds above and sparkling ocean below. I inch closer to Joe.

What a dream. A private jet to the Dominican Republic. I literally had no idea. After packing up and hustling to the airport to catch a flight that didn't actually exist, Joe surprised me with our exclusive transport. A "test run for our honeymoon," he said.

I couldn't wipe the smile off my face as we walked the tarmac to our awaiting jet, but I could feel the eyes of the passengers watching us from their cramped seats on the commercial planes. I could hear the whispers. *Who are they? Blake Lively and Ryan Reynolds? Taylor Swift and Travis Kelce?* It was perfect.

Except . . .

"Refill?"

I glance up to find our very curvy blonde stewardess with her hand outstretched, dangling a bottle of Dom Perignon. Her bright green eyes are trained squarely on my fiancé. The top button of her white blouse has inexplicably come undone. I grit my teeth, all the while keeping that same smile plastered on my face; surely, the stewardess is breaking *some* company protocol with her lacy black bra that's peeking out of her shirt like she's Britney Spears circa 1997. I'm tempted to call out her blatantly unprofessional behavior, but time has taught me to hold my tongue — and to tighten my grip on Joe's arm. If the stewardess wants him so badly, she'll have to pry him from my cold, dead fingers.

I shoot her a look that says, *Go ahead and try.*

"Yes, please," Joe answers much more amenably while holding out our champagne flutes, seemingly oblivious to her advances. "My *fiancée* and I would love a refill." Or not so oblivious.

My insides tingle as the stewardess averts her eyes to our glasses where they belong, the corners of her lips dipping. I can see the wrinkles forming. They're still ten years away, but whatever. Serves her right.

"She was totally checking you out," I say before taking an unnecessarily large gulp of champagne, once she's retreated again.

"Hadn't noticed," Joe replies with a wink.

I raise an eyebrow and study my fiancé's olive complexion. He *had* to have noticed. Women ogle my soon-to-be husband as if God put him on this planet for their eyes and their eyes alone. But at least I can take comfort in the fact that he is indisputably mine. I glance down at the four-carat rock on *that* finger for confirmation. It winks back at me.

"For as long as we both shall live." Joe clinks his glass against mine, shattering my thoughts.

"Till death do us part."

Champagne bubbles pop in my throat as I take another sip. I should slow down and save myself for when we get to the house, but the Dom Perignon is the only thing taming the butterflies fluttering around in my stomach.

"Private jets are the way to travel," I muse, staring out the window at the cotton candy cloud hugging our plane. Warmth spreads throughout my body like I'm wrapped in a fluffy, white robe. "The view is *so* much better," I continue. "Or, maybe it's all this champagne your *girlfriend* keeps feeding us." I wink, though behind every joke lies a kernel of truth. My gaze finds the stewardess watching us, sulking.

Joe taps a finger on the tip of my nose. "You're the only girlfriend for me, wife-to-be. Nothing but the best for my Britter-Bug."

I smile widely at him.

"You know," Joe says, lacing his fingers through mine and staring at my ring. A shiver skitters down my spine as I take in the serious expression on his face. He pauses a painfully long time before declaring, "I think I know what I'm getting you for your wedding gift."

"Wedding gift?" I squeal, my disquiet instantly turning to delight. "Isn't marrying you the gift?"

He laughs, crinkling the skin around his amber eyes. "That and our own private jet, so we can go wherever we want, whenever we want." Joe cocks an eyebrow, giving me his best *come hither* look. "And do *whatever* we want."

I feel my cheeks flush bright red. The airplane is suddenly very *hot.* A rivulet of sweat dances slowly down my back.

Joe takes both my hands in his, much to the chagrin of the stewardess, who watches us intently while pretending to scroll on her phone. "Just imagine it, Brit. Me and you traveling the world on our every whim."

"I think if you spoil me anymore, I'm going to rot." It already feels like my stomach is consuming my body from the inside out.

Joe smiles widely, dimples popping on his cheeks. We clink glasses again, but apparently, just a touch too hard, because the stem of my glass breaks off, nearly cutting into the flesh of my palm. Just like that, the warmth is gone, replaced by a chill. An inexplicable sense of foreboding. My eyes flick nervously around the jet and then up to the ceiling, where I catch sight of Joe's hand readjusting the air so that it's blowing straight at us. I breathe a frosty sigh of relief. Well, at least that explains the chill.

The inexplicable sense of foreboding, on the other hand . . .

The stewardess shoots me a look that could kill before cleaning up the mess and supplying a fresh champagne glass. If we purchase a private jet, I will be in charge of staffing it. Maybe I'll hire a male flight attendant. Or perhaps a female with a pronounced unibrow who can dress herself properly.

I'm relieved when we touch down in Punta Cana, several *unbroken* glasses later. The plane rises and falls like a rollercoaster ride as it connects with the runway. Steadying itself, it loudly screeches to a halt. The Caribbean sun beats hard against the window as we taxi to our gate. I half close the shade and turn to Joe. "I can't believe we're finally here."

Joe squeezes my hand. "This will be the weekend of your dreams, my love."

It should be all that and more, if everything goes according to plan. My stomach flips, the mixture of excitement and nerves tangled into one giant, indiscernible knot.

Joe continues to grip my hand tightly as we exit the plane and retrieve our matching Louis Vuitton travel luggage. One day, I was dreamily eyeing the luggage in the window display at Bloomingdale's on 59th Street, and the next, the bags had appeared on our doorstep seemingly out of the blue.

Joseph Briggs is *the* most thoughtful man I've ever met. And generous, too. We could have paid for the band *and* flowers for the cost of those two bags. Not that my husband-to-be would skimp on the band or flowers. Joseph Briggs never skimps on anything.

It's one of the many reasons I love him so very, very much.

It doesn't hurt that our car is already waiting for us outside the arrivals terminal, despite the long line of frazzled passengers standing in the taxi queue. I gasp as the mechanical doors to the airport close behind us, feeling like we've been shoved into a pressure cooker. The Caribbean humidity grips me like a hand closing around my neck. I struggle to take a deep breath, eventually steadying my pulse. Somehow, it's even more oppressive out here than it was when we exited the plane off the runway.

Joe holds open the Uber door and ensures I'm comfortably seated before sliding in beside me.

Such a gentleman. I internally swoon.

"How do you think everyone will get along?" I ask as our car navigates the rocky island roads. "Do you think we should have invited another guy? I mean, what if there's a love triangle between Darren, Lisa, and Brenda?"

Joe raises an amused eyebrow. "A *love triangle?* This isn't *Bachelor in Paradise*, Brit. Darren's got a girlfriend, anyhow."

Right. I roll my eyes. Where do I start with Darren's girlfriend, Tamara? I guess I start at the only place you can start: her breasts. God gave Tamara an abundance of breasts, but like the Scarecrow in *The Wizard of Oz*, he forgot the brains. Well, her plastic surgeon gave her an abundance of breasts. And she always wears those tight shirts that somehow make them look even bigger, though I'm not sure how that is even possible.

I considered inviting her; I'm not completely heartless. And it would have been useful to have a hairdresser on site for pictures, but Tamara had nothing else to bring to the table this weekend, so she didn't make the cut.

Only a very *select* few did.

Thankfully, Darren wasn't all that cut up about it, from what Joe has told me. Then again, Darren doesn't strike me as a one-woman kind of guy. But Joe knows Darren better than I do. Like Lisa and I, they've been friends since grade school.

"I don't know. It might be a little awkward. I want everyone to have fun. I want everything to be perfect."

"And it will be."

My stomach settles slightly.

"I thought Brenda would back out. She's been acting strange at work lately. I guess I would be too if my engagement, you know . . ."

Joe's voice brings me back to attention. "Good thing you don't have to worry about that." He's right. I — *we* — don't have to worry about that. There will be no separate bachelor-bachelorette parties. No opportunity for things to spiral out of control

I nod in agreement but still feel uncharacteristically anxious, as if there is an itch somewhere on my body that I can't scratch.

"True," I say slowly, willing the feeling of impending doom to go away. "And I think Lisa has things under control, but what if she doesn't, you know?"

Joe once again takes my hands in his. His fingers are the perfect combination of strong and manicured.

"I don't want to talk about Darren and Brenda and Lisa. I want to talk about which room we will christen first, before the rest of our party arrives." He winks and flashes those blindingly straight, white teeth. If Joe's lucrative career in finance fails, my fiancé could have a future as a veneer model. At least we have a backup plan.

Still, I regard my husband-to-be skeptically. How could Joe possibly think about sex at a time like this?

Then again, he has no idea what's coming next.

"Joe, I have to tell you something—"

His eyes grow wide with anticipation.

I open my mouth to speak, but I don't get a chance because a noise outside the car interrupts our conversation.

We both pull our gaze to the side of the road where a mangy dog sits, howling. Its fur is matted gray, with dirt and mud. It's looking straight at us through the glass — drooly mouth wide open, almost like it is trying to tell us something.

Or eat us.

The car slows to a painful crawl as we pass the dog, which is baring its teeth. It *definitely* wants to eat us.

"That's creepy," Joe says, wrapping an arm tightly around my shoulders. "He looks like he wants to maul us to death."

"*Es más que espeluznante*," our driver interjects. It's the first thing he's said the entire ride, and we've been in the car for a good twenty minutes. I'd almost forgotten we weren't alone. "*Es un presagio. Alguien va a morir*," he adds.

"*No hablo español*," Joe replies, looking quite proud of himself that he can say "I don't speak Spanish" in Spanish.

My fiancé may not speak Spanish, but I do. It is one of the many things Joe has yet to learn about me. It feels like we've been together forever. Still, you can't possibly know everything about another person in only four months.

Or maybe ever.

Yes, it happened *that* fast. And no, I do not have any reservations. Not about Joe, at least.

About this *trip*?

I should feel carefree, but I know what our driver said. It's probably just some silly local superstition, yet it chills me right down to the core.

It's more than just creepy, the driver had said. *It's an omen. It means someone is going to die.*

CHAPTER 2

Lisa

Maid of honor.

Such a lovely term, but fraught with so much responsibility. And yours truly is the recipient.

Brit provided me with a list — two pages long, single-spaced — of all the things I need to do to ensure everything is *just so* on her and Joe's wedding day. And not to be forgotten, this weekend. Brit's fiancé booked the accommodation for their joint bachelor-bachelorette party, but I've been tasked with planning all the pre-wedding activities. Since it's a Jack and Jill get-together, and two of the five guests are straight men, the go-to bachelorette party penis straws won't do. And though I've only just returned from my own holiday, I've been working hard to make the weekend extra special for my best friend and my soon-to-be best friend-in-law. I have loads of fun activities planned and, like a magician, a few tricks up my sleeve.

Brit and I have been inseparable since we were thirteen. She thinks she knows my every move, before I make it.

She will be very surprised to find out that she's wrong.

I'm thinking about all this during the four-hour flight from New York to Punta Cana, which is bumpier than expected. I am beyond grateful when the tires hit the runway and screech to a stop. The cabin erupts in loud applause — to which I join in, relieved to have made it safely and delighted to have arrived in paradise. I exhale a long sigh.

I hope the others encounter less turbulence. I'm not too optimistic, though, as their flights are scheduled later than mine, and the skies often become more unsettled as the day wears on. There is a silver lining though; the happy couple and their other guests will touch down well after I do. This gives me precious time to set everything in motion.

It's a forty-minute taxi ride from the airport to our villa. I sink back against the headrest as I drink in the scenery — vast landscapes of coconut palms, white sand, and turquoise ocean for as far as the eye can see. As we travel farther inland, the lush greenery gives way to dense patches of brush and extensive farmland before, eventually, I find myself looking at a whole lot of nothing as the area becomes increasingly desolate.

I hadn't realized our vacation destination was smack dab in the middle of nowhere.

Feeling a pinch of panic, I check the weather app on my phone. I've been checking it religiously for the past few days. It's currently a soupy ninety-nine, with a breeze rolling in from the southeast. Super humid, but sunny. I scroll down a few hours ahead, and . . . *ew*, things may be taking a turn for the worst. Tonight looks iffy, with the potential for some extreme weather. I examine the ten-day forecast, disappointed to find the rest of the weekend looks just as suspect. Potential storms Friday, Saturday, and Sunday, followed by blue skies and sunshine *after* we leave. A chill snakes up my spine as I study the warning: *Significant threat to persons and property.* What terrible luck.

Panic rises as I read the accompanying weather warning and fast facts, learning that the last significant hurricane in Punta Cana was back in September of 2002. More than twenty years ago, when we were barely teenagers! What are the chances? Hurricane Irene was only a Category 2, and over 700,000 islanders lost power. If Hurricane Ivy hits the Dominican Republic this weekend, experts are predicting it will roll in as a Category 3, or maybe even a 4.

I shudder at the thought, unable to wrap my head around the possibility of a hurricane interrupting our festivities.

I draw in a deep breath, trying to steady my nerves.

Brit has high expectations, but the weather is one thing that I simply cannot control. Hopefully, the weather gods will blow in our favor. And if not, well, we'll have to make the best of the worst.

It's what we always do.

Still, I'm uncharacteristically unraveled as we pull down the gravel drive leading to our rental. I grip the seat in front of me as the taxi jerks from side to side. I don't think this is what Robert Frost had in mind when he talked about the road less traveled. To be honest, it doesn't look like this road has been traveled *at all*. In fact, the word 'road' is generous. I'm pretty sure we just drove through a large oleander bush.

I'm relieved when the car comes to a standstill. The driver helps remove my luggage from the trunk and then practically sprints back to the driver's side of the vehicle.

"Wait," I shout after him as he jumps into the car. "I still have to pay you!"

He acknowledges my plea with a "*Sal mientras puedas*" and peels out quickly enough to leave a plume of kicked-up rocks and dirt in his wake. I catch a glimpse of his reflection in the sideview mirror as he disappears into the trees.

He looks . . . *spooked*.

Well, that was weird, I think, swatting away the bits of debris swirling around me like a twister. I have no clue what he said.

I wonder why he was in such a hurry to get out of here that he couldn't wait to get paid. Why he muttered something in Spanish when he'd spoken to me in broken English throughout the car ride over.

Once the dust settles and I convince myself the driver forgot that I hadn't paid him yet or was in a hurry to pick up his next fares — the only explanations I can come up with that *don't* leave me with impenetrable Boy Scout double knots in my stomach — I make my way up the smooth slate stairs to the front door.

As promised, the house key is tucked under the welcome mat. I take a moment to admire the pure white stucco that stretches three stories into the sky with a half dozen balconies. The house sits on a two-acre property encircled by a canopy of imposing fifty-foot-tall mahogany trees. The place looks like it's straight out of the pages of a storybook — picturesque, albeit a little too remote for my liking.

I stick the key into the lock and twist it, ready to explore the house. I'm intrigued to find out why this place won out over the other three hundred-plus vacation rentals in Punta Cana.

That reason becomes abundantly clear as I open the front door. My jaw drops, nearly unhinging as I step inside. The pictures did not do this place justice. For starters, the house is *massive.* Three of my apartments could fit into the front atrium, and it's not like I live in the Village in a shoebox; my apartment is twelve hundred square feet and on the Upper East Side. The front atrium I'm standing in is the size of a *house.*

The place is all stark white, shiny, and bright — from the walls to the ceiling to the floors covered in marble tiles. The effect is blindingly breathtaking, but I can't help but think it's a foolish choice of color for a rental property. I can almost picture the mess a rowdy crowd might leave behind — a flash of burgundy wine splashed against the white. It's a good thing I'm here to keep things in order.

I shake the thought of the cleaning bill and gasp as my eyes catch the glint of a crystal chandelier hanging twenty-five feet above my head. The thing is colossal. It must weigh at least two hundred fifty pounds. I instinctively move out of its range.

My gaze flits around the foyer, and it strikes me how utterly empty it is. There are no pictures, no accent pieces, no *nothing*— it's just a whole lot of white. Thankfully, I brought a suitcase full of decorations. It's a lot of responsibility to ensure the bride and groom have the time of their lives.

Good thing I am more than up for the task. I'm determined to make this a trip no one will forget.

I tour the first floor, locating a door that leads out to a spacious terrace with a steel dining table set for five and a private pool shaped like a kidney. Two marble lions shooting water from their mouths are perched at the far end. I wonder for a moment if there are any actual lions in this part of the world. Jaguars? Oh God, I bet there *are* jaguars. My eyes dart toward the trees, taking in the heavy rustling in the leaves.

It feels like something is out there, watching me. Despite the oppressive heat, I'm suddenly shivering. Goosebumps line my arms.

I take a deep, calming breath. *Probably a harmless little monkey*, I tell myself. I'm not convinced, but—

I quickly push away the thoughts. I think back to the gorgeous scenery I passed on the ride over and let my gaze dance across the pool. This place is great, really. Just perfect. Wildlife aside, if I were to conjure paradise, *this* would be it. We'll be lounging with drinks in hand in no time — weather permitting, of course.

And while I have a lot on my plate, I don't have to worry about feeding the guests. Joe has arranged for a private chef to come to the house tonight to cook us a fancy, five-course meal. My stomach grumbles just thinking about it. I haven't eaten much the past few days.

I take another look around in absolute awe. Everything is so *new*. We are only the second guests to stay here. Clearly, money is no object when it comes to Brit.

I may not know Joe from Adam, but on paper, he is precisely the man I'd expect my best friend to fall head over heels for — successful, filthy rich, and movie-star handsome. He easily checks all the boxes and then some. The way he fawns over Brit, you'd think she was next in line for the Crown.

I'm glad Brit has found her knight in shining armor, even if I miss my best friend like the loss of an appendage.

My shoulders relax. Why am I putting so much pressure on myself? Whether Brit likes the activities I have planned or not, it would be difficult not to have the time of your life here. It truly is paradise. I can't help but smile widely. Brit deserves it.

Unable to sit still, I pace around the tiled living room and busy myself with some to-dos while awaiting Joe and Brit's arrival. From what I've seen so far, every room in the house has the same white mosaic tile. Even the kitchen has a white-tiled backsplash. It's as if a tile factory regurgitated here. I wonder if it's a weather thing.

Speaking of which . . .

I pull out my phone to Google 'Punta Cana weather' and see if there are any updates. Meteorologists are always talking about the next big storm in the U.S., and it *usually* turns out to be a whole lot of worry over nothing. Hopefully the same can be said for the Dominican Republic, and *this* particular storm will take a different course. Perhaps we'll be spared after all. I huff out loud in frustration as the phone spins and spins, but nothing comes up. My eyes flit to the upper corner. Zero bars. Well, that's just great. The closest cell tower is probably back at the airport. We truly are in the middle of nowhere. I check my phone for a Wi-Fi connection, but it doesn't show any networks in the area. That's odd. One would think a house as glamorous as this would have Wi-Fi. I'll have to ask Joe about it when he arrives.

I find myself overcome with agitation, anxious for Joe and Brit to get here already. I take a deep breath, though it does little to soothe the tug in my gut.

Gosh, I'm being ridiculous. Joe and Brit should arrive any minute, followed by Joe's best man, Darren, and Brit's friend from work, Brenda.

More than likely, a rash of hangovers is the only thing to be concerned about.

Still, I'm feeling a bit lightheaded and out of sorts. I've already blown up about three dozen black and gold balloons and scattered them throughout the living room that leads out to the veranda. Scrawled across each balloon is a cheeky saying to get our guests in the party mood — *party in progress, bring on the shots, last night single.* And my personal favorite — *it's not too late to run.*

Cute, right?

The bar is fully stocked with champagne, wine, liquor, and an assortment of fancy beers I've never heard of. And while there are no penis straws on hand, the stacks of shot glasses should more than satisfy all the guests. With the obscene amount of alcohol on site, I highly doubt anyone will be sipping from a swizzle this weekend. But I do hope civility doesn't go entirely out the window.

The last thing I want is for the party to descend into complete chaos. Not when I've exhausted so much time and energy planning *everything.*

I set out a few questionnaires that I found online for one of our many party games — a series of questions testing how well the guests know the soon-to-be bride and groom.

Where did Joe and Brit meet?

How long have they been together?

Where were they working when they met?

It strikes me how little I know about Joe. My best friend has been uncharacteristically tight-lipped about her fiancé and their whirlwind courtship. I've never known Brit to be this secretive. Impulsive. It's completely out of character. If I looked up *whirlwind* in the dictionary, I wouldn't be surprised to find a picture of Joe and Brit, smiling widely with their movie-star faces and too-white teeth. They do make quite a handsome couple.

Thankfully, my extensive internet searches have enabled me to fill in some of the gaps. Joseph Briggs is quite the catch — Harvard graduate, a big-time money manager, and CrossFit fanatic (oh, does it show). I'm dying to get to know him better. Considering what I found online, I'd expect Brit to be shouting from the rooftops. But nope, crickets.

A thought suddenly goes off in my head, like a firecracker. Could this be a shotgun wedding? That would explain a lot. Brit usually tells me everything. Well, she *used to* tell me everything.

Still, I allow myself to feel a twinge of excitement. Maid of honor *and* godmother? Oh, I will be watching Brit like a hawk to see if she consumes any alcohol this weekend. If not, I have my answer. Brit is probably just waiting to tell me in person. We haven't seen each other in weeks.

The other non-negotiable agenda checkpoint for the weekend is getting to know Joe better over the next two days. And his best man, Darren. One thing Brit has been *very* transparent about is that she doesn't care for him all that much — something about a snarky comment his girlfriend made that put her on alert — but I'm sure the four of us will be spending lots of time together. At a minimum, I will have to walk down the aisle with the guy, and then there's the first dance as husband and wife when Joe and Brit call their wedding party (Darren and me) to the dance floor. So, I figure we should be at least somewhat acquainted before then.

Besides, Brit can be somewhat dramatic. I'm sure Darren is totally harmless.

What better than a carefree weekend in paradise to break the ice for everyone? Perhaps only a sparkling glass of bubbly.

I uncork the first bottle of the trip, startling myself with the loud pop. The cork goes flying, and champagne sprays everywhere. I should clean it up, but instead, I pour myself a hearty glass and take a big sip as I anxiously wait for the guests to arrive.

It's all coming together.

Finally.

CHAPTER 3

Darren

"Do you have to go?"

Tamara shoots me a pouty look, and for a moment, I don't want to leave. A perfect bronzed breast peeks out from beneath the sheets, and it takes every last ounce of strength I possess not to jump back into bed.

Do I have to go?

"Yeah, babe, I have to go. I'm the best man."

"Can't I come with you? I bet we could find a nude beach in Punta Cana." Tamara winks, and the urge to tangle myself with her grows stronger.

"Look, I wish you could. But Brit's maid of honor was *very* explicit in her instructions. No significant others. And I quote 'Exclamation point. Exclamation point. Exclamation point.'"

One of her many caveats for the trip.

"Sounds like a real shrew. So, Joe and Brit get to have sex all weekend while the rest of you sit back and twiddle your thumbs?"

It's cute that Tamara thinks that I'll be twiddling my thumbs. We've only been dating for a few months, and if the opportunity presented itself, I know I'd be hard-pressed to turn it away.

I've never been good at saying no. It's the crux of all my problems.

"It's one weekend." I flash her a megawatt smile and wink. That usually does the trick. "We can have lots of sex when I get home on Sunday." I say, attempting to appease her.

"And maybe *talk*?"

Just not *this* time. The smile instantly slides off my face, followed by what feels like a *nine-months pregnant* pause. When I don't say anything, Tamara adds, "How about a quickie for the road?"

She pulls the sheet down farther.

I check the time on my watch. Ten minutes until I need to leave for the airport. I unbutton my jeans. The party won't start without me.

But I do almost miss my flight.

After our quickie, Tamara resorts to begging me not to go on the trip. I have to practically peel her body from mine like a banana rind, only slicker. Tamara has been incredibly edgy lately, ever since I agreed to let her give me a Tarot reading.

It sounds even more ridiculous now than when I agreed to it. Tarot card reading is a silly little hobby of hers, but I thought I would entertain her and play along. I anticipated she would see lots of wild sex in our future.

Not so much.

It was all fun and games until Tamara pulled the Knight of Swords. Her face went sheet white, and she packed her cards without another word.

"Why are you so upset?" I asked. "What's the Knight of Swords?"

Tamara shook her head and proceeded to lock herself in my bathroom.

"What does it mean?" I asked again, banging my fists against the door, only stopping momentarily when my downstairs neighbor brought a broomstick handle to his ceiling.

That's what I get for owning a penthouse apartment.

Tamara refused to answer my question. But I'm a successful entrepreneur, not a moron, so I googled it. *Death*. The Knight of Swords represents physical death.

After fifteen minutes, I resumed thumping on the door, which resulted in more thumping from downstairs. This time, I ignored it. "It's just a stack of cards, Tamara. Open the damn door and talk to me."

"It's not *just* a stack of cards, Darren. I've done these readings before. Something really bad is going to happen. Like death, bad."

"*Death, bad?*" I parrot. Surely, she was joking. "I promise you, nothing *death bad* is going to happen, Tamara. I'm a grown man. I can take care of myself." *Famous last words.*

I came dangerously close to telling Tamara to *stick to hair*, but I wisely stopped myself at the last second. I may not be winning any boyfriend of the year awards, but I'm well-versed enough to know saying that was sure to end '*death, bad*' for me. Rule number one of dating: don't insult the woman you're sleeping with, *especially* when her profession revolves around cutting shears.

Fast-forward to this morning, and this trip seems to have intensified Tamara's fear that something terrible will happen to me. I'm not really one to buy into all this New Age shit, but the look on her face when I *finally* extracted myself from the apartment sits with me through my whole journey.

Still thinking about it, a slight chill snakes down my spine as I settle into my seat and click the seatbelt into place.

This is ridiculous. I'm going to Punta Cana, for goodness' sake. I'm sure this trip will be amazing. At the very least, it will be interesting. It probably isn't the best time to confront my best friend, but there never is a *good* time for confrontation, is there? At least I won't be ruining Joe's wedding day.

If there even is a wedding after this trip.

My niggle of nerves eases as an attractive brunette slips into the aisle seat beside me.

"Excuse me," I say, and her eyes whip up from fastening her seatbelt, red-rimmed and puffy, as if she's been crying.

"Are you okay?" I ask.

She stares at me as if I have three heads. Okay, so maybe not as amazing a start as I was expecting.

"Darren," I offer, extending a hand.

She shakes her head. "I'm sorry," she apologizes. "I was just . . . somewhere else for a minute. But, yes, I'm okay. Brenda."

I study her face, taking note of the pink circles that have popped up on her cheeks. I watch, slightly mesmerized, as she tucks a strand of straight dark hair behind her ear. There's something familiar about the gesture.

"Have we met before, Brenda?" I ask.

"Do you use that line on every girl you sit next to on an airplane?"

"Only you," I respond, the corners of my lips rising. But yes, I've used that line many times before. Only this time, I mean it. I'm almost positive that I know her from somewhere.

"I've been told I have a familiar face."

"I guess that must be it," I say, though I'm not entirely convinced. Have I slept with her? Definite possibility. How incredibly awkward this flight may be if such is the case.

But now I'm sort of dying to know.

"Where do you live?" I ask.

"I live in the city."

"Work?"

"I work in the city, too."

Sheesh, she's not giving anything away.

Before I can ask another question and Brenda can produce an answer that includes the phrase 'in the city' for a third freaking time, the plane accelerates and lurches into the air. My stomach drops into my feet. I suddenly feel incredibly nauseous, like I might be sick. It's an unusually bumpy ascent into the clouds.

"Sure is turbulent," I mumble, swallowing the lump in my throat and gripping the armrests so tightly that the veins in my hands pop.

Is all this turbulence normal? Are we going to crash?

That stupid tarot card. What complete mindfuckery. I wonder if Tamara *intentionally* did this to keep me on edge since she wasn't invited on the trip. Maybe she made up the whole '*death, bad*' scenario on the fly.

Death, bad? Come on . . .

Who am I kidding? Whether Tamara knew what she was doing or not, it worked. She's officially in my head like that rare brain-eating amoeba picked up in a stagnant sea of lake water. I fear I will be stuck with her for the entire trip.

The plane relentlessly tossing us like rag dolls certainly isn't helping dislodge her warning from my thoughts. I dig my nails into the flesh of my palms, nearly drawing blood. Then, after what feels like an eternity, I hear the familiar beep indicating we've survived our takeoff. I exhale loudly. The skies may be friendlier now, but I still have a knot in the pit of my stomach.

I glance around the crowded cabin. The flight attendants are making their rounds with drink carts and genial expressions, so things must be okay. From a safety perspective, at least.

But Brenda still looks like I felt a moment ago.

"Nervous?" I ask, attempting to lighten the mood, as much for myself as for my seatmate. "I promise I won't bite." I surprise myself with the humor I manage to summon. It sounds convincing. I *almost* feel it.

I'm still rattled, though. After that Wild West takeoff and with Tamara's stupid prediction in the back of my mind, it feels like

I'm cruising at an altitude of thirty thousand feet in a titanium death trap.

I draw a deep breath, trying to rid my mind of all things *death*.

Hopefully, the weather will hold, and we'll go out and about in the Dominican Republic. I hear there are some happening bars and clubs on the island. If not . . . I consider the single ladies who'll be on this trip. Not much of a selection, if I'm being honest. Judging by Lisa's emails, it's safe to say Brit's maid of honor has a stick permanently wedged up her ass. I'm not sure about Brit's work friend, but if she's anything like her maid of honor, and we *don't* get out, maybe I will be twiddling my thumbs all weekend.

That, and figuring out how to have a serious conversation with my best friend. If I don't stop thinking about it, I will drive myself mad.

"Where are you off to?" I ask Brenda, desperate to escape my thoughts.

Thankfully, the color has returned to Brenda's face. Perhaps it *was* just the turbulence that had her looking a pale shade of green, though I can't dismiss the possibility that she's imagined us having sex.

"Bachelorette party. You?"

"Bachelor party. I'm the best man."

What a coincidence, I think, leaning my chin on a fist. Well, maybe not *such* a coincidence. Punta Cana is a popular place for bachelor and bachelorette parties. Half the plane is probably en route to one.

"Was the Dominican Republic your choice?" She asks. "As the best man." She has a point. I should have been the one doing the planning.

But, "No, actually. I wanted to take Joe to Vegas, but the maid of honor pushed this joint bachelor-bachelorette party at a villa on the island. I mean . . . who does that?" I raise a shoulder. "A joint bachelor-bachelorette party?"

Brenda goes sheet white again. "Did you say Joe?"

I nod.

"As in Joe and Brit?"

I nod again, slower this time. "And you?" I ask.

"Same."

No way. No freaking way.

Well, this just got interesting in an enemies-to-lovers plot twist sort of way. Brenda must be Brit's work friend.

And it looks like we are going to the *same* party.

CHAPTER 4

Brenda

"You can do it."

I stare at myself in the forty-inch mirror of the cramped plane bathroom. I sound like a gosh darn Nike commercial. Except, I don't want to do it. I don't want to go. Make that, I *really* don't want to go. It's a bad idea. A *very* bad idea. What was I thinking when I said *yes* to this trip?

I consider all the ways I might be able to weasel my way out of it. I could call Brit from the terminal and tell her I'm not feeling well. It wouldn't be a complete lie. But the ticket is nonrefundable. And I know I won't hear the end of it from Brit or her maid of honor, not that I care much about what Lisa has to say on the matter. But Brit? Well, she is another story altogether.

There's also the fact that this was supposed to be *my* wedding weekend, and the thought of spending it alone is even less appealing than the thought of spending the weekend in the Dominican Republic with Brit and her friends.

Especially after the unceremonious way my engagement ended.

To be honest, I should be flattered, not terrified, by the invite. I'm not quite sure how I finagled my way onto Brit's list, even though now I wish I hadn't. We're friendly, yes. But we certainly aren't close. Brit has yet to even introduce me to her fiancé, which would seem a prerequisite to being invited on such a trip. Nevertheless, Brit seems to have taken to me over the past year, ever since she personally hired me to check copy at her ad agency, Bright Horizons.

Yup, Brit Jones is my *boss*.

I can't very well piss her off by not showing up for her special weekend, *can* I? I might as well not bother showing up for work on Monday. No, I need to be there this weekend. So that's why — when I let myself out of the bathroom — I walk to my seat, suck it up, and paste on my best party face.

Who knows? This weekend could be just what the doctor ordered — a trip I'll never forget.

It certainly will be for the bride and groom.

I'm hoping for a quiet flight of panicked introspection, but apparently that's not going to happen, thanks to my overzealous seatmate.

If the guy sitting next to me on the plane is trying to get my number, he has another thing coming. Although it quickly becomes clear, we will be spending *a lot* of time together this weekend.

My thoughts are racing a mile a minute, like a hamster on a wheel. I'm well past the point of second-guessing this trip. I'm third-guessing. Fourth-guessing. *Fifth*-guessing. I shouldn't have come.

My hands rest on my seatbelt. I could still back out, go home, and start looking for a new job. I'll never have to speak to Brit again, though I might one day need a reference. Someone will give me a reference. Probably not Brit, and definitely not my ex-fiancé, but surely there is *someone* out there.

Except, my plan has a fatal flaw. We are now cruising at thirty thousand feet. The bell has dinged, indicating it is safe to roam the cabin. What am I going to do? Scream for the pilot to land the plane? I'll probably get arrested on terrorism charges. That's just what I need — a feature on the ten o'clock news for inciting a disturbance on an international flight.

So, the fates have decided — I'm going to Punta Cana, Dominican Republic, whether I like it or not.

I suppose it could be worse. My seatmate definitely has the whole James Dean thing going for him, with his dark eyes, gelled hair, and leather jacket. His five o'clock shadow certainly adds to the rough around the edges vibe he has going on.

Now, if I could just remember his name.

Dudley? Dane? Darren?

Yes, that's it. Darren.

I push past the lump lodged in my throat and force myself to speak. "What are the chances we'd be going to the same party, sitting next to each other on the same flight?"

"Kismet." Darren winks.

It's a bit cheesy, though I don't say so. I've all but sworn off men since the breakup. But I must admit, it's refreshing to have one flirting with me. Maybe it is *kismet.* I wonder for a moment, though, if Brit had a hand in this and is discreetly trying to hook us up.

Is *that* why she invited me on this trip?

Either way, Darren is easy enough to talk to and even easier on the eyes. Anything is better than focusing on this bumpy flight. I feel the tension in my shoulders slowly release like air hissing from a punctured tire.

"Hey, can you keep an eye on my stuff for a minute? I've got to hit the head." Darren shoots a side-eye at the older man sitting by the window seat. I laugh despite myself. The guy is out cold, drool sliding out the corner of his mouth. He's not touching Darren's stuff. He's not touching anything other than the Ambien I watched him dry swallow before the flight.

Nonetheless, I nod and watch as Darren disappears down the aisle. I take a long, deep breath, sinking back against the headrest. The plane takes a sudden drop, and I instinctively move my hand to stop Darren's phone from falling to the floor.

"Sorry about that, folks," the pilot says.

A few minutes later, I pull my legs up to my chest so Darren can squeeze back into the middle seat.

Once he's settled in, I ask, "So, how do you know the bride and groom?"

Lisa sent an introductory email, but with all of the guests blind cc'd on it. You'd think she'd want to spark conversation — give us a way of communicating with each other and engaging in friendly pre-trip banter — but clearly, Lisa would rather maintain control of the narrative. Unless it was an honest mistake. I mean, cc and bcc are only one letter off. But if it *wasn't* an honest mistake, it's quite odd since we are all vacationing together. Then again, based on the times I've met Lisa, that's exactly how I would describe her: *odd.*

I glossed over that initial email and the many that followed. Just tell me where to be, and I'll be there. Albeit, regretfully so.

"Joe and I grew up together. We've known each other forever, since like grade school. We even went to the same college. Roomed together and all."

"Wow, you must be super close."

"Like brothers." Darren's jaw tenses as he says this. But just a moment later, his face appears relaxed.

"What about you, Brenda? How do you know Joe and Brit?"

"Well," I hesitate, pulling at a cuticle. It's a terrible habit I developed growing up, and it seems to be getting worse lately. A small bubble of blood pops from a half-healed scab. "I only know half of the happy couple. I work with . . . actually, I work for Brit. I'm a copy editor at her advertising agency."

A long silence follows. Painfully long. I can't imagine what I've said to turn the gregarious Darren into a mute. I examine his rugged features, searching for a clue. His lips are pursed, eyes narrowed, crinkled around the edges. He looks pensive, like he's attempting to solve a complex math equation in his head.

When he finally speaks, it's not what I'm expecting. Nor do I like it. "So let me get this straight. You work *for* Brit, and she invited you on this trip?"

I flinch at the question. I'm not sure if Darren meant it to sound critical, but it does. I'm helpless to fight the flush I imagine crawling up my neck and spreading across my cheeks like a rash. I wish I could crawl into a hole and disappear.

Or, at the very least, get off this goddamn plane.

When I respond, I can't help but sound defensive. "Technically, *she* didn't invite me. Her maid of honor did. And *I* helped out with the administrative aspects of the trip." In other words, the *paperwork*.

"Touché. You know what I mean."

Do I? "We're friendly, okay?"

"I'm friendly with a lot of people, but I don't think I'd invite them to my intimate bachelor party. Not that I'm getting married any time soon, but—"

I cock my head, slightly confused, super offended, waiting for what will come out of this man's mouth next. He's blunt like a dull razor's edge.

"I'm just saying, it seems a little strange that it's Joe, Brit, their lifelong best friends, and then you."

Darren isn't wrong. It *does* seem a little strange. And if I didn't already feel like I shouldn't be there this weekend, I sure as heck do now.

When I don't say anything, Darren changes the subject, though he's made his point loud and clear, short of hiring a blimp and streaking it across the sky. It's a bell that can't be unrung — validation for the thoughts that have been cycling on repeat since that email invitation came through.

"Hey listen, since we're going to the same place, do you want to share a cab?"

Surely this guy is kidding.

I shoot Darren a questioning look. Do I want to share a cab with the virtual stranger who told me I'm an interloper on this trip?

Do I?

Well, I am a twenty-something single woman traveling alone for the first time to a place I'm unfamiliar with. My Spanish vocabulary consists of *hola* and *agua*. What will I tell the Uber driver, who might not speak English? *Hello, water?*

So, for lack of a better option, I agree, hoping I won't regret my decision — or any of my decisions. "Sure, we can split a ride."

The sick feeling in my stomach only intensifies as our hired car navigates the bumpy roads leading to the rental. Unfortunately, it isn't just car sickness, although I wish it were. It isn't even what Darren said that has my intestines twisted into a knot. He's right. Brit must have other friends she's closer to. She definitely has better things to do than invite me to her bachelorette party for a pity hook-up with the best man. What exactly is her play?

As I stare out the Uber window, my eyes hone in on a ball of tumbleweed. *Tumbleweed.* We've passed a few pockets of houses and farms, but it's been at least ten minutes since I've spotted any real signs of civilization.

I live in the city for a reason. *I like civilization, thank you very much!*

I don't think we've seen another car, for that matter. Where the hell are we?

Lisa failed to mention that this place is smack dab in the middle of nowhere, despite rambling about any and everything in the five hundred emails she sent about this trip. I had to create a separate folder to keep track of them. It was utterly exhausting.

I turn my attention back to Darren, pushing the nagging thoughts from my mind. He's saying something, apologizing, apparently.

"I hope I didn't offend you on the plane. I . . . just . . ."

"You just what?"

"I've just had a lot of nerves about this trip."

"So, I'm not the only one?"

"No," he admits. "There's some backstory. And the truth is, I'm not sure how this trip will go."

Darren's confession doesn't make me feel better. If anything, I feel worse. I'm sick to my stomach. If the groom's best man is apprehensive, what does that say about what we are walking into? Nothing good.

But there's no way out now. We are already in the middle of swampland, twenty minutes into the forty-minute drive. There is nowhere to go. If I jumped out of the car, I'd probably fall into a sinkhole or get eaten by a ravenous animal. Maybe I'd get lucky and get tangled up in that tumbleweed.

Perhaps that wouldn't be such a bad thing.

Jeez, I need to stop thinking like this. It's a bachelor-bachelorette party! We'll enjoy some crystal-clear water, fine wine, and good food this weekend. It will be fun.

Everything will be fine.

From: lisamreynard@reynardaccounting.com
To: joseph.briggs@briggsfinancial.com
Subject: Villa rental

Hi Joe,

So, I have some exciting news. I found the absolute best villa for our trip. A client has a rental in the DR. Six bedrooms with balconies. Private pool with a waterfall and hot tub. Brand-spanking new. It sounds like a dream. And, she said we can have it for the weekend for free. *Free!* You can't beat the price lol. Thoughts?

xx
Lisa (Maid of Honor)

From: joseph.briggs@briggsfinancial.com
To: lisamreynard@reynardaccounting.com
Subject: Re: Villa rental

Hi Lisa,

That sounds amazing, but I wouldn't want Brit to think I'm being cheap. You know how she can be sometimes.

Thanks for your help,
Joe

From: lisamreynard@reynardaccounting.com
To: joseph.briggs@briggsfinancial.com
Subject: Re: Villa rental

It'll be our little secret. Consider it an early wedding gift. I'll send you the link so you can book. I've got the entertainment for the weekend covered. Punta Cana, here we come!

xx
Lisa (Maid of Honor)

CHAPTER 5

Brit

I jump out of the car before it comes to a complete stop, leaving Joe to settle the bill and navigate my overstuffed luggage. I know I should stick around to ensure the driver doesn't overcharge him, but then Joe will discover that I speak Spanish, and I'll have to tell him what our driver said. I don't even want to *think* about what our driver said, though I won't soon forget it. I certainly don't want to talk about it.

Thankfully, Joe doesn't seem to mind. "I love taking care of my Britter-Bug," he reminds me at least ten times daily, ever since he approached me at the club four months earlier. I wasn't looking for love, but, as they say, that's when love finds you. After spending a hot and heavy weekend together, we flew back to New York as a couple. I smile widely at the memory.

And now we could star in a Hallmark movie.

Joe, meanwhile, grunts as he pulls my bag from the trunk. It weighed in at a whopping sixty-five pounds. Good thing we didn't fly commercial. I may have overpacked just a wee bit for our weekend trip. But I thought it best to be prepared for anything this little island might throw at us. When I checked last night, the weather looked favorable, but a hurricane is forming out at sea that could make landfall.

I pause momentarily in front of our rental. Its white facade is even more impressive in person than on the computer screen. Coupled with its intricate, canopied roof, it could pass for a Buddhist temple.

A gush of warmth flows through me like I'm sinking into a steamy bubble bath. I love that Joe did this for me. For *us*.

That feeling quickly vanishes, though, as I rest my hand on the knob, ready and eager to explore, and the door abruptly flies open. I leap back, startled. My foot slips off the step behind me, and I'm barely able to grab the railing before toppling down the bluestone slabs to the gravel below. My heart thunders in my chest, blood whooshing in my ears as I struggle to catch my breath.

"Britter-Bug!!" Lisa rushes through the frame with her arms outstretched, seemingly oblivious to the fact that she almost killed the bride before the bachelorette party could even begin.

It takes a minute for my pulse to slow down. The tremor in my hands remains, not so easily shaken. There's nothing like a good old scare to kick off a dream vacation. Hopefully, this is the first and last of the good old scares. I want nothing more than to enjoy a lovely, relaxing weekend with Joe and our friends.

Starting now.

Because, despite the initial shock, it is *so* good to see Lisa. It's been just a few weeks since we last hung out, but it's felt like years. That's how it goes when you've known someone as long as we've known each other.

I breathe a sigh of relief as I take in her chocolate eyes and sensible polo and shorts set. Her familiar chestnut hair is pulled up into a tight bun, not a strand out of place, smudgeless sunglasses tucked neatly into the collar of her shirt. She's dressed for a game of golf, not that I imagine there are many — or *any* — courses nearby. There's not even a grocery store within a twenty-mile radius.

"Lisa!" I fold into my best friend's arms. "I wasn't expecting you to get here before us!" I steal a glance back at Joe, who has taken a break from deadlifting our bags to wipe the sweat from his brow. Based on our conversation about christening the house, I take it he wasn't expecting Lisa to arrive here before us, either. Oh well.

Lisa pulls back and looks me over. "You look gorgeous, as always, Brit." Her lip twitches. "If only we could all look good as effortlessly as you."

It's certainly not effortless, but I appreciate the sentiment. I run a hand through my hair, tousled from the flight. My cheeks, which were already heated from the champagne, feel like they've been set on fire after that ominous Uber ride.

Still, Lisa always has something nice to say. And if she doesn't, she usually keeps it to herself. These two qualities are invaluable in a best friend.

"You look great too! I can't believe how tan you are!" I exclaim. Lisa's usually pale skin looks like it's been kissed by the sun, though I can't miss the purple shadows bleeding like bruises beneath her eyes. Poor thing. She's spent the past month working tirelessly to help Joe set up this trip. And she only returned from her own vacation a day ago. She probably hasn't had a good rest in ages.

Bless her heart.

"So . . . did you meet anyone special?" I ask. "Where'd you go again? Aruba?"

"The Bahamas." Lisa rolls her eyes, jokingly annoyed. That's another thing I love about her — my best friend *never* seems to get mad at me. "But anyway, I didn't meet a soul. Every guy there was either spoken for, gay, or waiting for a Tinder date. Whatever happened to good old-fashioned hooking up with some random guy at a bar in New York City?"

I laugh out loud. "As if you would *ever* hook up with some random guy at a bar."

"Maybe I would," she challenges, jutting her lower lip.

"No, you wouldn't," I counter, because she would *never*. Joe would sooner fly economy.

"Okay, fine. I *wouldn't*. But you met Joe on vacation."

It was a work trip, but . . . "True," I agree.

"Anyway, I was hopeful I'd meet someone, but I guess it wasn't meant to be." She shrugs, then adds, "Maybe *this* trip?" Lisa widens her eyes expectantly as if I might be concealing a fully available, hunky bachelor behind my back.

I'm not sure what my friend is expecting. She already knows that the only other man attending is, according to Joe, off the market. I knew we should have invited another guy, but surprisingly, Joe doesn't have all that many close friends.

"You'll meet the right guy someday. I'm glad I didn't settle down before. Joe is everything I've ever dreamed of and more. He's perfect."

"No one is perfect, Brit."

I'm about to argue about my fiancé's perfection when we both startle at the crunch of gravel behind us. Joe is standing at the base of the stairs, wiping the sweat from his forehead. It's so freaking muggy out. Stifling. The humidity is wrapped around us like a double-knit blanket.

Oh God, it feels like rain. *No, no, no*. It can't rain. It just *can't*. Rain will ruin everything.

I slap a mosquito on my arm, the blood of its last meal splattering across my skin.

"Gross," Lisa says, pointing to the streak of blood on my arm. Her face grows serious, the corners of her lips dipping. "My driver said something really strange about mosquitoes on the car ride over . . ." her voice trails off as she chews on her lower lip, apparently disturbed by the memory of her driver.

I share the sentiment, not that I plan on telling her what *our* Uber driver said. Surely, what her driver said can't be any worse.

"What? That they're disgusting and carry like eight million different diseases?"

Lisa shakes her head, her expression still somber. The way her face has darkened and the furrow of her forehead makes me incredibly anxious and slightly irritated.

"Well, what is it? Are you going to tell me?"

She hesitates. "It's stupid, really. I shouldn't have even brought it up."

"But you did bring it up." I try to hide the annoyance in my voice.

"Fine," she relents, drawing a deep breath before speaking. "He just said that witches can shapeshift into the form of a mosquito. They get their power from the Devil, and if that power is released, well . . ." She throws her hands up and shakes her head, looking perturbed, almost as if she can see that power, as if it's a tangible thing.

Witches? Shapeshifting? Lisa can't actually believe this nonsense, can she? This is ridiculous. It's even more ridiculous than the superstition about the dog on the side of the road. I wonder for a moment if we had the *same* driver.

But still, Lisa is supposed to be the practical one here.

"By the way," Lisa deadpans. "Do you know what '*sal mientras puedas*' means?"

My stomach sours. "Who said that to you?"

"My driver. Why? What does it mean?"

I shake my head, wondering if her driver knows something we don't. I swallow against the lump in my throat. "It means get out while you can."

Why would he say that?

Lisa doesn't have a chance to react as Joe inserts himself into our conversation, offering a welcome interruption to talk of *getting out while we can*, and the black spirit I've evidently unleashed to avoid getting devoured by a disease-carrying mosquito.

"Your best friend sure knows how to pack," he pants, holding a hand to his chest as he attempts to catch his breath.

"Always has," Lisa agrees, wrinkling her nose and glancing down at my luggage. "Are you moving in?" She asks me, a wry grin on her face.

I stick my tongue out at her, all in good fun.

"It's nice to see you again, Lisa." Joe walks up the stone stairs, giving Lisa a quick kiss on the cheek. She instantly flushes red. I can't blame her. Joe is unusually good-looking, an anomaly of human genetics. Dark, wavy hair. Gold-flecked amber eyes. A jawline that looks like it was sculpted from stone. "Thanks for getting things set up for us."

"Anything for Brit, right?"

"As I always say."

"Ahem." I clear my throat. The way they are carrying on about me, it's almost as if I'm not standing here. "This is fun," I say, rolling my eyes in jest. "But I'm dying to see the place." With thoughts of the death-boding dog and the dark spirit-carrying mosquito in my head, I wonder for a moment if *dying* is the best choice of words. But I do *really* want to see the house.

"Right, of course." Lisa steps to the side, a grin spreading from ear to ear. "It's absolutely amazing. Stunning, really."

I interlace my fingers through Joe's and pull him inside the house. I can't wait another second. Joe can grab our luggage from outside later after we've taken a proper tour of our five-star accommodation.

"Shoes," Lisa says, motioning toward the floor. "The whole place is white marble. Even the bedrooms upstairs."

"How bougie," I observe as my eyes dance dreamily around the entryway. I'm enthralled but not surprised. My fiancé enjoys the finer things in life. Always has. Always will.

On that note, I carefully remove my studded Valentinos and place them neatly by the front door next to Joe's Ferragamo loafers and Lisa's boat shoes.

"Shall we?" Lisa beckons us with a flick of her wrist, and we eagerly follow her through the atrium into a living room the size of a football field. A warm breeze blows through the French doors that open up to a breathtaking veranda and a spectacular view of the lush tropical greenery.

My eyes focus inward, greedily devouring the space. A massive marble fireplace serves as the room's centerpiece, framed by an elegant leather wrap-around couch. A large mirror hangs above the fireplace, and a fully stocked bar encased in marble sits off to the right. There's a museum-esque quality to the space — opulent minimalism at its best.

And Lisa wasn't joking; it's *all* white.

I bet our accommodations served as inspiration for her White Lie Party.

"Holy wow," I say, my jaw dropping.

"I had the exact same reaction." Lisa claps her hands together in excitement.

"I'm so glad you love it. Only the best for my Britter-Bug." Joe snakes his arms snugly around my waist and smiles widely at Lisa. It's so nice to see them getting along already.

"It's just perfect, Joe. Except for one thing, darling—" The hair on the back of my neck shoot up. Goosebumps line my flesh. "Is it me, or is it freezing in here?"

At once, Joe and Lisa wrap their arms around their bodies. "Now that you mention it," Lisa adds, "it's like an icebox in here."

"An igloo."

"A chilly bin."

Lisa and I both laugh. We've been playing this game since our teens. The last person to come up with a catchy synonym wins. It has gotten us through some painfully long nights.

"On that note, I'll let you ladies settle in and catch up while I look for the thermostat."

I blow Joe a kiss, admiring the view as he walks away.

"You haven't told him, have you?" Lisa asks once Joe is out of earshot.

I glance toward the empty space where Joe stood just a moment ago, blissfully unknowing. "No—"

Lisa's smile slides off her face. "You have to tell him, Brit, or . . ."

"Or *what?*" My hands find my hips. She *wouldn't* . . .

"Look," she says, softening her tone while simultaneously flashing the *trust me, I know what's best for you* look she's been perfecting since we first met.

"Don't you think Joe will have questions when the wedding rolls around next week and you have no family there? Won't he wonder—"

Okay, so I may have embellished a tad about my pedigree.

Still, "You always do this." I clench my teeth hard, cutting her off, acutely aware of the throbbing pain in my jaw.

"Do *what?*" Lisa's eyes grow wide with feigned innocence.

"Remember my *last* boyfriend?"

"He was a loser."

"Says you."

"Says the twenty other girls who swiped right."

I fold my arms across my chest, annoyed. She's right. He *was* a loser. Six months, and then the guy just disappeared off the face of the planet. But still . . . "You're always meddling in my life."

There, I said it. Although I kind of wish I could *unsay* it.

Because Lisa's face falls, filling me instantly with guilt.

"Not that it's any of your concern, I was going to tell him on the way here. But—"

"But what?"

"There was this dog, and then the driver said it was some sort of omen and, anyway, it's a long story. I'll tell Joe every last detail about my family when the time is right. It doesn't change anything."

Other than the fact that I know she's right. I have to tell Joe sooner rather than later.

Just not this second. Not this weekend.

Lisa mirrors my posture, crossing her arms and jutting out her hip. "Fine, whatever you say, Brittany." I flinch at the sound of my full name. Lisa never calls me by my full name. She's the one who started calling me Brit in the first place, back in grade school. "You know best," she adds.

Despite the thin smile stretching her lips, I can tell she doesn't mean it.

CHAPTER 6

Lisa

I swear if I hear "only the best for my Britter-Bug" even one more time, I cannot be held responsible for my actions. Brit is beautiful and successful, and all that, but this guy is over the top. He's a caricature of a person — maybe even a caricature of a caricature.

And it's only been four months. They barely know each other at all. As I've just discovered, they know each other even less than I thought. I wonder what Joe would make of his precious Britter-Bug if he knew the truth. Who she really is.

I inhale a deep breath, recentering myself. Things are going as smoothly as a wooden roller coaster. It feels like my head is being jerked in every direction. I rub my palm along the back of my neck, massaging away the phantom pains.

Despite Brit's jab, as per usual, I relent, "I'm sorry I upset you. You know I only want what's best for you. You're like my sister, Brit." Truly, she's as close to a non-blood-related sister as one can get. "I've really missed you."

Brit's face lights up, and it's like the past two minutes of conversation never happened. My best friend is nothing if not mercurial.

"Awww, I've missed you, too, Li."

Did she, though? I study her expression. It looks sincere, but if it weren't for this trip and the wedding, I'm not sure I'd have heard from Brit at all. It's literally all we've talked about for the past month. Over the years, our relationship has become increasingly one-sided. Maybe it always was, and I've only just noticed. I feel my muscles tighten. My fingers involuntarily squeeze into fists behind my back.

"What did I miss?"

Brit and I jump at the sound of Joe's voice. I'm not sure how he managed to completely sneak up on us out of thin air. In addition to devastating good looks and a lucrative career in finance, Joe clearly has the role of stealth ninja down pat. All he needs is an all-black ensemble, and he'll be set for Halloween. Despite their outward displays of affection, I can't help but wonder if the happy couple will even make it to Halloween.

"Oh, nothing," I say, aware of the flush forming on my cheeks despite the chill in the air. "You weren't able to turn down the air conditioning? It feels like it's cranking even more now." I rub my hands up and down my arms for warmth.

"Unfortunately, no. I couldn't find any working thermostats on the main unit. This place isn't super user-friendly. I guess we're all going to be wearing sweaters this trip. Or sleeping outside."

"Joe, you can't be serious." Brit's blue eyes widen with panic. "Do you have any idea how many wild animals and bugs live in this part of the world? Or the diseases they carry? I am *not* contracting Diphtheria a week before our wedding."

My eyes momentarily flick to Brit's arm, where a tinge of blood remains from the mosquito she squashed outside. "Not to mention the fact that there's a hurricane watch," I mumble under my breath. I'm still holding out hope that the storm will pass.

"Don't worry, Brit, I'll keep you safe and warm," Joe croons. I mouth the words along with him — *only the best for my Britter-Bug*. I have a sinking feeling I'll hear those words in my sleep.

I watch uncomfortably as Joe brushes his lips against Brit's. The way they're staring so intently into each other's eyes, I might as well be in another room, on another island. This bachelor-bachelorette party was a horrible idea. They'd obviously much rather be alone. But it's too late for that now. What's done is done.

I need something, *anything*, to distract them.

"Shots!" I shout in a panicked, light-bulb moment. "Shots will warm us up. What do you think, Brit?"

Brit's lips stretch wide. "It's happy hour somewhere, right? Count me in."

Hmm, so it *isn't* a shotgun wedding. I'm not sure if I should be happy that Brit isn't hiding a pregnancy or unhappy that she might be hiding something else. I don't know how else to explain the widening chasm between us. It feels like the carpet has been ripped out from beneath our friendship.

My eyes narrow on Joe, as if I can see the fraying fabric in his hands.

I push down the thoughts and lead Joe and Brit through the living room to the wet bar. I slip behind the white marble opening and select a bottle of Jack Daniel's.

It feels like yesterday that we snuck our first sips of Jack Daniel's, even though it was well over a decade ago. Brit passed out in the closet *after* she confessed to making out with Tanner McDaniels, whom I had a massive crush on. The *biggest*. It was on that day I came to learn that Jack Daniel's is essentially Brit's truth serum.

Am I trying to sabotage this weekend by feeding her truth serum? The wedding? *Of course not.* But the truth will eventually come out, one way or another. It always does.

"Too early?" I ask, dangling the bottle in front of them.

"It's never too early to get the party started." Brit pumps an excited fist in the air. I feel a slight flicker of joy. *That's better.* The weekend could still turn out exactly how I pictured it would.

Except, I freeze with the bottle suspended in midair as a man and woman approach the bar. The bottle trembles in my hand, a sheen of sweat shooting across my forehead. I've been preparing for the past month, but I'm not ready for this.

I stand frozen as Joe greets the man, and Brit, the woman. By process of elimination — Darren and Brenda. *Well, duh.*

I feel a sharp stab of jealousy like a serrated knife to my side. Why have they come here *together*? Brit shouldn't have invited Brenda in the first place. It would have been a perfectly lovely trip with just the four of us. Not that I said as much to my best friend. Not that Brit would have taken my advice if I had. She never does, despite the fact that I am so obviously the voice of reason in this friendship.

Brit grabs my arm and pulls me toward them. I wish I could share in her excitement, but all I feel is *shook*.

"Lisa, this is Darren and Brenda." They each hold out a hand, which I dutifully shake. I find myself clutching Darren's hand for a beat longer than necessary. Funny, Brit never mentioned how devilishly good-looking he is. Come to think of it, she's not had much nice to say about him at all. If memory serves, her exact words were, "Arrogant womanizer who invents stupid shit that no one needs or uses." A glowing description, it was not.

"You're just in time," I say, forcing a smile for Brenda; the one for Darren, that's the real thing. I'm more interested in what Brit *hasn't* said than what she has, like how incredibly handsome he is. Now, I can't stop smiling. My cheeks pinch with pain. I quickly turn my back, hoping the flush blooming on my face goes unnoticed. "I was about to pour us some shots."

"I'm going to pass on this round." I flip back around at the sound of Brenda's voice, watching as she shakes her head and tucks a dark strand of hair behind her ear. "I won't make it to dinner if I start drinking now."

Hmm, would that be such a bad thing? I wonder.

Out loud, I ask, "So, how do you and Darren know each other?" I narrow my eyes at Brenda. It's only been two minutes, but her presence is already getting under my skin, like the damn bugs flying in through the open veranda doors.

Brenda glances at Darren quickly — as if they're in on a secret the rest of us aren't privy to — before answering. "We just met on the plane."

"We were sitting right next to each other. I know, what are the chances, right?" Darren adds, with a half-cocked grin. He is hot — if you have a thing for bad boys. Brit *used* to have a thing for bad boys until she met Joe. Joe is the total opposite of a bad boy. He would be the antonym of a bad boy in an illustrated thesaurus. He probably doesn't have a bad bone in his body. The guy is so far up Brit's ass you'd need a crowbar to get him loose.

I consider Darren's question: what *are* the odds? Smooth introductions may admittedly elude me, but numbers are my thing. Approximately seven direct flights to the Dominican Republic from New York daily, one hundred eighty-nine seats per plane. "Off the top of my head, I'd say it's thirty times less likely than getting struck by lightning. And everyone knows that's like one in a million."

The room goes quiet; the only noise is the maniacal whir of the A/C. Everyone is staring at me with wide eyes as if I've just sprouted a second head *and* it got struck by lightning. *But I'm right*, I want to shout. The odds of Darren and Brenda randomly sitting next to one another on the plane are slim to none at best.

But it's clear by their incredulous expressions that I should have kept my statistical observations to myself. I let out a muffled *hmph*.

After an awkward silence that stretches for far too long, Brit finally breaks it. She flips her silky blonde hair over her shoulder, deadpans, and says, "The universe works in mysterious ways, doesn't it?" I'm sure we're all familiar with the cliché, but I don't understand what exactly Brit is implying.

Does the universe want Brenda and Darren to spark a connection? Does the universe want me to spend my life alone?

Maybe it does.

I study my best friend as she leaves the room, presumably to grab that sweater Joe was talking about.

Maybe it wasn't the universe. Maybe Brit had something to do with this.

CHAPTER 7

Darren

Lisa is everything I expected and more — so, *so* much more. Brit's maid of honor is wound tighter than a spring. The tension is radiating off her in palpable waves. And she's staring at Brenda like she wants to wrap her hands around her neck and never let go.

What in the world have we walked into?

I don't have much time to ponder that thought as an air-splitting scream cuts through the room like a knife. It's come from outside.

We seem to realize this all at once, as we nearly topple over one another racing to the front door.

There, we find Brit standing at the base of the stairs with her head clutched in her hands, moaning loudly. I can't imagine what's happened to her. The only thought that comes to mind is an animal attack, though I don't see an animal circling her — or any blood, for that matter. Still, we are in the middle of the boondocks, surrounded by a veritable forest that could double as a fortress. There's not much else other than a wild animal that you could reasonably expect to encounter here.

"Oh my God, Brit, are you okay?" Lisa pushes past us all to Brit's side. I get the whole *best friend* thing — Joe has been a staple in my life through the years as well — but Lisa is a little over the top. Joe told me in confidence that it was Lisa's idea to do this whole joint bachelor-bachelorette party. I would have been more than happy to take Joe to Vegas for a normal bachelor party, with gambling and strippers. But Joe is so far gone that there is no coming back. I could say the same for Lisa, the way she's bowing and scraping over Brit.

She might as well pull out a fan and start feeding her grapes.

"Do I look *okay*?" Brit snaps, snapping me back to the present.

Lisa reels back as if she's been slapped across the face. I can almost see her heart shatter into a million pieces. I wonder how — *why* — they're even friends.

Brit quickly backtracks. "I'm so sorry, Lisa. It's just . . . it's our luggage."

"What about our luggage?" Joe interjects as we stare at Brit and Lisa standing on the gravel drive with hands pressed tightly against their bodies as if squaring off for a boxing match.

"It's gone. Everything . . . just *gone*."

"Don't be silly. It can't be gone, darling." Joe confidently walks down the steps, looking like a superhero ready to save the day. In fourth grade, we drew self-portraits for an art class. Even back then, Joe drew himself with a cape. Not much has changed.

I clench my teeth so hard I'm concerned I have cracked a tooth.

Everything has changed.

I flick my attention back to the drama playing out on the gravel. "I left our bags right here." Joe emphatically points to an empty spot in front of the house.

"Yes," Lisa agrees. "I saw them when you got here."

"Well, they're not here anymore," Brit huffs. "So where are they? Why didn't you bring them inside?"

"I was dealing with the air conditioning situation, and I forgot about them. I'm sorry, my love. I'm sure they're somewhere."

I examine the sheen of sweat forming on Joe's forehead. His brow is slightly furrowed, and his posture is statue-stiff. He doesn't *look* sure that they are somewhere.

Joe spins on his heels to face me. "Did you see our bags when you got here?"

"Ten minutes ago? No, there was nothing here but gravel."

"This doesn't make any sense at all," Joe huffs. "Why would someone take our luggage?"

"And *who?*" I add, stating the obvious. "If it's just the five of us. You three were inside, and Brenda and I just got here . . ."

Lisa clears her throat. "Except we weren't all inside. Joe went to check on the air conditioning," she says, shooting Joe a wild look as if he were the one who stole his own luggage. Why would he steal his own luggage? That's the most ridiculous thing I've heard all day — second only to Tamara's premonitions.

Great, now I'm thinking about that *again.*

But maybe it's a positive sign that this — whatever *this* is — has happened. Perhaps Tamara confused physical death with the death of Brit's weekend wardrobe.

"This is ridiculous," Joe complains, pacing in front of the house. "There has to be a logical explanation. Maybe your driver saw our luggage sitting here when he dropped you off and thought he could make a quick buck." He runs a hand across his chin. There's a subtle tremble in his fingers. "I mean, it is thousand-dollar luggage."

"But it wasn't sitting here," Brenda reminds him. "I'm certain there was no luggage here when we pulled up."

If I didn't already like Brenda, I do now. If I'm lucky, I'll spend most of my time with her this weekend.

"Well, that's just great." Brit dramatically throws her hands up in the air, exasperated. "And what am I supposed to wear all weekend, *hmmm*?"

And not with *her*.

"Come on," Lisa coos gently as if handling a baby. She places a palm on Brit's shoulder. "You can look through my suitcase. It'll be like the old times when we used to raid each other's closets!"

Or *her*.

Brit takes a deep breath and smooths the hem of her short dress. I try not to stare. Joe has done quite well for himself in more ways than one. Knowing him as I do, I wouldn't expect any less, though, at one time, I would have hoped for more. I guess it's true what they say: you never truly know anyone.

My gaze involuntarily lingers as Brit follows Lisa into the house, leaving Joe and me standing awkwardly with Brenda.

"I should probably go with them," she announces with little conviction, not seeming like she wants to go with them. I can't blame her. But then, she probably doesn't want to stay with us either.

Brenda doesn't seem like she wants to be here *at all*, come to think of it.

I'd like to unpack that. Later.

For now, I toss her a wave, slightly disappointed to watch her disappear into the house. But I know it's for the best so Joe and I can have some time alone. Best man and groom.

And . . . the other thing.

"So—" I say, getting ready to drop the bomb.

"So . . . listen, I need a favor, Darren." Joe looks around, presumably to make sure no one else is listening.

Not the conversation I was expecting to have, but I'm intrigued. "What kind of favor?"

"I need you to tell Brit you saw our luggage."

I'm confused. "But I just told her I *didn't* see your luggage. Why would I tell her I saw it? She's not going to believe me."

"I don't know, man. Make something up. Tell her you smoked a joint or something, and your memory was a little foggy."

"Seriously? You want me to pretend I was so high I forgot I saw your luggage outside the house?" I shake my head in disbelief. Joe's asked for a lot over the years, but this? "Dude, you *hid* your luggage?"

"Of course I didn't hide our luggage. I have no idea what happened to our luggage. All I know is that I can't have my fiancée falling apart this weekend."

"So, you want me to *lie* to her?"

He nods.

Well, my best friend is no stranger to lying.

"Alright. I'll tell her I might have been mistaken, okay?"

"You're the man, Darren. The M-A-N, man." Joe slaps me a little too hard on the back. It doesn't go unnoticed.

"God, you're fucking cheesy. Listen, there's something I need to talk to you about."

"Oh?" Joe arches an eyebrow, all wide-eyed and innocent. I pause, examining his expression closely. His face is now relaxed, posture loose, a stark contrast to my inner angst. I feel the rage simmering inside me, beginning to reach its boiling point. If I don't confront Joe soon, I am going to explode.

But as I open my mouth to broach the topic that has taken up permanent residence in my head, the ladies reappear in the doorway. My stomach sinks. This conversation will have to wait until later.

"Joseph, darling." Brit appears before us in the stucco archway with the sun shining down on her like she's an angel standing outside the gates of heaven. She's dressed in a maxi skirt with a thigh-high slit, a crop top, and a more amenable expression. I'm not sure how much warmer this outfit will be than the last since the slit travels so high up her leg that the lacy hem of her underwear is peeking through, but she does have a denim jacket draped over an arm. So, there's that.

My eyes flick to Lisa in her *soccer mom just squeezing in a round of golf* outfit. Funny, I *cannot* imagine her wearing Brit's sexy ensemble. It's almost as if she packed it just for Brit in case of an emergency like this.

"Wow," Joe says, looking Brit up and down appreciatively. "You look absolutely amazing, Britter-Bug."

Brit blushes. "Oh, this old thing." She flips her long blonde hair over her shoulder.

Something in my brain clicks. "I've got a new nickname for you," I offer, and they all glance in my direction. "Wait for it—" I pause, holding up both hands before bringing them down like a low-budget drum riff. "Brit — dun, dun, dun — Barbie."

Joe coughs loudly into his arm while Lisa lets out a strangled squeal.

"What's that supposed to mean?" Brit asks, her eyes narrowing on me as she folds her arms across her chest.

"You know, the long blonde hair, makeup, clothes."

"You're a real jerk, Darren." Brit thrusts an angry hand onto her hip and storms into the house in a plume of perfume.

Joe scowls at me. "Dude, why would you say something like that?"

"*What?*" I lift a shoulder. "It was just an observation."

"You compared my bride-to-be to a plastic doll. What woman wants to be called plastic, you moron?"

My cheeks redden. Maybe he has a point.

Joe wraps his arms across his body. "Considering what your girlfriend looks like, I hardly think you should be throwing stones," he mumbles, not quite under his breath.

Considering what you did, you shouldn't be talking at all, I almost say. He's lucky I don't clock him in the face right now and break his jaw.

While Brit has disappeared into the massive house, Lisa and Brenda are still standing at the door, mouths agape, watching our heated interaction. I can't very well say something — *do* something — now, not with an audience. I missed my opportunity. Again. But surely there will be others.

I'm just not sure how much longer I can wait.

CHAPTER 8

Brenda

"Do you think I look like . . . like *plastic?*" Brit pulls her face out of her hands, mascara streaking down like lightning bolts from her eyes. She's so striking; the heavy lines feel intentional.

"Of course, you don't look like plastic," Lisa soothes, rubbing the back of Brit's head. "Darren is a big jerk."

Darren may very well be a big jerk. I don't know him at all. Still, I can't help but note, "He didn't sound like he was trying to be mean. Maybe he meant it as a compliment." My voice lilts, and the observation becomes more of a question than a statement. "I mean, he definitely seemed surprised that you were upset."

It's immediately apparent that Brit and Lisa won't entertain the possibility of Darren having anything other than cruel intentions. They both stare at me in utter disbelief. "What?" I throw up my hands as if readying myself to ward off an attack. "Barbie is like a multi-billion-dollar industry. She's had every job under the sun. She lives in a dream house. And she even has her own movie with Margot Robbie starring as her alongside Ryan Gosling as Ken!"

"Seriously, Brenda? A *compliment?*" Lisa shakes her head in disapproval, then wraps a protective arm around a shaken Brit.

The way they are carrying on, you'd think Darren killed Brit's dog. *Goodness.*

The best friend duo walks away, leaving me standing alone in the foyer with my thoughts. For the fortieth time today, I ask myself why I came on this trip. And for the fortieth time today, I remind myself, *you just* had *to come on this trip.*

I jump at the sound of the front door swinging open. Joe and Darren walk casually through the frame.

"Oh, hey Bianca," Joe says, as if surprised to see me. It's a reaction I am rapidly becoming accustomed to on this trip. It wasn't hard to miss the disconcerted look on Lisa's face when Brit reintroduced us at the bar — yes, *re*introduced. The girl has met me at least a half dozen times. Thinking Brit had a stalker, I almost called security on her when she kept showing up at our office, only to find out that they were actually best friends.

I don't see it, to be honest.

"Where are Brit and Lisa?" Joe asks with an irritated expression on his face.

"I'm . . . I'm not sure." I shuffle nervously from foot to foot, feeling claustrophobic under the weight of Joe's glower. My insides twist and turn as if I'm being wrung out. In a weird nonsensical way, it's *kind* of my fault that Brit and Lisa stormed off. I was just trying to help. That backfired spectacularly. "Brit's pretty upset," I admit.

"And it's Brenda, by the way," I add, almost as an afterthought. It may as well be because that's how Joe treats it.

Ignoring my correction, Joe glares at Darren. "Dude," he barks. "You need to go apologize to my fiancé."

How about apologizing to me for butchering my name?

I'm not sure why Darren puts up with Joe. He seems like an asshole, if I'm being honest. Not that I'd dream of sharing my opinion with Brit. Certainly not after *that* reaction.

It would appear, though, that Darren isn't sure why he puts up with Joe either. I catch him rolling his eyes. A muscle in his jaw tenses before he gives in to Joe's demand.

"Okay, okay. I'll apologize."

For the record, I still don't think he did anything wrong.

"Tell her about the luggage, too."

"What about the luggage?" I ask Joe as Darren disappears into the living room. "Did you find it?"

"No, but Darren remembers seeing it. Guy needs to stop smoking so much." Joe shakes his head in displeasure, but I don't miss the smirk playing on his lips.

Tell me you're lying without telling me you're lying, I think. "But . . . I was with Darren the whole time. The luggage *wasn't* there, Joe. I'm sure of it."

"Maybe *you* need to stop smoking so much," Joe says with a laugh, but his eyes are hard. I glance down at Joe's hands, curled into fists at his sides. "Think about it. Do you remember seeing the luggage now, *Bianca?*" Despite the inflection in his voice, it's not a question.

My name's not fucking Bianca! I want to scream at the top of my lungs. This guy is actually driving me crazy.

But something tells me I should tread lightly. Perhaps it's the fact that the veins in his arms are bulging. Or maybe the way his lips are pressed firmly together in a thin, angry line.

"Right," I say, ironing my shirt, wishing I could smooth out the uneasiness in my voice. There is something decidedly unnerving about this guy. "The luggage was outside all along. And it's Brenda."

Joe's face relaxes with disturbing ease as if slipping on a mask.

"Now that we're on the same page, *Brenda* . . ."

I don't want to be in the same room with this guy, let alone on the same page, but I'm not about to say that out loud. The hair on my neck bristles; the dark look in his eyes has me chilled to the core. Despite the gold-flecked amber circling Joe's pupils, they're almost black.

Thankfully, the moment of panic dissipates as Joe spins on his heels to console his precious Britter-Bug. I exhale a sigh of relief. Note to self: stay out of the groom's way for the rest of the trip.

Which will be ending right about *now.*

I pull my phone from my pocket. This was a huge mistake. I shouldn't have come here. I shouldn't have agreed to this. I want to go home. And I can; I *can* go home. I'm an adult, goddamnit. I'll call an Uber to get me the hell out of here, and then I'll switch my flight. Heck, I'll sleep at the freaking airport for the next forty-eight hours if I have to.

I don't even *like* my job all that much.

I'll worry about the fallout later.

Except . . .

I can't do any of the above.

Not without service on my phone.

CHAPTER 9

Brit

Our rental is an icebox, and my luggage is missing.

Could things suck any more right now?

Apparently, they could and would. One look at Joe's frazzled expression is all the confirmation needed.

"Darling? What's wrong?"

"Oh, it's nothing," Joe says, with a broad smile that is so obviously fake.

I regard him skeptically, because . . . oh . . . it's *something*. He's lying. I have a knack for reading people. A sixth sense that tells me when something isn't right. And the fact that Joe's shoulders are almost to his ears tells me something is wrong. Either that, or he's got a major kink in his neck from the flight. But we had full-size pillows on our private jet, so . . .

"Are you sure?" I bring a hand to Joe's cheek, tilting his chin down so his eyes align with mine. It's much harder to lie while looking someone in the eyes, though by no means impossible. "You know you can tell me *anything*, right?"

Joe runs a hand across his chin, where a sexy five o'clock shadow is starting to form. It almost makes me want to end our party (which isn't feeling very much like a party) early tonight and head to our room.

To *not* worry about what has him perturbed.

But I *am* worried.

"The caterers were supposed to arrive thirty minutes ago," Joe admits. He shakes his head, displeasure dripping from his skin like sweat. Joe doesn't take well to tardiness. When you run a business where seconds mean the difference between astronomical gains or losses, there's no room for dragging your feet.

I've often wondered how he does it — managing other people's money with such composure. Apparently, the same can't be said for food, though. Joe doesn't look all that composed right now. Despite the icicles hanging from the Crown molding, he's sweating like he's spiked a fever.

Good thing he's not a caterer.

I place a soothing hand on Joe's chest. "Maybe they hit some traffic, darling."

Joe raises a dark eyebrow, incredulous. "*Traffic?*"

He's right, of course. There's a better chance of us winning the lottery than the caterers hitting traffic. We are in the middle of freaking nowhere. A shiver slithers down my spine like a snake. What if something happens here? The nearest house is miles away. What if there's an emergency? An accident?

Would anyone hear us scream?

I wrap my arms around myself, simultaneously feeling isolated and exposed.

"Maybe they got the time wrong." I lift a shoulder, grasping at whatever straws I can grab hold of, desperate for a reasonable explanation.

"You're probably right."

I beam, "Why don't you shoot them a text and find out their ETA? With all this alcohol . . ." It will get ugly fast with nothing to soak it up. There's already an underlying current running through the house that I can't quite put my finger on. Hunger certainly won't help the situation.

"What would I do without you, Britter-Bug? You're like the yin to my yang. The up to my down. The moon to my sun. The—"

"Okay, okay," I laugh, delighted to find I've successfully talked Joe off the ledge. "Go ahead. Text them."

Joe scrolls through his contacts list, locating the caterer's number. He types up a text and hits send.

Within seconds, his phone beeps.

"See," I say, relieved they've written him back so fast. All that worrying for nothing. Except, Joe doesn't look relieved at all. He looks the *opposite* of relieved. His face is pinched as if he's just received terrible news or sucked on a lemon. So, by process of elimination, since we don't have any food . . .

Realization sets in heavy, like rocks sitting in my gut. "The caterers aren't coming, are they?"

"I have no idea if they're coming," Joe says, pacing around me frantically like a shark circling its prey.

My face scrunches in confusion. "What do you mean?"

Joe stops pacing momentarily and flips his phone so I can see the screen for myself. My stomach sinks. The text didn't go through.

Because Joe has no service.

Okay, it's not the end of the world. I draw a deep breath. *This doesn't mean anything*, I tell myself with little conviction. "Come on," I say, leading my fiancé by the arm to the wet bar, where I left my purse — a Chanel crossbody that Joe surprised me with for our one-month anniversary.

Maybe I'm just being paranoid. Although I'm not imagining the fact that my luggage has mysteriously gone missing . . .

"Here," I pull out my phone and hand it to Joe. "Try my phone."

Joe turns my phone over in his hand, examining it like a bomb he's been asked to diffuse. His fingers tremble. A rush of cold air shoots out of a vent. I wouldn't have thought it possible, but it has gotten even colder inside. It's so frigid that we could safely store raw meat in the open. If, of course, we had any raw meat to store.

Joe's gaze meets mine as he hands back the phone. I glance down, panic rising in my gut, and a shudder runs through me that has nothing to do with the air.

No service.

From: lisamreynard@reynardaccounting.com
To: rodriguezcatering@outlook.com
Subject: Catering order — Briggs

This email is to notify you that we need to cancel the Briggs catering order effective immediately due to unforeseen circumstances.

Thank you for your understanding,

Lisa Reynard

CHAPTER 10

Then

I can't remember the last time I ate. My stomach is twisting and turning, writhing in protest, begging for something, anything, to make the gnawing pain stop.

"Wake up," Ginger shouts from the top of the stairs. I'd roll my eyes if I had the energy — as if I could possibly sleep when my insides are eating themselves. Did you know that sea squirts eat their own brains? Neither did I until Ginger told me. She said not to worry about it since I don't have any brains to eat. Surprisingly, it's not the meanest thing she's ever said to me.

I bet Ginger doesn't skip any meals. She's a dead ringer for Shamu and dresses the part of a whale woman to a tee. Her wardrobe consists of brightly colored mumus, each more shapeless than the last. The obnoxious patterns — peacock feathers, swan necks, oversized four-leaf clovers — make me dizzy and nauseous. Four-leaf clovers? There ain't nothing lucky about those dresses. At least, not for us.

Ginger's eyebrows are too thin and oddly lined, giving her a permanent angry expression, even when smiling. Not that she smiles often. Despite her thin lips, Ginger always wears the brightest red lipstick, making it look like she's smeared blood on the lower half of her face. Maybe she has. Someone should tell her that Red 40 causes cancer in lab rats and is already banned in a handful of countries. It won't be me. I'm anxiously waiting for those supposed effects to kick in, however long that takes.

I don't have much else to do down here other than wait.

Ginger and her husband Walter, who looks exactly as one would expect Shamu's husband to look, with a bald head and slick skin, are the smartest dumb people I've ever met. They've obviously done their research. The human body can survive three to five days without water and about a week without food. I learned that fact in elementary school. Ginger and Walter don't want us to die since we're their proverbial meal ticket. I'm pretty sure neither of them work. I've overheard snippets of conversation about the money the state pays them for every foster child they take in.

And clearly, Ginger likes to eat. I mean, she *really* likes to eat. They should be thanking me for their lobster dinners, as opposed to locking me in their dingy basement.

"Are you going to answer her?" a shaky voice on the floor next to me squeaks.

"Nah," I say, unmoving. "She'll drag her fat ass down here if it's important enough." I press my head into my makeshift pillow, a yellowed towel that's been down here for as long as time. I think it might be a relic from the Ice Age. Shamu doesn't do our laundry very often. Or ever.

"Well, what if it's food?" Her stomach lets out a long, painful growl as if to emphasize.

Damn it. She has a point; always the voice of reason.

The only time Shamu comes to the top of the stairs is when there are some leftovers for us to eat or the agency is coming by. On those days, Ginger and Walter are the absolute picture of perfect foster parents. On those rare days, they rub our heads and do all the things I imagine loving parents do. I can't understand how social services don't see through them. I guess Ginger and Walter deserve Oscars for their performances, along with a warm seat by the bonfire in the pits of hell.

"Coming," I manage, rising shakily to my feet. My legs are like Jell-O, weak from malnutrition and lack of movement. There's only so much exercise you can get when trapped in a twelve-by-twelve concrete basement with no shoes. I have become quite adept at pacing, though. I barely feel the bruises on the balls of my feet anymore.

Still, it's not easy to walk up the stairs. It feels like I'm walking a plank or getting ready to face a firing squad, which I suppose I am. With Ginger and Walter, you never know what you'll get. I take a deep breath and grip the handrail. The splinters of splitting wood cut into my fingers and the palm of my right hand. It momentarily dulls the ache in my stomach.

Disappointment floods me, though, as I reach the top of the stairs. Ginger's hands are empty — no food — not even a slice of stale bread for us to share.

And she's not alone. There's a young girl around my age with her — maybe twelve, thirteen? The girl smiles widely, displaying a crooked-toothed grin. I feel an actual stab of remorse for her. It's a physical pain that goes beyond my hunger.

Because I can guarantee you, she won't be smiling for long.

CHAPTER 11

Lisa

I am so *not* happy right now, and I have many regrets. Not least of which, I should have packed an extinguisher because — in addition to planning all of the activities for this weekend — my other job is, evidently, putting out fires. First, the missing luggage. Then, Darren's insult brought Brit to tears.

Now, *this*.

I watch as they all, one by one, check their phones. I don't need to check my phone. I already know there's no service. The reception here is pathetic — we couldn't even combine ours into one single bar. I've heard of spotty reception but come on!

Why would anyone build a house like this in a place with no Wi-Fi? In this day and age, *every* rental has Wi-Fi. Every rental except ours, apparently.

Adding insult to injury, the caterers are not coming. So, in addition to not having cell service or Wi-Fi, we also have no food. And accordingly, there is no way of contacting a car to take us out to eat or a delivery service to bring us food.

Not quite what I had planned.

I know what it's like to be hungry. This was so *not* on the agenda for this weekend. I exhale a heavy breath. I've trained myself not to dwell on those days, but every now and again, the past reminds me of where we've been and what we've been through.

One word: *Hell.*

"Is there a landline?" I ask Joe. Surely, there must be a landline somewhere in this mammoth house. There are at least twenty rooms that I've seen so far.

Joe shoots me a pointed glare as if I'm the cause of everything that's gone wrong today — like I somehow have control over the weather, cell service, and the caterers *he* insisted on hiring. Okay, maybe I have a *little* control. I am the one who suggested this trip and took responsibility for our activities. But I did it for Brit. I didn't want her to worry about her fiancé cheating on her at his bachelor party. She was incredibly rattled by Brenda and Nick's sudden breakup, and I suspect cheating was at the root of it. I didn't want anything or *anyone* to threaten her wedding, to jeopardize Brit's happiness. Of course, that was before I realized I don't very much like her husband-to-be. But I still want the best for her.

"How would I know?" Joe barks. As I was saying about *not* very much liking her husband-to-be.

"What are we going to do?" Brit cries into Joe's shoulder.

"Joe and Darren could try to walk into town?" I suggest. "Maybe someone has a working landline. Or cell service."

"And *where* exactly would that *town* be, Lisa? We're in no man's land. It took us forty minutes to get here from the airport, and I don't recall seeing another house for miles." Joe clenches his teeth, and a muscle in his jaw twitches.

"Besides," Darren adds a little more gently "The sun is setting. We can't exactly go out exploring in the dark. Not if we want to make it back here alive."

The thought of anyone *not* making it back alive fills me with cold dread. Death is not on the agenda for the weekend either.

Think, Lisa, think.

Lucky for our guests, in addition to being a phenomenal planner, I'm also a certified problem solver. Give me numbers, and I'll give you solutions. It's what makes me such a great accountant. No, I'm not in the glamorous field of advertising like my best friend, but it's people like me who shield their best friends from the wrath of the IRS.

"The fridge," I shout excitedly, smoothly slipping into problem-solving mode. "We're the *second* guests here. Maybe the first left some food behind." *Hopefully, the cleaning service didn't clean out the fridge*, I think, but I don't say.

"I can look," Brenda offers.

I nod in agreement. It's the least Brenda can do considering what she did — took Darren's side over Brit's. If I know my best friend (which I do, better than anyone, even — *especially* — her fiancé), Brenda will regret that decision. And you won't hear me complaining about Brenda taking an earlier flight home.

Not that anyone is going anywhere. Not now. Not tonight, when the sun has nearly dipped fully in the sky.

Or maybe it's the cloud cover that's sending out vibes of the end of days.

Either way . . . tomorrow. We will get out *tomorrow*. We just need to get through the night.

We've survived worse.

"Food!" Brenda screams from the kitchen, popping my thoughts of survival like a pin in a balloon. "I found food!"

"Yes!" Darren practically jumps for joy, as if he's stumbled upon an oasis in a desert. He sprints to the kitchen with Joe hot on his tail. If the way to a man's heart truly is through his stomach, Brenda just earned some major brownie points.

Because *she* found food. Even though it had been my idea to look for food in the first place. But hey, what do I know? Next, they'll all be lifting Brenda on their shoulders and praising her for her phenomenal foraging skills. *Jeez.*

"Come on, Lisa." Brit pulls me by the wrist, dragging me toward the kitchen. "Did you hear the good news? Brenda found food!"

My jaw tightens as I reluctantly follow Brit through the living room to the kitchen. Brit is humming to herself, and I can hear the enthusiastic chatter wafting from the kitchen. The way everyone is carrying on, you'd think Brenda discovered gold, not just sliced bread.

What about everything *else?* I don't recall seeing Brenda blowing up thirty-six party balloons for the bride and groom-to-be, planning all the party games, or comforting the bride in her time of need.

That's what maids of honor are for.

I feel my blood starting to boil. I need to calm down. This trip has me on edge. A little booze, some food, some party games, and the mood will lighten considerably. Everything will be okay.

It damn well better be.

Like the rest of the house, the kitchen is stark white, broken up only by the high-end stainless-steel appliances. And the *very* happy men enjoying a hearty snack on the island. I eye the spread, gobsmacked. When I suggested the former guests might have left *something* behind, I thought *maybe* a few slices of ham or a half-eaten jar of peanut butter. But *this?* It's like someone catered an actual buffet.

I'm not complaining that we won't starve to death. But, "Where did all this food come from?"

"Damned if I know," Joe says through a mouthful of food.

"Well, *you* made the reservation. Did it say anything about a stocked fridge?" I'm trying to be cordial, but this guy is *really* starting to piss me off. I'm no longer sure what Brit sees in him. He's kind of a big, chiseled jerk.

"No, but it didn't say anything about a frigid maid of honor either," Darren mutters.

And so is his best man. Figures.

My cheeks flush scarlet, not that anyone notices. They are too busy eating. Even Brit and Brenda are digging in ravenously like they're fresh off a juice cleanse.

"Come on," Brit cajoles, nudging a tray of food toward me.

"I have an idea," I say after begrudgingly shoving a slice of cheese on a cracker into my mouth. "We should play one of the icebreaker games now. Get to know each other a little better."

"That's a great idea, Lisa!"

I smile widely at Brit. It's nice to see my efforts appreciated. The truth is, I would do anything for that girl.

I already have.

CHAPTER 12

Darren

Despite the rocky start to the trip, the day has gotten exponentially better with Brenda's discovery of the feast in the refrigerator. I wonder if Joe rented the house with a fully stocked fridge without even realizing it. My best friend has never been shy about throwing money around. On a dare in college, he literally wiped his ass with a one-hundred-dollar bill.

We are all enjoying the food when Lisa suggests we kick things off with an icebreaker. I already know enough to know that I don't care to know Lisa any better than I already do. As for Brit, well, she's Joe's problem. One of his many problems.

Brenda, on the other hand . . .

Maybe I'm just missing Tamara. I shrug off the thought. It won't do any good to dwell too long or hard on that. I sense it will be a mind-numbingly *long* two days as it is.

Lisa hands out numbered index cards with questions printed on one side to each of us. *Laminated* numbered index cards. Talk about being persnickety. Did she even *shuffle* the deck? I swear I catch her peeking at a card before handing it to Brit. Maybe I'm paranoid. Lisa couldn't possibly be so anal as to hand-select who gets what question under the guise of it appearing random, could she? Then again, she did take the time to laminate them.

Not to mention the five hundred emails she sent. Despite her "cordial invite," I still don't know what the hell a White Lie Party is. To be honest, I'm slightly afraid to ask.

"Here's what we're going to do," Lisa says, a sly grin tugging her thin lips. "You each have a question in your hand. We'll take turns asking one person the question we're holding. It's up to you who you ask. Then, the person who got asked does the asking next. Get it?"

Oh my God, this is so lame. I suddenly find myself wanting to venture out into the unforgiving dark in search of that nonexistent town. Seriously.

"Why don't we just go around the room and introduce ourselves? Give a little fun fact?" I suggest.

Lisa's lips form a perfect scowl. "We could, Darren, but that wouldn't be nearly as much fun."

Says you. "We could take a vote," I say.

"I'm sorry," Lisa huffs with anger, crossing her arms. "I wasn't aware *you* had poured all your precious time and energy into planning this weekend's activities."

If Lisa were a cartoon character, she'd have smoke coming from her ears. Or her head would pop off and spin around like in *The Exorcist.*

"Moving on . . ." She holds her hand up like a stop sign, indicating our conversation is over. "I'll go first," she says.

Of course.

Brit's maid of honor seems to have the weekend planned down to the nanosecond. She also appears to have recovered from the potential food catastrophe with renewed gusto. I watch as her body vibrates with adrenaline.

"Without further ado . . ." Her words come hard and fast. Coupled with the wild-eyed expression on her face, Lisa looks like she's in the throes of a manic episode.

"Darren . . ."

Oh God. Do you know the feeling when you get called on in class completely unprepared? And all you can think is, *please don't call on me, please don't call on me.* Yeah, this is about ten thousand times worse. I try not to roll my eyes while Lisa reads her question aloud. "How did you and Joe meet?"

My shoulders relax slightly. It's an innocuous question, really. There's no secret there. "We met in elementary school. He threw a rock at my head during recess. It nearly blinded me. It was the beginning of our beautiful, lifelong friendship."

Joe laughs out loud. "I think you have that story mixed up, buddy. You threw the rock at me." His eyes gloss over the group as if preparing to deliver a monologue. He brings a hand dramatically to his chest. "Twelve stitches to close that bad boy up. Thank God for plastic surgeons." His gaze lands on mine, daring me to challenge.

The room grows quiet, everyone staring at me as if I've *just* thrown a rock at Joe's head right here and now. Heat crawls up the back of my neck. To know Joe is to love him and *hate* him. I know he threw the rock at my head, not vice versa. My parents probably still have the emergency room discharge papers to prove it. The only thing Joe got right was the twelve stitches. I still have the ghost of a scar above my eyebrow.

Still, I draw a deep breath. *This* isn't worth fighting over, not in front of everyone. It's his bachelor party.

Joe can have the moment.

It may be one of his last.

"Your turn, Darren." Lisa points a finger at me.

I turn over the card in my hand. "What's something no one knows about you?" My eyes dart from Joe to Brenda to Lisa before landing on Brit.

"*Me?*" Brit flips her hair over her shoulder. She does that often — at least twenty times since we've arrived. Her hair is the color and texture of spun silk, courtesy of my girlfriend. You'd think Brit would like me by mere association.

But nope.

I don't think she could like me any less. Perhaps I can find out why this weekend. But for now, "Yes, you. What's something *no one* knows about you?" I laser my eyes on Brit. She seems to cower under my stare.

Brit purses her lips as if giving my — well, Lisa's — question careful consideration. "I mean, I'm pretty much an open book, but there might be things people don't know about me. Gosh, this is such a hard question."

"Like what? *What* things do people *not* know about you?"

I try not to stare at Brit as she chews on her lower lip. She's a Victoria's Secret model hot. There's something else there too. What's her secret? *She only washes her hair once a week? She eats Rocky Road straight out of the carton? She killed a man once?*

I'm sort of dying to know.

Unfortunately, before Brit can answer, Lisa pipes in, "I know *everything* about you, Brit."

Now *this*, this grabs my attention. "Wait, you can answer for someone else?" Surely, this can't be in line with the rules of the game. Then, it is *Lisa's* game. So, the rules are: Lisa doesn't follow the rules. What is this? *Fight Club?*

I watch with keen interest as a look passes between Brit and Lisa. It's odd. Strained. Brit smiles at her best friend, but it doesn't stick. She visibly shifts in her seat, adjusting her clothing, though every stitch appears perfectly set in place.

"Hey Brit, like remember that time when we snuck out of the house and—"

Brit cuts Lisa off with a pointed glare.

And? And what?

What exactly did Lisa mean by that? Is she privy to some scandalous secret Brit doesn't want Joe or the rest of us to find out?

Maybe my best friend doesn't know his fiancée as well as he thought.

Then, I could say the same for how well his fiancée knows him.

"Come on, Brit. It seems like you've got something you're not sharing with us." I actually *need* to know what Lisa was about to say.

Brit again squirms in her seat. She narrows her eyes at Lisa, before Lisa announces, "Moving on."

I could argue the point, but I sense I'm not going to get anywhere right now with Brit's gatekeeper looking on. There's always later, I guess.

"Fine. Who's next?" I ask. According to the rules of the game, Brit should ask the next question. But since Brit technically didn't answer her question because Lisa interrupted, does that mean Lisa is the one who asks? God, this game is so stupid.

Still, it's no great surprise when Lisa's hand shoots up; ever the control freak, I'm quickly learning. "I got this one," she says, pulling a card from the deck. I watch her bypass one card in favor of another. Interesting.

"Joe," all eyes laser in on Joe, "what do you do for a living?"

"Other than taking care of my Britter-Bug?"

My throat suddenly feels dry. I cough into my arm, and take a long swig from the beer I grabbed from the bar.

Joe smiles widely at the group. "Professionally speaking, I'm in financial management — fifty clients strong. My man Darren is one of them. Always has the next great idea. I'm like the rainmaker to his umbrella. We've been working together since he invented that device that pulls the wax straight from your ears. What's that thing called again, Darren — ah yes, the Waxinator."

I cough again, louder this time; I can't stop myself. Something has lodged in my throat. Of the dozen gadgets I've invented that have gone to market, Joe just had to tell them about the Waxinator.

He couldn't have picked the jewelry cleaner that works on every single type of metal? Or the hot-to-cold gadget used in physical therapy offices around the world? I mean, seriously. I physically feel them all staring at my ears as if I invented the Waxinator just for my personal use.

Earwax is *every* person's problem; I want to scream. Though I did make a shit ton of money off of that invention. Money which Joe then invested and quadrupled for me, but still.

"Oh my God!" Brenda squeals. "You were on *Shark Tank*, weren't you? The hosts all doubled over when you did that Arnold Schwarzenegger *Terminator* impersonation. Ooh, can you do it for us now? Please, please, please!" An excited Brenda claps her hands together.

No, I cannot *do it for you now!* I try to appear unbothered, but my face is frozen in mortification. Not quite the fame I was chasing. I wish the floor would open up and swallow me whole.

"You all right, Bud?"

Damn, I think, as it dawns that I'm still here.

"I'm good," I lie. "I must have got a peanut or something stuck in my throat." That, and I would like to move the conversation as far away from wayward rocks and sticky earwax as possible. I'm not thrilled with the direction this icebreaker game has taken. "Your turn, Joe. What's your question?"

Joe flips the card in his hand, pausing dramatically before he asks his question. "Lisa, where was your last vacation before this one?"

"Aruba," she answers without skipping a beat.

"Wait, *what?*" At once, all eyes in the room land on Brit. "You said you went to the Bahamas," she interjects, her forehead wrinkling in confusion.

"No, I didn't." Lisa crinkles her eyes and shakes her head. "You must have heard me wrong, Brit."

Brit folds her arms across her chest. "No, I did *not* hear you wrong, Lisa. I literally asked outside if you went to Aruba, and you said you went to the Bahamas." Brit points an accusing finger at her.

"That's an odd thing to lie about." Brenda's eyes widen as she says this, and she clasps her hand over her mouth just as soon as the words have fallen out.

Lisa clenches her jaw, along with the stack of cards in her hand. Without flipping one over, she replies, "Must have been a misunderstanding. What about you, Brenda? Brit mentioned you've had some unfortunate luck in the love department lately. We're all friends here, right? How about you share with all of us why your engagement ended so abruptly?"

Well, that was unexpected. My jaw drops. I've never seen someone go from congenial to aggressive with such alarming speed.

Brenda's face grows red. I can almost feel the heat radiating off her from across the island.

But before Brenda can even open her mouth to respond or to defend herself against what sounds like an accusation, a loud vibrating noise booms from outside, where the doors to the veranda are still wide open. I imagine the warm breeze gently tickling our skin and this Caribbean wedding-moon would be lovely if the apocalypse weren't taking shape outside.

"What is *that?*" Lisa asks, a look of panic passing over her face like the dark storm clouds rolling outside.

"It's a weather siren," I respond. I'm quite familiar with the warning alarm, having spent a few months traveling through Thailand soon after my evidently infamous appearance on *Shark Tank*. That's where I met Tamara. We were staying at the same hostel and connected immediately. I can't help but wish at this moment that I had heeded her warning and stayed home. This trip has been nothing but painful so far, and that was before the weather siren sounded.

"Why would there be a weather siren going off?" Brit asks, interrupting my thoughts like a scratch on a DVD.

Hmm, why would *there be a weather siren?* To announce an island-wide bonfire on the beach? Because the circus is coming to town? *Really?* For a girl who runs a successful advertising agency, Brit is not too quick on the uptake. "There must be a storm blowing through. I'm sure it's fine."

The truth is I'm *not* sure that it's fine. We all knew coming into this that there was a chance the hurricane could make landfall. That siren wouldn't be bellowing if it hadn't.

And the trees outside wouldn't be bending as if about to break.

CHAPTER 13

Brenda

I am trying hard not to think about the fact that we are *trapped* inside this house. Okay, so we aren't literally trapped. Like, I could walk outside if I wanted to, but such an endeavor would be ill-advised, to say the least.

So yeah, *trapped.*

I try to convince myself it isn't so bad. We have alcohol, food, and a fireplace (thank goodness, because the air conditioner is on steroids). And while the company could be better, I suppose it could also be worse.

My best friend reminds me of that daily: it could always be *worse.* Spoiler alert: none of these people here are my best friends, nor do I expect them ever to be. Brit is all right, I suppose. Fine as bosses go. But Brit's husband-to-be? Her best friend? They say you are the company you keep. I'm not sure what to make of that.

"I'm going to look for supplies," Darren announces. "In case we lose power."

"You think we might lose power?" Brit cries out as if she's just suddenly taken heed of the ominous turn the weather has taken. Joe instinctively pulls her into him, petting her long blonde hair like she's his lap dog. It's surprising to see Brit so dependent on her fiancé for reassurance. She certainly doesn't act like this in the office, that's for sure.

Maybe *this* Brit is an act.

It could very well be an act.

"We'll be fine, darling. It's just a little storm."

I eye Joe curiously. Weather sirens don't sound for little storms. They sound for big storms. They sound for hurricanes. And the fact that it's *still* sounding doesn't bode well for us, or our prospects for a nice vacation weekend.

The room momentarily spins. It feels like I'm starring in a B-grade horror movie. Despite the living room's generous square footage, it's claustrophobic, like the walls are closing in. I need to get out of here. "I'll help you look, Darren."

Within minutes, the sirens are barely audible over the angry howl of the wind. It's as if someone has flicked a switch outside from tropical to apocalyptic.

Speaking of switches, the lights flicker, an ominous dance of *will they, won't they*, before stilling. I exhale a strangled breath. It's as if this island has wrapped itself around my neck.

The lights are still on, for now. But for how long will we have power? What happens if the lights go out?

I follow Darren into the kitchen, sticking as close to him as humanly possible, listening carefully as he rattles off directions.

"Look for batteries, candles, matches . . . anything to sustain us when the lights give out."

"*When?*" I arch a concerned eyebrow.

Maybe we'll get lucky? Perhaps there's a generator?

"Not a chance in the world the power is staying on."

As if to confirm, a large branch scrapes against the glass skylight, causing us both to jump. One of the windows beside us shakes but miraculously remains intact. I look around, my heart beating in my fingers. Pulsing. Throbbing. There are an obscene number of windows in the house. And trees outside. There are so many fucking trees.

Following Darren's lead, I quickly begin opening and closing drawers. There's an unspoken sense of urgency between us, knowing the power could give out at any moment. It's bad enough being stuck with these people *with* electricity; without it, it's downright terrifying.

"Jackpot!" Darren shouts, pulling a bag of flashlights and batteries from a drawer. He slides one out of the bag and hands it to me. "You're gonna need this." A loud clap of thunder echoes through his words, punctuating the statement. "Sooner rather than later," he finishes.

"Should we see if we can find anything else?"

"Good idea," Darren says, flashing a lopsided grin. He really is handsome. Too bad I've all but given up on men. And besides, I would *never* go after *another* woman's man. At least, I don't think I would ever go after another woman's man.

Something — *everything* — about this weekend has me doubting what I know. And it's only the first night. Not even twelve hours since we arrived.

I feel Darren's eyes on me as I play an intense game of mental gymnastics. My gaze shoots up, meeting his.

"It's getting worse out fast," he warns. "Come on. Let's keep looking."

Right. "There are a few closets over there." I point toward a mudroom and laundry area off the kitchen.

Footfall follows as we hurry toward the adjacent rooms, anxious to find whatever we can before we are plunged into darkness. I swing open a door with the word *pantry* scrawled across the glass in fancy script while Darren advances farther into the mudroom. Inside the pantry, I locate some bags of chips and a case of water sitting unopened on the floor. It's nothing compared to the feast de resistance in the refrigerator, but it would do nicely if munchies were to strike. And if we lose power — *when* we lose power — the fridge will no longer work, so that food will be the first thing to go.

I also find a board game on the top shelf.

The game feels like a bonus. We are going to need *something* to do if there's no electricity. I'd rather Lisa *not* choose our activities. Although, admittedly, I am curious about the White Lie Party she mentioned in some of her five hundred emails. If it's anything like that icebreaker game, though, I may have to fake a migraine.

I'm busy gathering as much as I can carry when I hear Darren calling my name. His voice is shaky, laced with panic.

"I found some chips and water," I announce, emerging from the pantry, proudly displaying the goods. "And a game—" I add before stopping dead in my tracks when I see him, the look on his face.

The water bottles slip from my hands. The caps fly off as they explode, soaking the tiled floor. It looks — *feels* — as if the storm has found its way inside the house. Though one might argue, it's been here all along. I can't quite wrap my head around it. It's just this feeling.

"What's wrong?" I ask, my forehead furrowing in concern.

"*This* door." Darren points to a door adjacent to the mudroom. He shakes his head, staring at the door. I follow his eyes, but all I see is a white door, like the other two dozen white doors in this house.

I raise an eyebrow, waiting to discover what's so special about *this* particular door.

"It's locked."

"*Locked?*" I repeat the word back to him as if that might somehow give me insight into why I should care.

He nods.

It doesn't sound like that big a deal. I nonetheless twist the knob, trying the door for myself. I'm not taking Darren's word for it. It strikes me that I hardly know him, *any* of them, for that matter. Darren seems like a nice guy, but so did Jeffrey Dahmer, and we all know how that one ended.

But Darren is obviously *not* Jeffrey Dahmer, and in his defense, the door is most definitely locked.

Still. "Don't rentals usually have a locked room where the owners keep their private stuff?" I ask, seeing no reason to make a mountain out of a molehill.

Darren, on the other hand, looks about ready to run from the house, screaming bloody murder. A lot of good that would do him.

"Yeah, but . . ." his words trail off.

"But *what?*" I can't hide the slight irritation in my voice. I also can't believe we are on the cusp of losing power and standing here debating the appropriateness of a locked door at a rental house.

"Well, I did some research before the trip. What can I say? I'm a bit of a nerd."

I stifle a giggle, feeling my cheeks grow hot. I would *not* call Darren *any* bit of a nerd. His biceps are freaking *huge. Locked and loaded*, my best friend would say, *should a gun show break out.* Something about the thought of a gun gives me pause. Maybe there's a gun hidden behind the locked door.

"Anyway," he continues. "This place was built solely for rental purposes. It's registered to an LLC."

"I'm sorry, meaning what?"

"Meaning it's owned by a company that does rentals. No one lives here, you know, like in the off-season. So, it's not like the owners are leaving *their* stuff here. So, why lock the door?"

Now, the locked door seems a teeny bit suspicious. But really, what could the rental company have locked in there? *A jet ski? Extra towels and linens? A dead body?*

Goosebumps jump down my flesh. And then an idea pops into my head, "If it's a rental property and Joe is the renter . . ."

Darren completes the thought. "He should have the key."

CHAPTER 14

Then

Ginger must be in an abnormally good mood. I can smell it in the air before she even unlocks the door. Tonight, she feeds us dinner. It's not just a pile of leftover mush. It's *real* food. I make out an actual piece of chicken, and I swear I could cry. I probably would, too, if I weren't so damn dehydrated.

Besides, I have to stay strong for her. And for the new girl. There are three of us now. Ginger must be getting paid a fortune to take care of us. She certainly eats like it. Her latest purchase — a mumu with elephant tusks — is starting to cinch around the waist.

"How long have you been here?" the new girl asks as she forks what resembles a carrot into her mouth. I want to tell her to pace herself. Who knows when we'll eat again? If I had to venture a guess . . . not for another six days. But I don't want to scare her, not while she's enjoying the only meal she'll be seeing for a while.

"Eight months, give or take," I tell her. I gesture toward our other roommate. "About six."

"How are they?" she asks, licking gravy off her lower lip. We've never had gravy. Not even on Thanksgiving. Not that I'd know Thanksgiving from Easter from Christmas down here. Every day is just another day, more of the same.

I gather by *they*, she means Ginger and Walter. Our accommodation speaks volumes, but maybe I've just been hardened by the cold concrete floor beneath me.

Day by day, slowly stripped of all hope.

Nope, it's pretty damn obvious. "Look around," I tell her, fighting the urge to roll my eyes at the obviousness of our dire situation.

The girl does what I say. Her eyes slowly move around the space. She takes in the unfinished basement with its uneven floors. The old, dirty towels that were converted into makeshift pillows and beds on the floor. She looks up at the exposed pipes overhead, dripping rusty liquid drops like bloody tears.

Then it hits her. I could pinpoint the exact moment recognition sets in, right before she jumps to her feet. Her eyes go wide, her mouth lax. Despite the shock on her face, there's a determination in her posture that wasn't there a moment ago. She's made up her mind; she's going to try to leave. I don't have the heart to tell her that the only way she's getting out of here is in a body bag.

She's not going anywhere.

The basement door is locked.

In the first few months here, I did the same thing: I tried to open the basement door. I banged and screamed until my fists were bloody and my lungs were raw.

Every. Single. Night.

Finally, I gave up. She will too.

But for now, I watch silently as she runs up the stairs. She wraps a hand around the knob, twisting gently at first. Then, when the door doesn't open, she begins turning the thing back and forth frantically. I know what's coming next before she does: bare fists pounding against wood.

"Don't bother," I tell her, pushing against a nail sticking out of the floor. "There's no way out. They won't come. They don't care."

Not only that, but I have a sinking suspicion that the room above us is soundproofed. We can hear them, but they can't hear us. Or more likely, they just ignore us.

After banging frantically for a few more moments, the girl recoils in horror. Her legs appear to give out, and she sinks down to the top stair, burying her head in her lap. Big fat tears fall from her doll-like eyes.

"Come back down," I tell her. "It'll be okay."

I don't mean it.

CHAPTER 15

Brit

Things are not okay.

I'm still crashing out over the luggage. I had the absolute cutest outfits planned out for the weekend, not to mention the drugstore of skincare products and makeup I packed. The minuscule amount of money we'll recoup from our travel insurance won't touch that. Not that money is an issue, but it's going to be a royal pain in the ass to replace everything. Things are just not going as expected.

For the first time, I wonder if this is an omen for the wedding.

I don't have any reservations about how quickly things have moved between Joe and me, but I can't get the broken wine glass out of my head. Or that damn Uber driver, the missing luggage, and the storm.

It feels like the universe is trying to tell me something.

Personal. It feels *personal.*

In addition to partying the night away with friends, I was hoping to get the perfect picture for Bright Horizon's website this weekend. Perhaps out on the veranda or in the infinity pool with the sun beaming down and amplifying all the brilliant hues of this tropical paradise. Except, it's so incredibly dark and stormy out I can no longer *see* the veranda or the infinity pool, let alone pose by it. For all I know, the veranda is now fully submerged in the infinity pool.

Speaking of which, I turn to my fiancé. "Joe, darling. Do you think we should board up the doors or something?" Or maybe even just *close* them? The veranda doors are still wide open, the glass rattling against itself with every gust of wind. Water has sprayed across the living room floor, creating a shiny, slick surface. If the storm gets any stronger, which I strongly suspect it will, the white couches will soon be covered in a salty mixture of water and muddy debris. Then there won't be anywhere for me to take a decent picture.

Pictures probably shouldn't be my top concern, but I've worked my ass off to build up my business, and I need to capitalize on every opportunity that presents itself. This scene would make for a highly effective advertising campaign for travelers' insurance. Too bad none of my clients are insurance providers. At least, not yet. Maybe after this trip.

We just have to weather the storm and make it through this trip.

Joe nods in agreement, then quickly springs into action. I watch with bated breath as he fights against the wind, pushing his way out onto the veranda. At one point, there's a gust so strong that I squeeze my eyes shut, worried it has carried my fiancé away with it. But thanks to all the hours he logs in the gym and his resulting upper body strength, Joe manages to cling to the flailing door. When the wind momentarily abates, he pulls the door closed. Only after the second door is secure do I exhale deeply, feeling better.

Momentarily.

We may be shielded from the storm outside, but we still have no service. And there's no television or radio that I've seen. There is no way to monitor the storm other than by eyeballing it. And my eyeballs tell me it's getting worse by the second. We need to figure out a plan — *fast*.

I'm about to say as much when Darren and Brenda blow back in from their supply-hunting mission, looking flushed and slightly disheveled.

As I was saying about Darren . . .

Joe seems unfazed by their frazzled state and what might have led to it. Then, Joe doesn't worry about much. Except for food, apparently. He was *very* worried about the food. Still, I don't know how he's keeping so calm in the face of this hurricane. We can barely hear one another over the howl of the wind and the crack of limbs raining down on us. As if I don't have enough to worry about, I'm literally worrying about Joe not worrying right now.

"Did you find anything of use?" Joe asks, his face completely relaxed, albeit wet.

"Some flashlights and batteries," Darren says. "And, and we found a locked storage room or something. Can we get the key?"

"The *key?*" Joe's forehead wrinkles in confusion. "What key? I don't have a key."

"How do you not have a key?" Darren asks, the edge to his voice razor sharp.

"Lisa," Joe shouts. "Where's the house key?"

Lisa waves a hand in his direction. "I'm right here. You don't need to yell. I left it by the front door. It was under the welcome mat, as per the villa instructions."

"See," Joe says, visibly irritated. "*I* don't have the key."

It seems like semantics, but whatever. We follow Joe through the house to the front door. He looks around — surveying the window ledges, the tiled floor, even the bottom stairs. But there's no key.

"Where did you leave it Lisa?"

"Right there on the windowsill."

Joe folds his arms across his chest. "Well, it's not there."

"Are you sure?"

"Yes, I'm sure. I'm not blind."

"Well, I don't have dementia. I know where I left it."

Joe and Lisa argue back and forth. I can't help but think Lisa misplaced it and is embarrassed to admit it to us. She's clearly exhausted from her back-to-back trips. Irritable, even.

And not having the key doesn't seem the biggest of deals. Who cares what's in the storage room? I'm more interested in what happened between Darren and Brenda, to be honest.

While Joe and Lisa continue to duke it out, I turn to Darren and Brenda. "Wait, let me get this straight. All you found the whole time you were gone was a few flashlights and batteries? You were gone for a quite a while." I let my insinuation hang midair.

"And some chips, water, and a board game," Brenda adds, motioning with her head toward the chips and game cradled in her arms.

My eyes zero in on it. A Ouija board. First, that mangled dog outside the car warning of death. Then, the shapeshifting mosquitoes. Now *this?* Seriously?

Anyway . . . their story. "Where's the water?" I ask, casting a suspicious glance in Darren and Brenda's direction.

"I, um . . ." Brenda stutters. "I dropped the bottles. They exploded everywhere."

Really? I can't help but wonder if chips and water are a euphemism for belt buckle and zipper. And if this Ouija board is a terrible idea.

I don't have long to ponder these questions or to ask them — not that I'd ever just come out and ask; I'd have Lisa do that for me.

But I can't even do that.

Because just then, the lights flicker again. Only this time, they fully go out.

From: lisanreynard@reynardaccounting.com
To: lisanreynard@reynardaccounting.com
BCC: joseph.briggs@briggsfinancial.com, brit.jones@brighthorizons.com, brenda.peterson@brighthorizons.com, darrenljost@hotmail.com
Subject: Re: Brit and Joe's White Lie Party — Countdown

Only two days to GO time!

I don't know about you, but I am super excited to celebrate these lovely people!

A few gentle reminders: please, let's try to keep this party as PG as possible. No unexpected guests. No hard drugs. No need to bring anything other than yourselves.

We've got LOTS of games!

And I promise, *yes* to lots of fun!

xx
Lisa (Maid of Honor)

CHAPTER 16

Lisa

I can't decide if I'm relieved that the lights went out so that no one can see my dumbstruck expression, or panicked because, *duh*, the lights went out. I'm not holding my breath that they'd be coming back on anytime soon considering the complete pandemonium unfolding outside.

What took Darren and Brenda so long? What *were* they doing while we waited on pins and needles?

I was too busy arguing with Joe about the key he couldn't find to hear what they had to say.

This is just great. My original plans are going to hell in a handbasket. It's as if the storm has trickled in, wreaking havoc on the house. The mood inside is just as turbulent and chaotic as outside. If not *more*.

After a few moments of beetle blackness that feel more like minutes, Darren's face lights up — *literally* — then Brenda's. I breathe a sigh of relief, taking note of the flashlights in their hands. Thank God they found flashlights. The thought of being trapped in the dark in this place with these people fills me with cold dread.

"Look what Brenda found," Darren says.

My fingers individually curl into tight fists at my side.

"Okay, someone cue the creepy music," Brenda says slowly, in a low, chilling voice. "It's a . . . Ouija board." She holds out the box so we can all see. Well, so we can all kind of see. Even with the flashlights, it's still pretty dark. "We are gonna have so much fun with this."

"I don't know . . ." Brit wraps her arms around herself. "A Ouija board in the middle of a hurricane with no power?"

"Yeah," I quickly agree, jumping to my best friend's aid. "It does seem like asking for trouble."

Brenda laughs. "It's a game, Lisa."

I spent the past month planning our games, Brenda. You haven't seen anything yet. I bite my lip to stop the words from spilling out. It's only our first night; I don't need to lay all my cards on the table just yet. Besides, maybe she's right. Perhaps this will be fun. "Okay," I relent.

We move our party to the kitchen, each settling at the circular table, which is, unsurprisingly, made from white marble. Darren positions his flashlight so it's aimed up. Our shadows dance across the ceiling above us. Brenda, meanwhile, points her flashlight at the game. Would you qualify a Ouija board as a *game?*

"Has everyone done this before?" she asks, pulling the wooden board and planchette from the box.

I nod, then gulp loudly. Brit and I experimented with a Ouija board once. I can still feel the planchette sliding beneath our fingers as it spelled out . . . *evil.* She would never admit it, but I'm sure Brit was playing a joke on me. She had to be.

I glance around the table, my gaze landing on Darren. He has an unreadable expression on his face. "I don't know if we should do this," he says, catching me off guard. If earlier was any indication, I'd think Darren would be happy to play *any* game I didn't plan. I mean, considering how argumentative he was over an icebreaker. Especially after I took the time to laminate the question cards.

"Why not?" Brenda asks as she casually places the planchette in the center of the board, as if she's not attempting to summon spirits in the midst of a blackout and hurricane. "Are you *scared?*"

Darren quickly shakes his head. "No, I'm not scared." I examine his face, the slight quiver of his lip as he says this. He sure *looks* scared.

"Great," Brenda exclaims, clapping her hands together. "Everyone put your pointer and middle fingers on the edge of the planchette and try to clear your mind."

A loud crack of thunder booms, shaking the room. *Try to clear your mind.* That should be easy. *Not!*

Still, we each do as we're told, resting our fingers on the border of the heart-shaped pointer.

"Are there any spirits here with us tonight?" Brenda asks, the room silent save for the hurricane outside and our heavy breaths.

"Please," she continues. "If you are here, reveal yourself to us."

I roll my eyes. This is so silly. Everyone knows ghosts aren't real. Except for my cab driver and Brenda, apparently.

But then the strangest thing happens; the planchette starts to move. It scrapes across the board slowly. It doesn't look like anyone is purposefully guiding it in a specific direction. My heart starts beating frantically in my chest. My eyes flit nervously around the table.

But that can't be.

My breath lodges in my throat as I watch the planchette spell out:

I-A-M-H-E-R-E.

Brenda smiles widely. "Guys, it's working."

"Are we supposed to be happy about this?" I mumble, but no one seems to be listening, just like no one listened to Darren when he voiced his reservations about playing this stupid game in the first place.

Undeterred, Brenda continues, "Do you have a message for us?"

Within seconds, the planchette is back on the move. It crawls to the upper left-hand corner:

YES.

"Cut the crap," Darren demands, his voice shaking. "Who's doing this?"

Brenda shushes him. "Don't disturb the spirit. Let it say what it wants to say."

"This is really stupid," Darren insists. "We shouldn't be doing this."

Brenda ignores him and asks her final question: "What is your message for us?"

Sweat gathers in my armpits and the small of my back as my fingers follow the letters around the board. I watch in horror as it strings together a warning.

Y-O-U-A-R-E-I-N-D-A-N-G-E-R.

CHAPTER 17

Lisa

Brenda's fingers fly off the planchette like it's given her an electric shock. Her hands shake. She looks like she's seen a ghost.

I had assumed Brenda was the one staging the messages — just like Brit did all those years ago when she spelled out *evil* — but Brenda appears genuinely surprised and sufficiently freaked out.

Now, *I'm* sufficiently freaked out as well.

We sit momentarily in stunned silence, broken by a noise from above — almost like footsteps. But that's impossible.

"Did you hear that?" I ask.

"The storm," Joe answers, rather quickly. *Too* quickly.

"It sounded like footsteps upstairs," I add, my heart thundering in my chest.

Joe rolls his eyes. "In case you haven't noticed, we're in the middle of a *hurricane*, Lisa. Get used to it — we're going to hear lots of uncomfortable noises."

He's probably right.

But still . . . "I'd feel much better if someone checked."

Joe grits his teeth. "Fine." He stands up abruptly, rattling his chair. "I'll go make sure no one trudged through the superstorm outside and snuck into the house." He mumbles to himself as he stomps away.

It does sound like a ridiculous impossibility, but you never know.

It's somewhat silent until Brit asks, "So what now, Brenda? Will your spirit tell us *how* we're in danger? What to *do* about it?"

My best friend is visibly shivering, and I don't think it's from the cold. Even her lips are trembling.

"I honestly don't know what to do with this." Brenda lifts a noncommittal shoulder, but her forehead furrows with concern. She pushes her chair back a few inches, putting some distance between her and the game. "I played this a bunch of times in high school and college, and I've never had a message like that."

We all glance at the board as if danger might jump off the wood and take us all out. The possibility of one of us *not* being responsible for this hangs in the air between us.

Joe returns from his intruder-finding mission looking even more pissed than he did before he left. "There's no one else in the house," he says definitively. "Are you *happy* now?"

I don't respond, because *no*, I am not happy.

"Could that thing be right, Joe? Do you think we're in *danger?*" Brit flicks a shaky wrist toward the Ouija board.

I hone in on Joe, trying to picture how Brit sees him — riding on a white horse as he comes to her rescue and saves the day. Maybe even shirtless with a cape. The more time I spend with him, the less real he seems to me.

I always thought Brit and I would fall in love with best friends, buy houses next door to one another, and raise our kids together. I glance at Darren — well, that's clearly not happening. So I guess what they say is true: always the bridesmaid and never the bride.

Joe still hasn't answered Brit's question. *Does* he think we're in danger? More importantly, does anyone other than Brit give a hoot about what Joe thinks? Finally, when the silence stretches so tight it feels like it might snap, Joe tells her, "The storm is bad, yes, but I think we are safe as long as we stay inside together. I'll protect you, Britter-Bug."

His lip twitches as he says this. He's obviously lying. I get the feeling it wouldn't be the first time.

Brit's face relaxes. I'm glad *she* feels better about our situation.

As for the rest of us . . .

"But what if it wasn't talking about the storm?" Brenda asks, just loud enough that we all hear her. "What if there's something *else?*"

"What else would it be talking about, *Bianca?*" Joe's face twists as he says this. We let out a collective gasp. "You want to know what I think?" He leans across the table, narrowing the space between him and Brenda. His eyes are like slits in the semi-darkness. All I can think is, *I'm so happy I'm not Brenda right now.* That, and, *for the love of God, her name is* Brenda! "I think you're messing with us. That's what I think."

Brenda pushes back even farther from the table, her chair screeching against the tiled floor like nails on a chalkboard. "*Wha . . . what?*" Her eyebrows shoot up. Her voice shakes as she asks, "Why would I mess with you?"

"I don't know, why *would* you mess with us? I'm not even sure what you're doing here." Joe slams his palms against the table, shaking the board. His Adam's apple bobs mercilessly in his throat.

Meanwhile, Brenda's face reddens. Her eyes go glassy. But this time, she doesn't respond. She shakes her head and disappears from the room as quickly as the spirit conjured by the Ouija board.

"Wow, that was a doozy," I offer, trying to ease the tension. I'm sure Brenda will be fine. Well, I'm reasonably sure. She just needs to calm down. Besides, she's not the one I'm concerned about.

Brit taps her finger rhythmically against her chin as she conjures a response. "A sockdaloger," she replies, and I feel my shoulders relax.

Game on. "A ripsnorter."

Brit smiles widely. "Killer," she adds. "A killer."

Sometimes, the simplest words pack the strongest punch. "You win, Brit. Killer."

"You two are weird," Darren observes, his gaze darting back and forth between us like we're a pair of psychopaths because of our shared affinity for synonyms.

"Lisa?" Darren picks up the flashlight and aims it at me like a spotlight. He's chewing on his lower lip as if thinking hard about something. He looks incredibly determined to shift our conversation away from synonyms. It's not the first time mine and Brit's telepathic closeness has made someone else uneasy. It won't be the last. "I don't suppose any of your party games involve glow sticks or a disco ball, do they?"

If we were playing *my* party games in the order I wanted to play them, nothing like this would have happened. I worked incredibly hard to make this weekend perfect. "Now that you mention it . . . I have half a suitcase full of glow sticks."

"There's no need for sarcasm," Darren remarks, his voice stern, lips pulled taut in a straight line. "It was a joke."

"I'm serious." *Jerk*, I almost add, stopping myself. The last thing I want to do is cause more drama and upset Brit, especially when her dream vacation is already somewhat of a nightmare. "I brought glow sticks."

"Sorry," Darren offers with an apologetic smile. I examine the shadow of his face. He does have quite a disarming smile.

"That's great, Lisa," he adds. "We should have as much light on reserve as possible."

I can't help but think the Ouija board's message may be fueling his concern. That and the loud smash of a tree limb as it swats the side of the house like a baseball bat.

My heart skips a beat. What Darren *didn't* say, but what we're surely all thinking, is 'who knows how long we will be without power.'

And without cell service.

Stranded, like sitting ducks in this house.

"If there's no power then why is it so cold in here? What's powering the air conditioner?" Brit wraps her arms around her body, shivering.

"Yeah," I agree. "That does seem to defy logic."

"Probably because of the storm," Joe conjectures. But that doesn't make sense either. We're in the tropics. Hurricane or not, it's still at least seventy-five degrees outside. My guess is it's about fifty in here. And that's a *generous* guess.

Upon mention of the storm, Darren says, "Let's go find Brenda."

Great, he sounds like he's actually *worried* about her. It feels like I've taken a kick to the gut. I'd hoped he'd forgotten about Brenda, at least for tonight. I roll my eyes, not that anyone can see them.

"How about I make us a round of shooters to warm us up, and then I'll get those glow sticks with you, Lisa?"

Now, that's more like it.

My face grows hot at the thought of being alone in my bedroom with Darren. Despite Brit's accurate assessment that I would not go home with some random guy from a bar in New York City, we're clearly *not* in New York City anymore. And Darren is not some random guy. Okay, he's a couple of degrees of separation from being some random guy, but still. It's just a weekend. It's not like I want to marry him or anything.

Watching Brit and Joe together has soured my stomach — I am *never* getting married.

"So, are we all on board? Shooters?"

I snap back to attention at the sound of Darren's voice. A shot is just the thing to soothe my nerves and quiet the thoughts thundering through my brain louder than the *actual* thunder outside.

Evidently, I'm not the only one looking for liquid courage. One by one, we all agree. Then we move from the kitchen to the wet bar in the living room.

"Hey," I hear Brenda say once we reach the bar. "Sorry I stormed out of the kitchen. I'm incredibly rattled. You were right, Darren. We shouldn't have played that game."

Darren places a hand on her shoulder, and every last muscle in my body tenses up. "Don't worry about it," he says. "I'm just glad you're okay," That makes *one* of him.

"I'm making us shots. Are you in?" he asks her as he eases behind the bar.

"I'm definitely in."

I grit my teeth. Now I'm *really* in desperate need of that shot. Thankfully, a few moments later, I hear the clink of a glass being placed on the bar in front of me.

I knew we wouldn't need swizzle sticks.

I suck down the contents, wincing at the burn. Despite the frost spreading across the windows, my body already feels warmer. I think I may only have frostbite in a few of my toes now, as opposed to all ten.

"Come on, Lisa." I feel the heat of Darren's breath in my ear. "Let's go get those glow sticks."

Maybe it's just the alcohol talking, but as Darren gently places his hand on the small of my back and guides me out of the living room toward the front stairs, I wonder if it's about to get a hell of a lot hotter in here.

My legs tingle as we ascend the long, winding staircase. It almost feels like they've been dipped in hot wax. I lean my weight against the banister, feeling a dulled sense of panic as the railing wobbles.

I suck in a sharp breath. There must be some loose screws. Or maybe I'm the one with a screw loose. No, I'm *mostly* sure it's the stairwell.

That's odd.

This whole scene feels so surreal. Out of body. I didn't drink *that* much, did I?

With my free hand, I grasp Darren's arm to hold myself upright.

All the champagne and shots on an empty stomach must be getting to me. I haven't eaten much in spite of myself. And the stress of planning this weekend, the storm, the blackout. My last trip.

That has to be it. I can't imagine what else would have me feeling like I'm balancing on stilts. I'm so woozy I don't know if I'll even make it back downstairs tonight. My eyelids suddenly feel too heavy to keep open, like lead weights on my face.

But surprisingly, *that's* not what worries me. I'm much more concerned about the direction this evening will take.

I can't help but wonder what our guests will do for entertainment without me.

CHAPTER 18

Then

I've been trying to make the best of a bad situation. I had hoped, maybe, that having a new basement-mate would make our lives a little more entertaining. Dying of boredom seems like an awful way to go.

But the new girl is quiet. I finally get what people mean when they say quiet as a mouse. They're talking about her, or people like her. We've tried to engage her in conversation, but since our predicament became clear to her, it's been like crickets down here.

Other than the crying. There's a constant stream of tears, like a river that's never seen a drought. I'm worried we might drown down here if she doesn't *stop* crying. At least she's not a dramatic sobber, though, which I strongly suspected she might be, based on the way she hooted and hollered while banging on the basement door that first night. But no. First impressions aren't always correct. The new girl is more of a silent weeper.

Silent in general. Or maybe, she doesn't want to talk to *us*.

Perhaps it's my fault. I can't help but feel guilty, like somehow I made it worse while trying to protect her from what I learned the hard way — we are prisoners here. Ginger and Walter are our wardens.

Still, I could have been gentler. She's clearly frightened, lonely, and sad — cycling through the same emotions I went through not long ago. It's like the stages of grief I experienced after my parents died before I was dropped off at this hellhole: denial, anger, bargaining, depression, and acceptance.

The new girl doesn't have a choice. She'll find acceptance eventually.

She seems to be getting there, albeit slowly. Given our shared space and subpar living conditions, it was awkward at first, but now we're kind of used to each other. We keep on keeping on, doing what we do. Surviving day by gut-wrenching day.

As expected, six long days pass before Ginger brings us more food. And it's not just food she brings, but news, too.

"Apparently," she announces from the top of the stairs with a hand on her hip, clucking her tongue, "I have to send you misfits to school, or I'm contributing to your truancy. If I find out who reported me—"

I stick a finger in my ear, trying to remove the wax. If only there were a gadget to do that for you. Wouldn't that be nice? Because right now, I can't be sure I heard her correctly. Did she say we are going to *school?* As in, we will be *leaving* the house? This *room?*

I pinch myself to see if I'm dreaming. For the first time in eight months, I'm happy to be awake.

Ginger keeps talking and talking, but I don't hear a word she says after that. Sometimes, I think she talks just so that she can hear the sound of her own voice. It's surprisingly singsongy for a witch. But her voice isn't grating on me as it usually does. I'm too lost thinking about getting out of this house, even if just for a few hours. It feels like the equivalent of freedom.

"Are you listening to me?" Ginger shouts, breaking me from my trance.

As my eyes flick up to meet hers, I see she's talking to me.

"Yes, ma'am."

"If you so much as breathe a word of this," she gestures a hand around to indicate, well, everything, "you won't live to see another day."

I swallow the lump in my throat, nodding.

"Tomorrow is your first day of school. Remember, if I get so much as a call from the school or see the flashing lights of a police car, you'll all wish you were dead."

I can't help but think we're already half dead.

She lectures us for another twenty minutes on the proper way to conduct ourselves at school, as if *she* would know anything about being proper.

"Now go to bed," she shouts, slamming the basement door behind her. Then comes the familiar click.

I have no idea what time it is, but it must be evening. The small window in the basement reveals the shadows of a setting sun.

Despite Ginger's ominous threats, for the first time in as long as I can remember, I embrace the darkness and sleep.

From: lisamreynard@reynardaccounting.com
To: sanchezsupplies@hotmail.com
Subject: Party supplies

Good afternoon,

I'd like to place an order for the following supplies, delivered to [ADDRESS REDACTED]: waters, chips, cups, flashlights, batteries, plain white t-shirts, black Sharpie marker, tissue paper, and one Ouija board.

Thank you,

Lisa Reynard

CHAPTER 19

Darren

Lisa wasn't joking. She literally brought half a suitcase full of glow sticks. I can't begin to unpack what she planned on doing with all these glow sticks for five people. *Did she invite hundreds of surprise guests and a DJ for a pop-up rave?* Considering what I've seen of Lisa thus far, I highly doubt it. Besides, given the tumultuous turn the weather has taken, the only way any other guests could arrive here would be by boat, and clearly that wouldn't be the safest endeavor. But I can only speculate on Lisa's intentions, anyway, given her current state of absurd inebriation.

"I'm a little dizzy," Lisa giggles as she attempts to rise on wobbly legs from the floor. She sways in place, nearly falling into her suitcase, which she finds incredibly amusing. Her giggles morph into belly laughs, and she clutches her side, folding in half. Whatever she drank — or *took* — she should have more of it. It's the first time I've seen her resting bitch face abate this entire trip.

When her laughing fit subsides, Lisa whispers, "I think I need to lie down." Her hand brushes against my arm, sending a chill skittering up my spine.

Oh God, does she want me to 'lie down' with her? Was *that* what she thought when I offered to accompany her to her room to retrieve the glow sticks? By glow sticks, I meant literal glow sticks. I would sooner venture out into the raging storm than hook up with Lisa. Brenda, maybe. But Lisa? No freaking way. I'm all for a good time, but in no alternate universe would I categorize Brit's maid of honor as a *good time*.

Yet, despite my reputation, I'm not a complete asshole. I assist (*carry*) Lisa to the full-size bed, rolling her onto her side in case she gets sick. I wouldn't want her to choke on her vomit. Like I said, I'm no monster. I tuck her into place under the crisp white duvet, overjoyed as she nearly instantly dissolves into snores.

Lisa is out cold. Not even a hurricane could wake her. To the contrary, I'm pretty sure it's lulled her into the sleep of the dead.

Still, I tiptoe away from the bed, wanting anything other than to rouse her. I shine my flashlight into Lisa's suitcase, tossing aside clothing and papers, so I can grab the glow sticks. There's a bunch of tax documents, a few pictures, an airline ticket, another airline ticket. I examine the tickets side-by-side. Two seat assignments for flights to Punta Cana. I check the dates. One is from today. The other is from a week ago.

What was Lisa doing in Punta Cana a week ago?

Didn't she say she went to Aruba? And didn't Brit say Lisa went to the Bahamas?

Where the hell was she?

I think about the locked door.

Was Lisa actually *here*, setting this up? Whatever *this* is.

God, this trip is getting stranger by the minute. I leave the room, incredibly confused, but with glow sticks in hand and my dignity intact.

Thankfully, the mood is slightly less weird and catatonic downstairs. Someone is playing music from their phone. I can't help but think it would be wise to conserve our batteries, but then, no one has any service anyway, so what does it really matter?

Through the muted darkness, I can just make out the silhouettes of Joe and Brit going at it in a corner of the room, and Brenda seated on a stool at the bar. I'm about to join her when, seeming to have eyes in the back of her head or a sixth sense registering my presence, Brit rips her lips from Joe's and spins around to face me. Well, what she can see of me.

"Where's Lisa?"

I should have seen this one coming from a mile away and prepared myself for the third degree. Two go up, one comes down. Brit and Lisa seem weirdly protective of each other.

"She's lying down in bed upstairs. She said she was tired."

Brit cocks her head to the side as if considering the validity of what I've just told her. My best friend's fiancé doesn't seem to like me all that much. I've barely hung out with her — or *him* — since they started dating. Maybe two or three times, max. We had one double date, but all Brit wanted to talk about was her hair. She must have opened and closed her Chanel purse at least thirty times, I suspect so we could covet it. Needless to say, Tamara found her to be a snob, not that she let on at dinner — our first and last *double* date.

Tamara wanted to *kill* me when Brit showed up at her salon the following week for a dye job. Of course, she didn't turn her away. But she did tell me it was as painful as a full-body wax.

Still, I never told Joe anything to indicate as much. I wouldn't dream of it.

But here . . . now . . . it's getting a hell of a lot harder to hold my tongue.

"What did you say to her, Darren? Why would she lie down in the middle of the party she put together?" Brit's hands move to her hips. Her words are loaded, dripping with accusation. The thing is, I'm not even sure what exactly I'm being accused of.

I've had women dislike me before, but hot damn, this is like another level.

My eyebrows shoot up. "How would I know? She's *your* friend."

"Who went upstairs with *you!*"

"She said she wanted to lie down. What was I supposed to do? Throw her over my shoulder and force her to come back downstairs?"

Brit glares at me, flashing her teeth like a dog readying itself to attack.

"Okay, enough, enough." Joe steps between us. He shoots me a pointed glare, the muscle in his jaw pulsing. "No need to get aggressive."

Me? Aggressive?

I throw my hands up in surrender. I'm getting awfully tired of being painted as the bad guy here. And I don't like what Brit is implying. Why in the world would I lie about Lisa lying down? What does she think I did to her? *Tie* her to the bed? For Christ's sake, this is ridiculous. No, it's borderline insane.

With hot cheeks, I sulk to the bar, plopping down on the stool next to Brenda. She is the only one I can tolerate among the unsavory cast of characters on this vacation.

"Tough crowd," she says, elbowing me gently in the ribs.

I smile. A genuine smile, one where it reaches my eyes, and, I assume, they crinkle around the corners and all that good shit.

Brenda tips her head back and laughs. There it is again, that glint of recognition. I'm convinced I know her from somewhere. But *where?* I could ask her again, but I don't want her to think I'm crazy. Or creepy. Or crazy creepy.

Brenda feels like my only ally in the house. Like this is a twisted reality show, and the outcome of this trip hinges on our alliance.

Maybe I'm just imagining things. Brenda would *definitely* remember if we spent a night together. And examining her striking features in the dim glow of the flashlight, I'm certain I would, too.

I tap my fingers anxiously against the bar, thinking. Whether or not I know Brenda from some past life isn't all that important right now, anyway. What's important is weathering this storm, which is growing in intensity with every passing minute. The wind and rain rhythmically smash against the house like a battering ram. It feels like the entire structure is shaking on its foundation.

I glance down at my hands. *I* am shaking on my foundation.

I grab the bottle of Jack Daniel's off the bar and take a nice, long swig. The alcohol warms my body as it flows through my veins, but it does little to quell my sense of unease.

All I can think about is Tamara's tarot card premonition: *death, bad.* And the Ouija board warning: *you are in danger.*

The storm, the service, the suspicion . . . are they right?

Because weather aside, it feels like we are on the precipice of something happening.

Something *very bad.*

CHAPTER 20

Brenda

I haven't known Darren for long, but I am seriously starting to worry about him. The cool confidence he wore on the plane is all but gone. In its place is a shaky shell of a man. I rest a hand on Darren's leg to stop it from pulsing up and down. It's making me nervous. He jerks dramatically, my gentle touch somehow igniting a firestorm inside of him.

He's probably just edgy because we have no power and because the wind and rain are lashing at us like whips, trying to break through the stucco.

Surely, things will look better in the morning.

Assuming we make it through the night. The storm seems to be taking on a life of its own. It feels like there are no guarantees.

Just as I attempt to process this thought, a large branch or some other debris decides to smash against the roof above us. Talk about perfect timing.

Darren's eyebrows furrow, creating a shadow across his face. "The storm," he says. "It's getting worse."

"Is that the *only* reason you're so jumpy?" I ask, feeling equally on edge, unable to shake this overwhelming sense of impending doom. Is it *just* the storm that has Darren so rattled? Or is there something else? Something he's not telling me.

I can't explain it, but I *feel* it, just as sure as I feel the draft still blowing from the air conditioner. It's impossible since we have no power. But tell that to the fine hairs popping up like miniature icicles all over my body.

"Did something happen with you and Lisa?"

Darren's eyes darken. "Why does everyone keep asking me about Lisa?"

I tuck a strand of loose hair behind my ear. "I don't know. Maybe because you went upstairs with her, and she didn't come back down?"

"So, you automatically assume that I *did* something to her?"

I'm not sure what I think, but I can't stop my face from contorting into a troubled expression. "*Did* you?" I arch an eyebrow, still unsure of what to make of him.

"Of course not." Darren visibly shudders. "I think she was trying to make a move on me before she passed out though."

"Why didn't you do it?"

"Why didn't I, *do what?*"

This time, my lips involuntarily curl into a smirk. "Give the girl what she wants."

Darren wrinkles his nose in disgust. "Have you met her?"

He makes a very valid point.

"Besides," he adds. "I sort of have a girlfriend."

"You *sort of* have a *girlfriend?*" I air quote the "sort of." What does that even mean? I knew Darren was taken. I'd overheard Brit at the office talking on the phone, presumably to Joe, about Darren's girlfriend — although she didn't qualify it with "sort of." Darren doesn't strike me (or Brit, apparently) as the boyfriend type. It's difficult to misconstrue the way he's been looking at me since I sat in the seat beside him on the plane. He hasn't made a move yet, but let's be real here; it seems like it's only a matter of time.

I can't help but wonder if, somewhere, deep down, all men are the same. Maybe it's built into their DNA, like eye color.

I focus on the man sitting next to me, not wanting to think about the one I was supposed to be saying "I do" to this weekend. Tonight would have been our rehearsal dinner. I had the simple white strapless dress picked out and everything; hair and makeup, scheduled. Unfortunately, Vegas had other plans.

Darren runs a hand through his thick, dark hair. Is he downplaying his relationship as some twisted hook to bait me? I've found men are liars, too.

"Yes. No," he says.

See, *liars.*

"I mean, I'm seeing someone, but I'm not sure about her, to be honest. I guess I was hoping this weekend would bring me some clarity."

I chew on my lower lip, thinking about the turn this trip has taken. We all came here to celebrate Joe and Brit's upcoming nuptials. But it feels like more than that. A storm brewing beneath the surface.

"Has it?" I ask, trying to shake the dread pooling in my stomach. If I focus on Darren, I won't have to think about *everything* else. "You know, has it given you clarity?"

Darren stares deeply into my eyes, sending a chill down my body. The hair on my arms shoot up once again. "I'm getting there. I guess it remains to be seen."

He leans in closer, as if about to kiss me. Dude just said he "sort of" had a girlfriend. I mean, seriously? "Listen," he whispers, his tongue mere centimeters from my ear.

"Y . . . y . . . yes?"

"Can you do me a favor?"

A favor? I inhale sharply. What the hell just happened? It felt like he was about to . . . Did I misconstrue *that?* Lord have mercy. I'm *sure* I don't want Darren to kiss me, but at this moment, feeling like an outsider and vulnerable from the storm, I'm also *not sure* I don't want Darren to kiss me. Quite the conundrum, just like this trip. I try unsuccessfully to push aside the thoughts.

Kissing Darren would be a huge mistake. I don't even like the guy all that much.

"What kind of favor?" I ask, grateful for the darkness because these wild thoughts have my cheeks burning like two hot tamales.

"Can you distract Brit? I need to talk to Joe."

I glance over to the corner of the room where Joe now has Brit pinned against the wall, her arms secured tightly behind her back. She looks like she's his prisoner.

I can't fathom interrupting them, but there's something about the pleading look on Darren's face and my own morbid curiosity. So, I reluctantly agree.

I wonder what this is all about. What could Darren need to talk to Joe about in *private during* a raging hurricane? During his bachelor-bachelorette party? What is it that can't wait?

And *was* he about to kiss me?

I wrap my arms around my body, trying to ward off a chill. It's not just the air conditioning.

Something is going on here.

CHAPTER 21

Brit

Joe abruptly stops kissing me. His entire body stiffens against mine, and his hand flies out from beneath my blouse as if someone has set my breasts on fire.

What the—?

Joe spins around, his right hand clenched into a fist. "Dude, seriously?"

It takes a minute for my eyes to adjust to the darkness.

Darren is there, standing *too* close to us. Brenda cowers behind him, her hand pressed against his back. I'm struck by the feeling that something terrible has happened.

"What is it?" I gasp, fumbling to right my clothing.

"Sorry, man," Darren says, holding up his hands. "Just wanted to spend some time with the groom-to-be. It's your bachelor party, not your honeymoon." He shoots me a look, as if I can help the fact that my fiancé can't keep his hands off of me.

I sigh with a mixture of annoyance and relief.

As much as I'd never admit it out loud, Darren is right. We should be doing less making out and more *hanging out* with our friends. Speaking of friends, Lisa *still* hasn't come back downstairs. Joe insisted that I shouldn't worry and distracted me in that way he does so well, but now, Lisa is all I can think about.

Why *hasn't* she come back downstairs?

She's been acting so strangely. I can't put my finger on it. I also can't stop wondering why she would lie to me about her vacation destination. I'm certain I heard her right the first time. Where *was* Lisa last week?

Two questions that require immediate clarification.

"It's fine, darling." I place a hand on Joe's chiseled chest. Somehow, during our steamy make-out session, all the buttons on his shirt came undone. I'm reminded of the stewardess on the plane. Perhaps that should have been the first sign that this trip was veering on a dangerous flight path. "I should check on Lisa."

"Why do you need to check on Lisa?" Darren asks rather aggressively. A vein throbs in his temple. Even with his arms hanging by his sides, Darren's biceps are impossible to miss. Joe says he throws one hell of a punch. Apparently, Darren had tossed around the idea of launching a fitness empire before he hit it big with the Waxinator. He could retire and maintain the same lifestyle.

"I told you she's sleeping," he said, emphatically, crossing his giant arms across his chest.

Well, *duh*. This is *precisely* why I need to check on Lisa. It's not like her to bow out so early, unless it's tax season. Not without telling me she was going up for the night. She tells me everything. Or so I thought.

Still, she had gushed for at least twenty minutes after we got here about all the fun stuff we'd be doing tonight. And all those emails about games and this being a White Lie Party. We haven't done much since we arrived. And Lisa, asleep in bed upstairs, doesn't seem like much fun.

"I want to make sure she's feeling okay."

"Whatever. It just seems silly if she's out for the night. You're going to wake her up."

I examine Darren's face. A muscle in his jaw twitches. His eyes flicker like a pendulum between me and the atrium. The *stairs.* Why is he so hellbent on me *not* checking on Lisa? Has he done something to *upset* her? Has he done something *to* her?

A sudden wave of panic rushes through me as thoughts of what Darren could have done to Lisa come flooding in, unrelenting and unforgiving, much like the waves thrashing against the house. Is it my imagination or are those waves getting *stronger?* Hitting *higher?* My chest constricts, making it difficult to breathe.

I'm not sure what's worse: the storm or my suspicions about Joe's best man.

Because there's something decidedly off about Darren; I felt it when we met a few months back at a Michelin-starred restaurant on the Upper West Side. It was a poor choice of establishment, in retrospect. When Darren walked in with Tamara on his arm, I thought he might have hired a hooker for the night. I tried my best to make conversation. When I found out she was a hairstylist, I attempted to engage her in small talk about her trade. I kept feeling his eyes on me, like lasers. It made me incredibly uncomfortable; I could only fiddle with my purse to pass the time.

I have been doing my damnedest to avoid him ever since. I know this joint celebration was meant to mend fences and have us all holding hands and singing Kumbaya at the wedding, but I can't shake the fear that this was a horrible mistake.

"I'll go with you," Brenda offers.

"Thanks, Brenda. I'm glad you're here."

I eye Brenda with gratitude and adoration. I can't help but notice the look of sadness on her face as she glances back at me. I've been so wrapped up in this evening, I've barely thought about how Brenda must be feeling. I mean, tonight was to be her rehearsal dinner. Instead, she's helping me look for my missing friend while a Category 4 hurricane rages outside. I'd be on the floor sobbing if I were her. I want to collapse on the floor sobbing, and I'm *not* her.

"Can I ask you a personal question?" I ask as we make our way from the living room to the atrium. It's none of my business, but . . ."

"Sure, have at it," she says, pausing before adding, "I'm an open book, just like you, Brit." I bristle at the comment, thinking about my earlier conversation with Lisa. But this isn't about my secrets. It's about hers.

"What happened with you and Nick? You seemed so happy. I just . . . I feel bad, I guess. This must be hard for you."

"I'm fine," Brenda says, not sounding fine. She's pointed the flashlight at the ground, so I can no longer make out her face, but she draws an audible breath. "Look, I appreciate your concern. I'm not ready to talk about it, okay? But if you need to know, there was cheating involved, and it didn't end well." Her tone is clipped. Apparently, I've hit a nerve.

"Men," I say.

"Men," she agrees.

"Well, again, I just want you to know how happy I am to have you here." I reach out and squeeze her hand. If Brenda weren't here, I would be going upstairs in the darkness alone to check on Lisa. The thought of doing *that* is enough to paralyze me with fear. I tell myself that everything is fine. I'm sure I will find my best friend curled up in bed, fast asleep, just like Darren said. Lisa probably had too much to drink. She's tired, no doubt crashing from her back-to-back excursions . . . to Aruba, the Bahamas, or wherever the hell she went.

Actually, I'm not sure of *any* of that.

My legs shake as I follow Brenda carefully up the stairs toward Lisa's bedroom, guided only by the circle of light from Brenda's flashlight.

About three-quarters of the way to the top, Brenda stops dead in her tracks. I nearly topple into her, barely catching myself on the railing. It wobbles for a moment before righting itself.

"Oh my God," Brenda gasps, clutching her chest.

"What? What is it?"

Brenda stands frozen in place two stairs up from me. Gripping the banister tightly, I take a large step and close the distance between us. My heart hammers like a drum in my chest.

And then I see it.

Brenda's flashlight is trained on the floor at the white marble step above us. Only it isn't white. For a moment, I think — *hope* — it might be a trick of the light.

But no.

The step is *red.*

And we've only been drinking champagne and hard liquor. No one here is drinking red wine.

"Is that . . . ?" I don't finish the thought. I *can't* finish the thought.

"It sure looks like it," Brenda says, her voice quivering as we stare at the ominous pool of crimson.

I scream at the top of my lungs.

Because why the fuck is there *blood* on the stairs?

CHAPTER 22

Darren

I *finally* have Joe right where I want him: *alone*. I've been waiting for this moment since we arrived. What am I so afraid of? *I'm* not the one in the wrong here.

Maybe it's the high likelihood that our friendship is about to reach an abrupt and dramatic end. We've been through so much together. I'm not sure how we will bounce back from this. Maybe doing this now is foolish, but I can't hold it in anymore. Nothing will ever be the same. It *can't* be the same. It's as if Joe has taken a sledgehammer to our friendship and hit it repeatedly until there was nothing left but fragments of what once was.

One could argue, though, that our friendship all but ended a week ago, when I received a series of emails from an untraceable sender with the evidence of Joe's betrayal.

It has been a long fucking week.

I'm as prepared as I can be for what will surely be a heated conversation. I'm glad the women have gone upstairs so they don't have to witness it.

As I open my mouth to speak, Brit's high-pitched scream pierces the silence. *Again*. But unlike the *I can't find our luggage* scream from earlier today, this scream is one of sheer terror. And it isn't just *a* scream in the singular. Brit doesn't stop screaming. It keeps going and going.

Tamara's words echo in my head. *Death, bad.* Panic jolts through my body.

Joe pushes me out of the way, and I stumble and nearly fall. Regaining my lost footing, I follow the sound of Brit's anguished cries. Dread curdles in my gut like spoiled milk.

This is all my fault. I asked Brenda to distract Brit. What if something has happened to her? I'm not sure I could forgive myself if something has happened to her.

My heart whooshes in my ears as I round the corner into the atrium. I'm flooded with instant relief at the sight of Brit and Brenda standing on the stairs, looking rattled but unharmed.

They are both safe and sound. So why is Brit screaming like a maniac?

"Brit!" Joe scales the stairs two at a time until he nears the top, pulling Brit into his arms. Her screams are muffled when she buries her face in Joe's chest.

I follow, at a far more modest pace, fear coursing through my body. If it isn't Brenda or Brit, is it *Lisa?*

"You!" Brit disentangles herself from Joe's embrace and jabs a finger toward me. "*You!*" she shouts again, louder, her lips twisting with unbridled rage.

I glance around as if there might be someone else she's pointing at. But no, her gaze is steeled on me and me alone.

I turn to Joe and find his eyes trained on the steps. I follow his gaze, landing on the marble. Everything around me momentarily stills, the voices mute, as I take in the white tile stained with red.

Stained with what looks like wet, fresh *blood.*

What in the world?

Has something happened to Lisa? I assume I would have noticed if this blood was there when we came upstairs.

And then another thought: Do they think *I* had something to do with that blood? But I didn't. Surely, they couldn't . . .

"Maybe it was there before," I offer, unsure what to say. Of *where* it came from. Of *when*. Of *who*. The room spins around me. I grab the railing for support, gasping aloud as it wobbles against my weight.

"Don't you think one of us would have noticed blood on the stairs earlier in broad daylight? The whole house is fucking white." Joe kicks a bare foot against the step and curses under his breath.

"You went upstairs before, too, Joe. Remember?"

"Exactly," he scoffs. "And there was *no* blood on the stairs then."

"Besides," Brit adds. "It's still *wet*. Something must have just happened — to *Lisa*. What did you do to her, Darren? What did you *do?*"

They all stare at me as if I'm some sort of monster. They're judge and jury, convicting me of a crime I didn't commit. Clearly, these people don't realize how difficult it is to try a case with no body. And there may be blood, but until I see a bloody *body*, well, there's no reason to assume one exists. As if attempting to manifest my thoughts, I suggest, "What if Lisa tried to come back downstairs to the party, fell, and returned injured to her room to sleep it off."

Joe huffs, "Seriously, Darren? You expect us to believe that?"

I don't know what I expect from *him*.

"I swear I've no idea where that came from. How could you even — Why would I hurt Lisa? I barely even know her." I stumble over my words as if they're physical obstacles. "Come on, we don't even know that she's hurt!"

Still in shock at the accusation, I watch as Brit runs up the remaining stairs. She truly hates me, I think, though I have no idea why. Joe and Brenda follow, leaving me alone with my thoughts and the blood on the stairs. I hesitate a little longer, giving Brit space and delaying the inevitable: what we might find up there.

Some trip this is turning out to be.

A spark of irritation flickers. I swear, you try to be a nice guy and where does it get you? If anything, I did them all a huge favor by getting Lisa into bed. Who knows what kind of trouble she would have started had I not, what with all these "party games" she couldn't stop talking about? Someone should tell her not to quit her day job as an accountant. This is by far the worst freaking party ever.

I flash back to the icebreaker in the kitchen, the way Lisa seemed to hand-select who got which question. What was that about? It was almost as if she were setting the stage, getting us to reveal information to make us turn on each other one by one. And then, there was the ticket in her luggage. The locked storage closet. This is ridiculous. But Lisa hardly strikes me as diabolical. My best friend, on the other hand . . .

My thoughts are interrupted by more screams and a fist pounding against wood. I climb the remaining stairs, taking note of the trail of blood splatter, then round the corner of the landing to find Brit banging on Lisa's door, with Joe and Brenda taking turns demanding that Lisa open it.

I think about how I left her: snoring peacefully in bed, tucked snugly under the crisp white duvet, with no blood outside her door, or on the landing, or stairs. Something irks me.

"Try the knob," I suggest.

Brit whips around and throws me a look of pure disgust. "Obviously, we tried the knob, Darren. The door is locked. But I suppose you knew that already."

No, that can't be possible.

This door was *not* locked.

CHAPTER 23

Brenda

"Wait, wait, wait."

I watch as a disheveled Darren holds his hands up in the air as if fending off an attack. I have the sinking sensation that if he doesn't offer Brit a reasonable explanation soon, he will have to do just that. The claws are out.

"Now you're accusing me of *locking* Lisa inside of her room? That's literally not even possible! How would I have gotten out?"

"Very easily. The lock is on the outside of the door."

Darren exhales a flustered breath. "And how could I possibly lock the door with no keys?"

"I'm sure you could figure a way. You're inventive like that," Brit huffs.

We are all now staring at Darren. The whole thing seems crazy, but how else do we explain the blood on the stairs?

"You are making a big deal over what is probably nothing." Darren shakes his head, looking annoyed and seemingly unwilling to admit the possibility that Lisa injured herself or has met with foul play.

"Over *nothing?* There's blood all over the freaking stairs, and Lisa isn't answering the door." Brit's nostrils flare.

I wouldn't be shocked if she started blowing fire out of them.

"I heard you tell her to go upstairs with you to get the glowsticks. Why couldn't you go *alone?* Why do we even need glowsticks?"

Our eyes simultaneously swivel to Darren. Why couldn't he go upstairs *alone?* Why *do* we need glowsticks?

"Ask your friend," he says, pausing as the ridiculousness of his response sinks in. It's difficult to ask someone a question when they're non-responsive. After a few beats of heated silence, he adds, "Look, I'm worried about what happens if the flashlights go out. And I didn't know where the glowsticks were. Because they're *her* glowsticks." Darren rolls his eyes, clearly over his soon-to-be friend-in-law's antics.

His expression hardens. "Move out of the way. Let me try the door."

"Be my guest." Brit steps aside so Darren can have a go at unlocking the door.

I'm not exactly sure *how* he's planning to do that without the keys, but—

First, he twists the knob. Of course, there's no give because the door is locked.

Just like it was when Brit and I tried to open it thirty seconds ago.

Next, Darren raps his fists sharply against the wood. "Lisa, wake up. Answer the door."

Again, unsurprisingly, there's no answer.

In what I can only presume is one final act of desperation, with Brit and Joe looking on angrily, Darren slams his body against the white wood. He immediately reels back, wincing in pain as he grips his shoulder. The door doesn't let out so much as a creak.

Darren turns back to us, his face a mask of panic despite the calmness of his words. "She's obviously in a deep sleep, and if all this commotion isn't stirring her, maybe she just needs to sleep it off."

"Sleep it off?" Brit barks. "She could be bleeding out in there right now."

Brit isn't wrong. How else do we explain the blood on the staircase leading up to her room?

"Why don't you try, Joe?" Brit suggests, nudging Joe toward the door.

Brit thinks *Joe* can break open this door? He's a good-looking guy, but Darren has both height and weight on him. Darren would definitely take Joe in a fight. He'd one hundred percent outdo Joe in a shoulder-door-slamming contest, so that seems quite an ill-advised endeavor.

Because a) there's no orthopedic surgeon on hand; and b) that door is not budging.

"Guys, we're wasting time," I point out. "If Lisa needs our help, we need to figure out another way in."

The commotion in the hallway momentarily stills as everyone turns to look at me. I continue, "There are balconies outside each of the bedrooms. What if one of us climbs up and tries to get in through her window?"

Joe starts pacing back and forth like a caged animal. "In case you hadn't noticed, there's a hurricane raging out there, *Bianca*."

I roll my eyes. How hard is it to remember the name *Brenda? Seriously?* Did Joe not own a television growing up? *Hello*, Brenda Walsh, *90210*.

Joe isn't wrong, though, aside from my name. *Brenda. Brenda. Brenda.* We'd have to be a little crazy to scale the side of this house in the middle of what must be at least a Cat 3. Still, "Well, we can't call for help, and we can't get in through the door. So, the only option I can see is to get in through the window. Unless—"

"Unless what?" Darren asks. "Do you have another idea?"

"Unless we find the missing key. It must be a universal key if the doors lock from the outside, right?"

"We already looked for it, *remember?*" Joe narrows his eyes at me. Despite the dim light provided by our flashlights, his eyes are filled with darkness. Once again, they look like little black holes.

"Well, it has to be *somewhere*. How else would Lisa have gotten in the house in the first place?"

"For the last time, *Bianca*, I don't have it!" Spittle flies from Joe's mouth as he says this.

I shiver, wondering if the purpose of these doors is to keep people out or to keep them in. If perhaps Joe *does* have the key, after all.

It feels like we're stuck in a standoff. Thankfully, it's Darren who breaks the heated silence. "Dude, her name is Brenda. And yeah, it's weird that the doors lock from the outside, and that we can't find the key. But whatever, it is what it is, so we need to figure this out."

"No," Joe says, angrily folding his arms across his chest. "*You* need to figure this out. You're the one who came up here with her."

"I don't think you want to do this here, Joe—"

"Do *what?* Are you threatening me, man?"

Something about the way Darren is glaring at Joe makes it sound like a threat. Darren looks about to say something, but a crack overhead sends us scurrying down the hallway like mice.

"Look," I offer, trying to smooth out the tension that is becoming so thick, I worry it will be impossible to cut through. It's almost as if we've invited Hurricane Ivy in. "I'm sure Lisa is fine," I say. My voice wobbles, and it's clear I don't mean it.

Obviously, I'm not sure that Lisa is fine. But we need a voice of reason before things escalate past the point of no return. "Someone just needs to check on her, and we can all relax."

Brit looks at me like I've gone off the deep end. Her face twists, and her arms thrust to her hips. "*Relax?*"

"Fighting isn't going to do anything."

"You're awfully calm, Brenda. A little *too* calm. When we found the blood, with all of this—" Brit waves her hand around.

Too calm? Tell that to my heart, which is practically beating out of my chest. I'm two beats away from crashing out. Surely Brit can't suspect *I've* done something to Lisa.

Or maybe she can. "Wait—" I take a step back, away from Brit. "Do you think *I* did something to Lisa?" My voice rises several octaves as I ask this. "I was downstairs with you the entire time. When could I have possibly done something to her?"

This is getting ridiculous. Lisa is probably freaking fine. Okay, *maybe* she's freaking fine.

Either way, we are in uncharted territory here. And until we find Lisa safe and sound in that bedroom, things are only going to get worse.

CHAPTER 24

Then

Things just keep getting better and better. Although when you've hit rock bottom, I guess the only direction to go is up.

Ginger gives us each a pile of *clean* clothes and allows us to take a five-minute shower before the bus comes to pick us up. It takes me the whole duration of the shower to absorb the fact that she actually did laundry. I'd just assumed she didn't know how. I don't think I've ever seen her in the same mumu twice.

One by one, Ginger instructs us to march up the creaky stairs to the only full bathroom in their ranch. She shouts out our names from the top step like a drill sergeant. I don't think Ginger has ever been down here, not that I can blame her for *that*.

When it's my turn, I excitedly walk up the stairs, anxious to leave this house. Ginger leads me to the bathroom, where Walter is waiting. He stays perched outside the door, just in case I, and I quote, "Even think of trying something." It's a good thing Walter can't read my thoughts. My eyes flit around the bathroom desperately, looking for something, *anything*, that might double as a weapon. But unless I'm going to poison Ginger and Walter with a bar of soap, it's a lost cause.

This isn't *A Christmas Story*, anyhow. I used to love that movie. Every year on Christmas Eve, TNT would run a twenty-four-hour Christmas story marathon. I'd spend the whole day snuggled up between my parents, hot cocoa with marshmallows and whipped cream in hand. I couldn't help but think I was the luckiest kid in the world.

Only I wasn't, because before my thirteenth New Year rolled around, my parents were both dead, killed in a horrific car accident. That's how I wound up here — orphaned and left in the care of two heartless sociopaths who would eat my insides and use my skin for hides if they could get away with it.

Maybe they could. I wonder if anyone would even notice if I disappeared.

I try not to think about the life I had before this God forsaken place or the life I have now. I only let myself think about the life I'll have after. Surely, there must be an *after*. This can't be it for me. I may have lost sight of hope for a while, but now, as I get ready to go to actual school, hope has wormed its way back in and snaked its way around my insides.

I imagine we are all feeling it, this shared sensation of breaking free.

We just don't talk about it. Or at all, for that matter.

We don't say a word to one another on the bus. It's like sensory overload between the rumble of the engine, the high-pitched squeals of kids, and the baritone warnings of the bus driver. I'm nervous and scared in a way I can't understand. Excitement has morphed into something else altogether. Something more like *fear*.

It doesn't help that our peers are staring at us like we have three heads. Maybe it's because we're new. Perhaps they've been told we're foster kids. Or maybe it's that inner Spidey sense telling them we're different.

We *are* different.

We are all in different classes to boot. I'd feel better if I weren't alone. I wonder if Ginger and Walter planned it that way. There's less chance of us talking if we're separated. The only thing they couldn't control was lunch. All the seventh-grade classes have lunch together.

I scan through the crowded cafeteria, searching for the others. I find one of my roommates alone at a table, and I quickly hurry to join her. Needless to say, neither of us brought any food or money to buy food. I hope someone will sit down next to us and offer to share. Wishful thinking. Kids are mean. Worse than adults. Worst case, I'm not adverse to inconspicuously slipping my hand into a garbage can and grabbing whatever I can without getting noticed.

Apparently, a few kids clean up the mess left by their classmates when lunch ends. There are several dustpans and cleaning clothes in the corner. I will be volunteering for that job any chance I get.

I'm lost in thought when I spot our missing housemate. Surprisingly, she's *not* alone. She's sitting across the cafeteria at a table with a gaggle of girls who appear to be hanging on her every word. You heard me right — hanging on *her* every word. Surely, my eyes are deceiving me. From where we sit, it looks like Little Miss Nothing To Say is talking up a freaking storm.

And *eating*.

She looks up, meeting my gaze.

I offer a weak smile and a wave. She must be so uncomfortable over there. Surely, she'll want to join us.

Her eyes linger on me for a moment, and then she turns to whisper into the ear of the girl sitting next to her. That girl says something to the next, starting a game of telephone, culminating in *all* eyes being on me.

She might as well have walked over here and smashed me in the face with a mashed potato-laden food tray. I'd still be the laughing stock of the cafeteria, but at least then, I'd have lunch.

But no.

They're all laughing. Each and every one of them — *laughing*.

Especially the new girl.

From: lisamreynard@reynardaccounting.com
To: lisamreynard@reynardaccounting.com
BCC: joseph.briggs@briggsfinancial.com, brit.jones@brighthorizons.com, brenda.peterson@brighthorizons.com, darrenljost@hotmail.com
Subject: White Lie

On the agenda for this weekend — lots of laughs. Give me your best white lie about yourself. And go . . .

xx
Lisa (Maid of Honor)

From: lisamreynard@reynardaccounting.com
To: lisamreynard@reynardaccounting.com
BCC: joseph.briggs@briggsfinancial.com, brit.jones@brighthorizons.com, brenda.peterson@brighthorizons.com, darrenljost@hotmail.com
Subject: Re: Brit & Joe's White Lie Party

Come on, guys! Surely you must have a little secret you can share???

xx
Lisa (Maid of Honor)

From: lisamreynard@reynardaccounting.com
To: lisamreynard@reynardaccounting.com
BCC: joseph.briggs@briggsfinancial.com, brit.jones@brighthorizons.com, brenda.peterson@brighthorizons.com, darrenljost@hotmail.com
Subject: Re: Brit & Joe's White Lie Party

Well, I haven't received any responses, so I guess you'll all just have to wait and see what I choose for you! I won't disappoint ;)

xx
Lisa (Maid of Honor)

CHAPTER 25

Brit

Despite the fact that I'm supposedly built like a Barbie doll, as Darren so rudely pointed out, I'm not a fucking idiot. I worked extremely hard to get where I am. My advertising agency is in the top ten in New York City and has received global recognition. This year, we've landed some big-name clients that will surely put Bright Horizons on the map.

Something happened to Lisa. Blood doesn't just magically appear out of nowhere. And why would Lisa lock herself away in the room when she was even more excited for this weekend than I was?

Darren isn't telling us *something*. It's him; I know it. I shouldn't have accused Brenda of playing a part in whatever happened to Lisa. Brenda has been nothing but kind. Supportive. Bright Horizons has doubled in productivity since I hired her. She's going places. People who are going places don't hurt other people and lock them away where they can bleed out. Just ask Elle Woods.

I'm panicking, and rightfully so. Despite Darren and Joe giving it their best Boy Scout try, the bedroom door is not opening. They could shoulder smash all night, but it's not coming down. Brenda was right. We have to find another way in. And it would seem the only other way involves pulling a Spider-Man and scaling the building.

Go, web, go.

"Joseph, darling." I turn to my fiancé, flashing him the doe eyes that he simply cannot resist.

"Yes, Britter-Bug?"

"Please, I *need* you to do this for me. I won't be able to rest or have any fun if I'm worried about Lisa. You and Darren need to figure out how to get onto the balcony upstairs."

Joe's eyes widen momentarily as if horrified by the suggestion of him trudging through a hurricane to break into Lisa's bedroom. I guess it does sound all sorts of horrific. But I'm serious. *Dead serious.* And as expected, Joe's face eventually relaxes, and he agrees. "Of course, I'll do it."

He turns to Darren. "Let's go."

"Wait a second! I never said *I* would do it." Darren shakes his head emphatically as a crash of thunder booms from outside like an exclamation point.

"You're the one she was last with. You are *absolutely* doing it." I angrily fold my arms across my chest.

This is all Darren's fault. Why couldn't my soon-to-be husband have a *normal* best man? I can almost feel the daggers shooting from my eyes, like tiny needles piercing through the lenses.

Darren grits his teeth. A muscle twitches in his jaw while we look on with bated breath, waiting for him to decide. Even the wind seems to have momentarily stilled, the ambient noises in the house silenced.

Okay, fine, climbing up the side of a three-story home during a hurricane isn't the *best* idea, but it's not like we have a playbook full of options. The clock is ticking. *Literally.* I catch sight of a clock in the hallway. The pit in my stomach grows with each tick of the hand.

"I think I saw a ladder downstairs," Brenda announces. She hastens down the hall to the stairs. Oh God, I should warn her about the railing, but it's too late now.

Joe and Darren look to the door, then to each other, before following her down the hallway.

I should warn them, too, but I can't seem to talk.

I pause momentarily, placing an open palm against the door as though it might open with a simple push, and I'll find Lisa okay. Though the reality is it's out of my hands now.

Reluctantly, I abandon Lisa and make my way downstairs. I use the wall for support, though thankfully, the banister still appears intact. I follow the sound of voices to the laundry room, where I find Brenda pulling a ladder out from behind the washing machine. *Dragging* is more like it. The ladder scrapes across the white, tiled floor (even the laundry room has white, tiled floors) like squeaking Styrofoam, sending the hairs on my arms on end. The thing is massive, double the size of Brenda. I watch as a line of perspiration shoots across her forehead.

I've watched Brenda do many things over the past year — organize a conference, oversee a major advertising layout with less than twenty-four hours to print, and remember every single employee's Starbucks order down to the *light ice* and the *extra hot*, but manual labor is not her forte.

Having built Bright Horizons from the ground up, I do all the heavy lifting. Despite all my delegating and having a fiancé who treats me like a princess, I'm not afraid to get my hands dirty. But I'm also not about to scale the stucco of a three-story house in the middle of a goddamn hurricane.

There's courageous, and then there's crazy.

"Here, let me take that." Darren grabs the ladder from Brenda. She smiles widely with gratitude. Darren reciprocates with a broad grin. *What* is happening between the two of them? I can almost see sparks flying, zings of electric energy zapping through the air. I suspect Darren's girlfriend wouldn't be overjoyed to see this. Perhaps *that's* why he didn't fuss about her not coming.

But I'm not worried about Tamara. I'm concerned about Lisa. This whole handoff, operation climb-the-house and rescue-my-maid-of-honor is taking way too long. Whatever optimism I had left is rapidly fading. Darren is struggling under the weight of the ladder. Joe takes one side in his hands, and together, they hoist it up. Their labored breaths are audible as they haul the ladder to the front of the house, then lean it against the wall so they can slip into their shoes and take a physical and mental break, I suspect. I'm sure neither of them is looking forward to walking out into Armageddon.

Who would be? The wind is howling as loud as ever, and all I can think about at this moment is the mangy dog and the cab driver's warning: *someone is going to die.*

CHAPTER 26

Darren

I can't believe I've agreed to this insanity. It's pitch black outside and the moon is completely obscured by the dark, angry clouds unleashing a relentless torrent of rain. I can't make out so much as a silhouette of the countless trees dotting the property in the darkness, but I know they're there. I'm reminded of their presence by the whoosh of the wind through their leaves, and the crackle of branches and bark.

I think back to one of my first inventions — a novel umbrella hat with battery-operated wipers. It sure would come in handy right about now. Without it, we're pelted with bitter raindrops and biting detritus as we struggle to drag the ladder out to the front of the house. We fight against the unabating gusts of wind and streams of rain, estimating in the darkness where Lisa's balcony should lie. Once we've managed to maneuver the ladder into place, resting it against the stucco, I pull the flashlight out from my back pocket and aim it up at the house.

"Are you sure about this?" I scream to Joe, unsure if he'll hear me over the haunting wail of the wind.

"No, I'm *not* sure about this," he bites back. "But we don't have a choice. Unless you want to tell me what happened to Lisa and save us a trip up there."

I can't see his face, but I can picture the smug expression on it. My hands curl into fists at my side. I heard *that* loud and clear.

I open my mouth to form a comeback, to put Joe in his place. I've spent the past week imagining every scenario in which I might confront my once best friend, the best way to do it, the right words to say — all the while acting as if everything was fine and dandy. I should have done it when I first found out instead of waiting until now, where it seems like the world is coming to a brutal and bitter end.

I'm not even sure what I've been waiting for. *Some show of remorse? Some sign that the person I've trusted for the best part of my life isn't a sociopath?*

Once again, my words are cut off, this time as a flash of lightning streaks across the sky. It's followed by the loud crack of a tree crashing to the ground close to us. *Too close.* All conversation immediately comes to a halt.

We need to get this done *now*. Get up the ladder and into the house and find Lisa safe and sound. I will deal with Joe later.

Oh, will I ever.

"Try not to break your neck," I say. Despite everything, I mean it.

"Hold it steady," Joe screams as he grips the sides of the ladder with each of his hands. The metal shakes as he hoists himself onto a step. I press my foot firmly into the bottom rung, looping my free hand around a side rail. With my other hand, I shine the light up toward the balcony. What little good it does. It illuminates the first few steps, but the rest of the ladder has disappeared into the blackness above. Within a few moments, Joe has vanished along with the rungs.

My hands tremble against the wind as I fight to keep the ladder from swaying. The only sign of Joe's progress is the distant creak of his weight pushing against the steel. At some point, the sounds disappear altogether, and the vibrations still, leaving me to assume Joe has made it safely to the top.

I take a deep breath, preparing for my ascent into the darkness. The metal side rails slip in my fingers as I grip the ladder, beginning the climb. Try as I might, I can't climb with the flashlight in hand. It slips from my grasp, falling to the gravel below with a thud. Within moments, my only source of light is gone. I can't see a thing. The darkness feels endless.

Above. Below. Everywhere.

The dense fog wraps itself around the ladder like a closing fist while the rain incessantly beats down. I try to silence the voice in my head, screaming — *turn around.*

Time crawls as I pull myself higher into the unknown, blindly feeling my way through the darkness. This house that looked so beautiful in the light is a nightmare in the dark.

I scream to Joe, but my voice is lost in the wind. And with it, my balance.

I gasp as the unthinkable happens. The ladder violently shakes.

First, my foot slips; next, a hand.

Within a matter of terror-laden moments, I find myself free-falling to the ground below, my scream carried off into the night.

CHAPTER 27

Brenda

My body tenses at the sound. It's distant but distinct. Unmistakable. "Did you hear that?" I ask, my eyes darting toward the front window.

Brit freezes in place. It's rather jarring, after the past twenty minutes she's spent pacing in a circle by the front door. Every now and again, she had stopped by one of the windows flanking the door, and cupped her face against the glass, trying to look outside. It was painfully obvious, even to an outside observer, that Brit couldn't see a blessed thing. She might as well have opened her eyes without goggles while deep-sea diving. She probably could go deep-sea diving with the volume of rain pounding outside.

I'm grateful now that stillness has settled. All the frenzied movement was only fueling my anxiety.

But that sound . . .

"Hear what?" She asks after what feels like an eternity of silence.

"A scream. I heard a scream."

Brit's eyebrows bend in, and her lips turn down. "It was probably just the wind. I didn't hear anything."

Could it have been the wind? Maybe I imagined it. But what if I *didn't?* I certainly *didn't* imagine the blood on the stairs.

"I'm worried, Brit. Aren't you? I think Darren may have hurt Lisa, and now, what if he's out there hurting Joe as well?"

"He wouldn't," Brit exclaims, but I don't miss the look of fear in her eyes.

"We should check on them," I say, knowing we should, but that we can't. Not right now. The wind is blowing too fiercely. The snap, crackle, and pop of the trees is deafening.

Still, it feels like we need to do *something*.

Anything is better than nothing.

"Brit." I place a hand on Brit's elbow, causing her to jump.

She looks at me, saucer-eyed, lips parted. I suspect she might be in shock. I think about the blood, about Lisa being unresponsive in her locked bedroom.

"We should try to find a first-aid kit for when they get into Lisa's room, don't you think?" It's safe to assume that if Lisa is alive, she'll require some sort of medical intervention.

Anyway, Lisa aside, what if something happened to Darren or Joe outside? I swear I heard a scream.

Brit's eyes shift from me to the door, from the door to me. Finally, she nods her head in agreement. "Yeah, you're probably right."

"I'm thinking kitchen, bathroom, laundry room . . . probably somewhere on this floor." Just, hopefully, *not* in the locked storage room, because we *still* haven't found the freaking key.

"Okay."

I aim my flashlight in front of us and head down the hallway leading to the kitchen. Brit trails closely behind. On the marble island sits the bag of flashlights Darren had located earlier. I slip a flashlight from the bag and hand it to Brit. "Do you want to look in here? And I'll go check out there?" I motion with my flashlight toward the mud room and laundry area.

Brit's blonde head bobs as she takes the flashlight, quickly flipping the switch to illuminate the space around her, a beam of light dancing around the room like a strobe as Brit surveys the area. There are at least twenty drawers. Surely, there must be a first-aid kit in one of them.

I leave Brit in the kitchen, hastening to the mudroom. The floor is still wet, the bottles splayed out on tile where I abandoned them.

My eyes move up the wall, settling on the door. Why was Joe so evasive about the keys? *Dodgy*, even? Morbid curiosity getting the best of me, I reach out and wrap my free hand around the handle. I twist, feeling the knob give against my palm. *Did it turn like that before when I'd tried it with Darren?* I think not, but I can't remember for sure. So much has happened since then. Time has become one big blur, lost in the swirls of the hurricane.

I take a deep breath and give the door a sharp pull. It flies open, and I fall back, losing my footing. The flashlight slips from my grasp to the tile below and shatters, batteries and the lens from the light scatter across the marble. My heart thunders in my chest, giving the storm outside a run for its money.

Panic hits like a freight train. Fingers trembling, I fall to my knees, frantically trying to piece the flashlight together in the darkness. What little good it seems to do.

"Brenda!" I hear the sound of Brit's voice, the tap of bare feet making their way toward me before the light hits. Brit stops short and brings a hand up to her chest when she sees me on the floor, picking up shards of the broken flashlight. Her eyes fly wildly around the space. "What happened?"

"The door."

Brit wrinkles her brow in confusion. She has no idea what I'm talking about. She probably wasn't even listening when we brought up the locked door in the first place.

"This is the door Darren and I found locked before."

"*Okay . . .*" Brit lifts a shoulder nonchalantly. I'm not sensing she gets it.

"It was locked before, Brit. And now it's . . . it's just not."

Brit steps around the glass, standing next to me outside the door. "Maybe you guys were mistaken. I mean, Darren remembered seeing our luggage when, at first, he thought he hadn't, right? Maybe the door was unlocked all along." She shrugs. "You guys were probably panicked about the lights going out. People make mistakes when they're panicking."

Her casual appraisal of the situation only makes me feel worse. Because that's another thing: *what* happened to Brit's luggage?

I look around as if Joe might hear me from the balcony outside. I lean closer to Brit and place a hand on her arm. "Darren *didn't* see the luggage, Brit. I was there. Joe told him to say that. And this door," I pull my hand away, motioning toward the door, "*was* locked." I am one hundred percent certain that it was locked. As certain as I am that it is now *unlocked.* As certain as I am that I should *not* have come on this trip.

None of us should have.

A look of pure rage flashes across Brit's face. I can't tell if the look is because of Joe or me. Her fiancé *lied* to her. He instructed his best man to lie to her. I'd be angry as hell. Heck, I am angry as hell on her behalf. "That's ridiculous, Brenda. You expect me to believe Joe told Darren to lie about our luggage?"

But nope, it's directed at *me.* There goes my year-end bonus.

"Well, yeah," I counter, "because it's true."

"I don't know what is going on with you, Brenda. Making something up like that. I'm sorry your fiancé cheated on you. But Joe is not your fiancé. Not all men are shit."

I reel back as if I've been slapped across the face. "He didn't cheat on me," I scoff. "And there *was* no luggage."

Brit widens her eyes sympathetically. "Bless your heart, Brenda. Really, what reason would Joe have to lie about that?"

"I don't know. Maybe to keep you calm."

"Whatever," Brit huffs, appearing anything but calm as she turns her back to me and moves into the now *unlocked* room. I take a deep breath and step inside behind her, surprised to catch sight of — of all things — a jet ski. Some towels, extra linens. No dead body. Thankfully, there's not that.

It's precisely what I'd told Darren was likely behind the door, but something is not sitting right. Perhaps the fact that the door miraculously unlocked itself?

"What's this?" Brit asks, shining her light on a medium-sized brown box on the floor in the middle of the closet.

I lean down to examine the box. It has each of our names written on it in black marker.

"I don't know," I run my tongue along the roof of my mouth, thinking. "Maybe Lisa brought it for one of her party games?" I suggest.

"She must have," Brit agrees. "Unless the rental company left it for us." She pauses, chewing on her lower lip. "Although, I doubt the rental agency has all our names. I'm sure Joe booked it under himself, with four adult guests."

"You're probably right. And besides," I add, "why would they leave a cardboard box in a downstairs closet in a tropical climate? Everyone knows cardboard attracts rodents and spiders."

Brit raises a brow, eyeballing me like I'm some weirdo with a box obsession.

"What? Come on, you knew that. I mean, we work in advertising. We're . . . well, *I'm* opening boxes all day and taking them from our office to the recycling bin."

"Right," Brit agrees, still regarding me skeptically. She's definitely *not* convinced that she should have known this at all.

"But . . ." A thought strikes like a lightning bolt.

"But what?"

"Well, if the door was locked, how did Lisa get the box inside?" I wring my hands together, suddenly very skeptical about the practicality of Lisa accomplishing that feat. Unless *she* has the key?

Brit's eyes lift as she seems to mull this over. "You must have been mistaken, Brenda. The door had to have been open. You've seemed a little unhinged since you got here. Maybe you and Darren were distracted?"

Unhinged? Distracted? She glances at me over her heavy eyelashes, and I almost can't believe what she's implying. No, we were not too *distracted* that we'd mistake an unlocked door for a locked one. *Sheesh.*

But I don't want to argue. I want to know what's inside that box. So, "Should we open it and find out what it is?" I ask, deftly changing the subject.

Brit nods and looks around the room for something she can use to slice through the packing tape. Finding nothing of use inside, she steps into the hallway and picks up a long, jagged shard of glass from the flashlight. I eye her curiously, a knot forming in my stomach. Brit is very hands-on at work, but *this* — grabbing a shard of broken glass with her bare hand — feels so out of character, given her diva-like behavior so far on this trip. It makes me wonder which version of her is the real one. "This should work," she says, kneeling in front of the box.

Now, that doesn't seem wise. "Maybe you should grab a pair of oven mitts or something. That glass looks awfully sharp."

Brit ignores me, pushing the glass fragment into the glossy tan adhesive. She blows a lock of hair from her face, exhaling through pursed lips. My own breath catches in my throat as I watch her move the glass back and forth, her fingers red from the pressure.

I sure hope she doesn't slice a finger; we never did find that first-aid kit.

But it's not just Brit's fingers I'm concerned about. I'm nervous in a way I don't like and can't explain.

Unhinged?

Back and forth, back and forth. Slowly but surely, the tape rips, and before I can utter another, *Be careful,* Brit has gotten the box open.

I squat down to the floor so that I'm at eye level with her.

Except we aren't looking at each other.

We're both just staring into the box.

CHAPTER 28

Brit

I don't think I've ever seen so much tissue paper in my entire life, and a few months ago, I ran an ad campaign for a small chain of stores selling greeting cards, gifts, gift wraps, and festive decor. So, I know tissue paper intimately.

This tissue paper is pretty — a dusty pink with speckles of silver throughout. It's certainly a lovely presentation for whatever is concealed beneath it.

But something doesn't feel right. Where *did* it come from? *Lisa?* Why would Lisa hide the box here and not in her room? How could she have even gotten the box in here in the first place if the room was locked? And did my fiancé really tell his dimwit best man to lie about our luggage? Okay, that has nothing to do with the box, but still.

What in the world is going on? This is pretty much the exact opposite of a vacation. It feels more like a punishment. At this rate, there won't be a wedding. After this debacle of a weekend, I'm all but certain we will elope.

It's not like I'd have any family there, anyway.

I push the thought aside as my stomach roils with a mixture of anger and anxiety — a dangerous cocktail. Despite what I said to

Brenda, I feel myself starting to unhinge, the carefully tightened lug nuts of the perfectly curated facade slipping off.

"Should we open them?" I glance up to find Brenda staring at me with dark puppy-dog eyes and a lost expression. I clench my jaw, sucking in a breath through my teeth. I'm sick and tired of making all the decisions. This weekend was supposed to be a break, a chance for everyone else to do all the planning.

On Monday morning, I'll be back in the office, negotiating ad space for a well-known multi-million-dollar purse company. I don't want to think about injured maids of honor, shady best men, or tissue paper unless there's a ten-thousand-dollar handbag wrapped up in it.

Monday can't come soon enough. All of a sudden, a terrible thought spikes like a fever. What if the storm isn't over by the time of our flight home on Sunday night? It only seems to be getting worse. Even from within the confines of this interior room, I can still hear the wind moaning and the glass ominously rattling.

The hair on my neck shoots up. Brenda is *still* staring at me.

"So, what do you think, Brit? Should we unwrap them?" She asks again.

I chew on my lower lip, giving the question careful consideration. I lower a hand into the box, retrieving a tissue-wrapped package. I roll it over in my palms. If I were forced to place a wager, I'd guess it's an article of clothing, based on the weight. If we'd gone to Vegas, had a normal bachelor-bachelorette party, I'd be placing wagers right now, not involving our secrets or our lives. Our biggest problem would be the dry heat.

"I don't know." I hold the package carefully as if handling a newborn baby. Or an explosive device. "Lisa probably wants us to open them together."

"Yeah, but Lisa . . ." Brenda doesn't finish the thought. She doesn't need to.

I won't entertain the possibility. *Can't.* "I'm sure Lisa will be back with us soon." I gently lower the tissue-wrapped item back into the box. Lisa is fine. She has to be. We should wait for her. For Joe and Darren.

I gasp and recoil as something slices through my hand. I pull the offending culprit from the box.

A paper cut. A freaking paper cut.

I bring a finger to my mouth, sucking on the wound to stop the bleeding.

But it barely helps. Bold drops of crimson bloom like small flowers, staining the paper in my hand red. I push back away from the box so as not to drip blood on its contents.

"What does it say?" Brenda asks, her voice shaking nearly as much as my hands.

I take a deep breath, trying to fight the wave of dizziness that has washed over me. Then I clear my throat and begin to read.

> *Welcome to Brit and Joe's White Lie Party.*
>
> *Fun fact — the white lie game is my absolute favorite game of all time. To keep things interesting, I've taken artistic liberty and incorporated an unexpected twist.*
>
> *Inside this box, you'll each find a wrapped T-shirt. Your task — should you choose to take it — figure out which shirt belongs to whom.*
>
> *There's nothing like a little white lie to help us all get to know each other better.*

What a sweet gesture, I think. Lisa put so much time and energy into planning this party. Though I can't shake the feeling we weren't meant to find this yet. And truthfully, this leaves me with more questions than answers.

Like, why would Lisa go to bed before nine and miss all the festivities? She couldn't have been *that* drunk. Despite her being the measured one in our relationship, she does have a heavy tolerance for prosecco.

And, "Hey Brenda, did you respond to that email from Lisa?"

"Which one?" She raises an eyebrow. She's right. There were *many* emails from Lisa. Too many to count.

"The one about this being a White Lie Party. The one that asked us each for a white lie for her to use for the game."

Brenda shakes her head. "I didn't. Come to think of it, I'm not sure if anyone did. Not that I would have a clue if someone did," she continues. "Considering she had us all blind cc'd on the emails."

Sweat beads on my forehead as I recall Lisa's follow-up emails just the following day letting us know that she would be choosing for us.

Panic begins to settle in. An awful, sinking feeling emanates from deep within. There's something about this box hidden away in the closet, Lisa's mysterious departure upstairs, the *blood* on the stairs. It feels interconnected. I don't think we're going to find cheeky sayings on these shirts. I think of Lisa pressuring me to tell Joe about my past. She wouldn't tell him herself. *Would* she? Well, she wouldn't have to if it's spelled out on a shirt. A part of me wants to rip open the gift right now. Maybe I'm just being paranoid. But what if I'm not? I can't open this now. Not in front of Brenda.

I squint my eyes, taking in the last line, written in small, fine print: *What's your secret?* I nearly choke on my breath. The room spins; the closet is suddenly too small for the two of us. Claustrophobic.

"What is it? What's wrong?" Brenda asks, her voice tremulous.

"They're T-shirts," I say, my eyes unwavering from the letter.

"Please tell me she didn't get us all matching shirts . . ."

"Not quite. I—"

Before I can explain, a loud bang emanates from the atrium, followed by harried shouts. A surge of adrenaline jolts through me like an electric current.

I drop the letter and jump to my feet. Hurdling the glass in the black hallway, I push through the darkness, following the shouting. My heart is beating out of my chest. I feel sick. I round the corner, sliding on the marble floor of the atrium, but catching myself before I fall.

I exhale a sigh of relief as I see them, though my heart still beats like I've just finished a marathon.

"Thank God, you're okay," I soothe, momentarily forgetting about the White Lie Party letter and its ominous message as I dash full steam toward my fiancé and maid of honor, grateful to have them both back in one piece.

Well, sort of in one piece.

As I get closer, I notice Lisa clutching a towel to her head. Joe is holding her upright with an arm wrapped tightly around her waist. She looks just about ready to collapse.

"Are you hurt?" I cry out.

"She's lost quite a bit of blood," Joe answers, his breath coming hard and quick. "I found her like this in her bed. We need to take care of that." He motions with his free arm to Lisa's head. Even in the faint glow of Joe's flashlight, the blood is visible on Lisa's hand, saturating the once white towel and oozing through her fingers, beneath which there must be a rather large, painful gash.

"What happened?" Brenda screams from behind me, having caught up to the drama unfolding in the atrium.

Because *why* is Lisa bleeding from her head?

"I . . . I don't know. I was with Darren. We were laughing, and then I was suddenly so tired. I literally couldn't keep my eyes open. Next thing I know, something — *someone* — hit me over the head."

"That bastard!" I shout. "I swear I'll kill him."

I mean it; I *will* kill him. Just as soon as I find him. Because it quickly registers that Darren is *not* with Joe and Lisa.

Unlike them, he hasn't come back.

CHAPTER 29

Lisa

My head is throbbing as if my brain is trying to claw its way out. The blood is warm like bath water in my hands. There are loose pieces of skin surrounding the gash. It's like someone pulled a Halloween prank on my face and left behind a hodgepodge of spaghetti submerged in slime where my features should be.

I think I might be sick.

I rack my brain, trying to remember what happened. I distinctly recall falling into bed. Darren, pulling the duvet up over my shoulders. And then, searing pain in my head followed by inky blackness. I flinch at the recall. There's no possible way I cracked my skull on the mattress. It's memory foam, for goodness' sake.

"Where's Darren?" I ask Joe. Darren is the last person I remember clearly.

Joe shakes his head. "I have no clue."

"Wait, he didn't go to Lisa's room with you?" Brenda chimes in, her eyebrows shooting up.

"No, I waited for a while for him on the balcony. When he didn't come up, I just assumed he chickened out and came back to the house through the front door."

"Well, where *is* he?" Brit asks.

I consider the questions. If Darren knows what's good for him, he's probably out in the storm searching for that nonexistent town. I don't get the feeling things will end well for him here. Brit looks just about ready to pull out a pitchfork.

"He's probably hiding out somewhere upstairs," she huffs, answering the question for herself. "I guess I would be, too, if I were him. That guy has quite a bit of explaining to do." She motions toward my head. The bleeding has stopped, but somehow, the throbbing has intensified. It feels like there is a full high school band marching across my scalp.

"Am I the only one not drinking the Kool-Aid here?" Brenda blurts out. "He's obviously not inside. You would have seen him come through the window if he was behind you, Joe. And we would have heard him if he came through the door. He's still out there somewhere. He could be hurt. In *danger*." Her panicked eyes flick to the front door.

I follow her gaze. I've got to side with her on this one — *just* this one time.

On that note, Brenda brushes past us, hastening toward the door. I watch as she wraps her slim fingers around the knob and pulls. The door flies open, nearly knocking her off her feet. It then smashes into the wall, leaving a nasty hole in its wake.

"Fucking Brenda," Joe huffs.

"*Joseph Briggs*," Brit gasps.

My eyes don't know where to land — on Brenda, cowering by the front door; on Brit, side-eyeing her fiancé with horrified disbelief; or on Joe, looking like a man who just got caught doing something very bad.

"How could you say something like that to my friend? To any woman, for that matter?"

"I'm sorry," Joe apologizes, wrapping Brit's perfectly manicured hands in his. "It's just . . . I'm worried about Darren now. And there's a hole in the wall. Look, it came out all wrong. I'm sorry, Brenda." He doesn't even look at her as he says this. He's definitely *not* sorry.

On the plus side, Joe finally seems to have remembered her name.

Recovering from the near fall and verbal assault, Brenda shakes her head and disappears out the front door, not bothering to close it behind her. The wind churns outside, twigs and branches hurtling through the archway like catapults.

Joe walks to the door to follow her. I think maybe he's going to apologize, to *help*, but then he closes it right behind her. He strolls — yes, *strolls* — back over to Brit and cradles her face in his hands. "You have no idea how bad it is out there. We need to stay inside. I barely made it back. I'm not risking my life again. Or yours."

Not even for his *best* friend? This pretty much tells us everything we need to know about Joe.

"But Darren risked his life to help me," I pipe up. "You're going to just let him *die* out there?" This guy has officially been downgraded from jerk to complete asshole in my book, and that's not a word I use lightly. The sooner they break up, the better.

Joe's ears turn bright red as he shoots me a nasty look. "Darren is the one who got us into this situation in the first place," he says sharply. "Have you looked at your head?"

He's not wrong, but I feel a prick of satisfaction having gotten under his skin. I hope Brit is taking notice. Mr. Nice Guy isn't all that nice.

"Do we know that as fact?" My lip twitches as I try to stop it from shifting into a smirk.

"What do you mean?" Brit asks, inching away from her fiancé. It's such a subtle movement that I almost don't notice it. But I am adept at decoding Brit's every mood. I can read that girl like an account ledger.

"Look, all I'm saying is that I didn't actually see Darren hit me over the head. It could have been anyone." It *probably* was Darren, but really, it *could* have been anyone. "That's the thing. I honestly don't remember, so . . ."

Joe throws his hands in the air. "You have to be kidding me! He was the only one in the room with you. Either he hit you, or you did this to yourself."

Joe runs a frustrated hand through his hair. He seems a whole lot less sure of himself than he did when we got here. And now he has a giant cowlick on the top of his head. Between his eyes darting around the room and his heavy breathing, he looks less like a leading man and more like a horror movie extra.

"What do you suggest we do, Joe?" Brit folds her arms across her chest and rubs hard against her skin as if trying to ward off a chill. A flash of lightning shoots through the sky, sending ominous shadows across the ceiling and walls.

"We wait," Joe responds, going to Brit and wrapping his arms tightly around her from behind. If I didn't know any better, I'd say he was taking her hostage. "Darren is a tough guy. I'm sure he's fine."

I stare at Joe in disbelief. He can't be serious. He can't *actually* believe that Darren is fine out there. I wouldn't believe it even if his best man were the Incredible Hulk.

They say there are two sides to every story, and then there's the truth. I'm guessing the truth is closer to: Joe doesn't care if Darren is fine. I can't help but find that incredibly strange. If something happened to Brit, I'd . . . I don't know what I'd do, only that I'd be capable of anything.

Joe moves the arm that was resting precariously close to Brit's neck to her lower back, steering her away from the front door toward the living room to *wait*, I presume.

What is he waiting for? Darren to reappear out of the storm completely unscathed and shirtless, cradling a hefty load of dry firewood in his lumberjack arms? I'd pay to see it, but what are the chances of *that?* I can't imagine he's still out there by *choice.* No freaking way.

And there's basically nothing we can do. With no houses nearby, we can't go for help, and with no cell service, we can't even call for help.

Not wanting to be left alone in the darkness or physically able to venture out into the storm, I reluctantly follow Joe and Brit.

I find Joe pacing around the living room like a dog in heat. Brit is slumped on the couch, her head clutched between her hands as she leans on her knees for support. I fall into the space beside her, resting my head on her shoulder, my nostrils filling with her signature floral scent.

That's one thing that's never changed about Brit — she's always worn the same perfume, a delicate and powdery aroma, ever since the first time she shoplifted it. She can afford it now. But back then, we'd cut class at least once a week and sneak over to the local mall. Brit would casually slip the elixir into her backpack. No one suspects you of stealing when you're gorgeous. I never tried. I wouldn't have been so lucky. Lightheaded and giggly, we'd run like the wind to catch the bus back to school. To this day, I shudder to think of the repercussions of not making it back on time.

Memories are funny things. They live in the recesses of your mind and pop up when you least expect them. They hide out. Almost as if they never happened. *Almost.*

"This is a really sucky bachelorette party," I say, for lack of anything better to say. "Who would have thought everything that could go wrong *would* go wrong? I'm so sorry. I know how much you were looking forward to this."

She and I both.

Brit shakes her head, her sun-kissed blonde waves still full of shine and bounce despite the inclement weather and stress of the evening. I reach a hand to my head, expecting to find a frizzy rat's nest, but all I come up with is a disturbingly large scab of caked blood. Well, at least it's clotting. And I always secretly wanted to be a redhead. So, there's that.

"It's not your fault, Lisa. I know you tried. The shirts, wrapped up like presents," she adds. "That was a really nice touch." There's an unfamiliar cadence to her voice.

I feel my face scrunch up, like I've just tasted something *really* disgusting. "Presents? What presents?"

"Ha, ha. I bet you didn't think we'd find them, did you? Don't worry, though; we waited for you so we can open them together."

I rip my head from Brit's shoulder, eyeing my friend with utter confusion. My pulse speeds up. *Oh no!* Was I supposed to bring presents? I bought Joe and Brit a beautiful, personalized picture frame for their engagement, and I already have the entire bed set ordered off their registry for the wedding. I organized this whole weekend. Is that not enough? Maybe I'm just confused. My head is killing me.

But seriously. "What are you talking about, Brit?"

CHAPTER 30

Then

By the time we get home from school, I feel like a powder keg ready to blow. I don't recall ever feeling this angry in my entire life. Not even after the time I got dropped off here, not even when Ginger forgot to feed us for six and a *half* days.

My chest is on fire. How could she do that to me? I've been nothing but warm and welcoming. And *this* is how she repays my kindness? By making me the laughingstock of the school? I could kill her for putting me through that, on top of everything else that I've been through. I'm done trying to help her. From here on out, the new girl is on her own.

I sink deeper into the bus seat; my hands balled into tight fists in my lap. At every stop, I debate getting off the bus and running away. But where would I go? I have no family. No friends.

And then I think of how Ginger and Walter would react. They might take it out on the two of them. The new girl can go to hell, but the other? She's the only one I care about. I'd do anything for her.

So, before I know it, we are pulling onto the dirt road leading to Ginger and Walter's house. *Both* of my foster parents are waiting for us on the street as the bus pulls to a stop, as though they're inside my head, anticipating the bold escape plan I'd considered. They are waving so forcefully that I'm worried their arms might dislocate. No. I'm not actually worried. It would serve them right.

I feel sick just looking at them — Ginger and Walter — portly and kind with their three foster kids. Except, it's all a show. Smoke and mirrors. Only we know what's waiting for us inside.

I get off the bus with my head hung low.

"Smile," Ginger orders, discreetly pinching my elbow between two fat fingers.

I turn around and smile at the bus driver. Ginger pokes me in the back with a pointy red nail, and I wave. Only then does she let go.

Once inside the house, Walter marches us back to the basement. He locks the door behind us.

My blood is boiling in my ears. I want to say something so badly, but my jaw is clenched so tightly I can't even open it. My mind is running too fast and furious to find the words, anyhow.

I simply stare at her, wondering how a person could be so cruel.

And then she looks back at me and smiles. *Smiles.* The look is sharper than silence. It's like the cafeteria never happened.

But it did, and something *else* will happen. Maybe not today or tomorrow, but one day.

One day can't come soon enough.

From: lisanreynard@reynardaccounting.com
To: lisanreynard@reynardaccounting.com
BCC: brenda.peterson@brighthorizons.com, darrenljost@hotmail.com
Subject: Go Time!

It's GO time!

Let's make this a weekend no one will ever forget!

xx
Lisa (Maid of Honor)

CHAPTER 31

Brenda

As the wind whips through my hair and slashes at my face, all I can think is that these people suck. They *really* suck. Darren is a human being. A friend. The freaking best man in their wedding. Yet, I'm the only one out here looking for him. As much as I dislike Lisa, I'll give her a pass since she's bleeding out from the head.

But Brit? Joe? *They* should definitely be out here. Not me. I just met the guy, even if there is a bit of an electric current flowing between us.

Yet, I find myself alone, pressed against the house as I push past the roaring wind. The stucco, which looked so lovely in the light of day, is cold and slick. My fingers slip repeatedly as I try to grasp onto something, anything, to moor myself. It feels like I'm a gale away from becoming a casualty of Hurricane Ivy.

A thought erupts, hot and heavy, like an active volcano. How many casualties will there be by the time this storm is over? This *trip?*

"Darren," I scream, my voice barely audible above the ambient sounds of a Category 3. A large tree limb snaps and crashes to the ground in the near distance. Make that . . . the ambient sounds of a Category 4. "Are you out there?"

Silence greets my question. At first, imposing but serene, the trees now look like gnarled hands reaching out to grab me. The branches cackle as if laughing at me. Like this is all some kind of sick fucking joke. Giving Brit whole milk instead of skim in her Starbucks latte is a joke. But *this?* We're talking about life and death here.

I momentarily think about the box of gifts. The concerned look on Brit's face. This feels bigger than the storm. Bigger than all of us.

I feel my way around the house, taking small, deliberate steps in the darkness. I should have brought a flashlight. Except for the flares of lightning slicing through the sky like fiery swords, it's the blackest night I've ever seen, like the darkness is bubble-wrapped in darkness.

But what can I do? It's too late to turn back now. From here. From the trip. I wish I never had to see any of those people inside this house again.

But we're trapped.

And I have to find Darren.

I continue inching along the perimeter of the house when my foot connects with something hard on the ground. My heart thumps frantically in my chest. It's so loud I can actually hear it.

No, no, no.

Maybe a tree is down, I think. Yes, it could be the lost limb of one of the eight thousand trees surrounding the house. I swear, it's as if this house were carved into the center of a rainforest.

Using the siding for support, I lower myself down to the ground, kneeling on the drenched grass. I take a deep breath and slowly reach out a hand. Tentatively, I move it, hovering above the object.

Three, two, one.

I place my hand onto the object, expecting — *hoping* — to connect with jagged bark.

But it's not bark.

It's flesh.

Human flesh.

"Darren!" I cry. His body is still warm. I fumble with both hands to find his wrist to search for a pulse. He has to be alive. *Has to.*

Darren doesn't answer, but I feel it — the gentle *thump, thump, thump* of his heart still pumping blood through his body. It's faint, but there.

Another flash of lightning. I take in the awkward position of his body, the curve of his neck, the bends of bones where they shouldn't be bent. The ladder is lying beside his badly injured body. He must have fallen from the ladder.

How could Joe not have noticed the ladder falling to the ground with Darren on it?

Unless he did.

Feeling sick, I push against the ground to rise to my feet. I need to get help, but gravity wraps around my wrist and attempts to pull me back down. To my surprise, gravity has fingers.

"Oh my God. *Darren.*"

My knees buckle, and I fall back down to the ground. I lean my head toward his. "Brenda," he whispers, his voice so strangled I barely make out my name.

"You're alive," I say. "I wasn't sure . . ." my words trail off.

Darren pulls me closer until my face is practically touching his. His breathing is quick and raspy. "I need you . . ." he coughs violently, a long spasm that seems to last forever. I wait for the fit to subside. "There's a folder in my suitcase," he wheezes. "Hold on to it. If something happens to me . . ."

My eyes spring with warm tears. "Nothing is going to happen to you. You're going to be just fine," I say with little conviction.

Because he sure doesn't sound like he's going to be fine. Another flash of lightning casts an eerie glow on his face. He doesn't look it, either.

"Please, if I don't make it . . . you have to get it to the authorities."

"The *authorities?* What are you talking about? You're scaring me."

"Please, Brenda. I'm begging . . ." *Cough. Cough. Cough.* "I'm begging you."

"Okay, okay," I promise. "I'll do it. But I'm getting help."

Darren starts to argue, but I cut him off. "It's not up for debate. We need to get you inside. I can't do it on my own."

And with that, I extract myself from his grasp. I scramble to my feet, determined and frantic.

This time, I don't walk gingerly, I break into an all-out sprint. Darren's moans of pain trail me to the house like a dark shadow.

With all I have left, I cling to the front door, wedging it open and screaming, "Help me." The door smashes against the wall, widening the hole.

Fuck Joseph Briggs, I think. This is all his fault. Maybe more so than I even know. What does Darren have hidden in his luggage? What could possibly be inside that folder that warrants a trip to the authorities? I can't help but think it has something to do with Joe . . . with this weekend, perhaps.

I push through the doorframe, nearly smacking straight into Lisa. The poor thing looks awful. Blood crusted on her head. Purple bags under her eyes.

But I can't worry about Brit's maid of honor right now.

"*Help!*" I scream at the top of my lungs. "Joe, Brit!"

"What's happened?" Lisa asks, rubbing her head with her hands. My screaming seems to have exacerbated her current condition. Probably the least of our problems.

I'm about to answer when Joe and Brit come running into the atrium.

"What's happened? Did you find him?"

"I did," I gasp. "Darren's alive — just barely. We need to get him inside."

The news doesn't land with the sense of urgency one would expect. Joe doesn't move toward the front door to help his friend. He doesn't shout out instructions for us to help his friend, either. He doesn't even breathe a sigh of relief or exhale that breath he didn't know he was holding.

There's something else.

Maybe I'm imagining it, but Joe does *not* look happy about the news that Darren is alive.

CHAPTER 32

Brit

My fiancé looks like he's seen a ghost. Within seconds, his complexion has shifted from a rich olive to a pasty white.

I think about Lisa's earlier talk of evil shapeshifters, and I shiver.

Add to this the fact that Joe is statue-still. His best friend is outside, clinging to life. Why is he just *standing* there like that?

"Aren't you going to help?" I ask, gently nudging Joe in the back. He flinches at my touch like I've shocked him. He doesn't say anything but walks toward the front door. It's almost as if he's in a trance. All I can think of is *shapeshifters*. It's like there's a voice in the room whispering, *Shapeshifters, shapeshifters*, reminding me of the drivers' ominous warnings.

"Did you hear what I said?" Lisa asks, interrupting my inner monologue.

"What?"

"I can't stop thinking about what the cab driver said about *shapeshifters*. All the crazy things that seem to be happening."

So, I'm *not* imagining things.

Twelve hours ago, I'd have told you our drivers were crazy locals with wild superstitions. Now, I'm no longer entirely convinced.

All I can do is nod my head in agreement as Brenda follows Joe outside. Her plea, "Hurry, please," is just barely audible above the wind.

I do hope they make it back unscathed.

My gaze falls back on Lisa. I suck in a sharp breath. *Shapeshifters* didn't bring that box. They didn't lie about where they went last week on vacation. And they certainly didn't steal my luggage.

"We need to talk, Lisa," I say, once certain that we are alone.

She simply nods but doesn't say anything.

"Where were you last week? Don't lie to me."

Lisa drops her head into her hands. "I was here, Brit."

"*Here?* Like in this house?"

"No, here, like on the island. I was trying to find the house."

This doesn't make any sense. "But why? And why wouldn't you just tell me?"

Lisa's cheeks grow hot. "I was embarrassed, okay. I didn't want you to think I was pathetic. I know I can be anal, and I just wanted to be as prepared as I could be for the trip. Then I got caught in my lie. I'm sorry, Brit. It was stupid. I should have just told you."

"You should have," I agree, only slightly relieved.

Lisa and I don't keep secrets; we know everything about one another. But it still feels like she's hiding something from me. That box. The tissue-wrapped gifts. The White Lie Party. I'm going to get to the bottom of it right now, while no one else is here to witness what trouble may be lurking inside those dainty packages.

Lisa chews on her lower lip as if thinking hard about something. "Now that we have that out of the way, you mentioned something about presents. I'm sorry, Brit, I didn't realize I was supposed to bring presents to the bachelorette party. I bought you guys a really nice wedding gift. And you know, I tried so hard to make this weekend special . . ."

I raise an incredulous eyebrow and tune Lisa out as she rambles on about all the activities she *did* plan. What does she take me for? An *idiot?* Lisa should know better. "We found the box you left in the storage closet, Lisa. With the wrapped — *whatever* — I won't call them presents. The wrapped *game*. The typed note. The White Lie Party. Ring a bell?"

Lisa scrunches her face. It looks painful. She has black eyes forming, and her forehead has turned a crusty reddish brown. "What in the world is a White Lie Party?" she asks, without a hint of recognition in her battered expression.

"Seriously, Lisa? You sent a whole damn chain of emails about it, for goodness' sake. What do you take me for, a moron?"

"I didn't send—" she starts to say, but I immediately cut her off.

"Don't play dumb. You know what a White Lie Party is. Everyone wears a white T-shirt with a white lie written on it. Tanner McDaniels had one in high school. I wore the *I have NOT had sex* shirt." At the time, Lisa warned me that it was a bad idea, and as usual, she was right. Someone took a picture and sent it to the principal. I almost got suspended. "You wore the *Brit is NOT my best friend* shirt. Remember?"

Lisa flinches at the mention of Tanner McDaniels. She had *the* biggest crush on him. It's a good thing she never found out that I made out with him at that party. God, she would have been so pissed!

"A White Lie Party, hmmm . . ." Her eyebrows fold in. "Why didn't I think of that?"

"But you did. You *did* think of that!" I feel my voice rising along with my blood pressure. Why won't she just freaking admit it? This is ridiculous.

Lisa shakes her head, a look of consternation on her face. "I have no idea what you're talking about, Brit. Honestly. I didn't send any emails. Can I see the shirts?"

She's doubling down. The thought makes my insides churn. I think about everything that could be written on those shirts, and my heart palpitates violently.

"Fine, I'll show you," I relent. Lisa clearly isn't going to admit to anything until I do. The quicker we get in that room and open the gifts, the quicker I can get rid of them before anyone gets back from outside.

I hurry toward the storage room, with Lisa following closely behind. I'm expecting to find it exactly how we left it. But the door is now shut. Brenda must have closed it after I hightailed it out of there. For a moment, I feel a prick of panic that it's locked.

But that's impossible.

I twist the knob, relieved when it easily turns and opens. I shine my flashlight on the box in the center of the room.

And then I examine Lisa's expression. I'm not the only one who can be read like a book. But she doesn't look all that guilty, if I'm being honest. If anything, she seems genuinely confused. Well, at least she's *acting* like she's genuinely confused.

I know a thing or two about acting.

Lisa lowers herself to the floor and begins rummaging through the box. She reads the note, splattered with the dried blood from my paper cut. "Oh my God, Brit. Do you honestly think I would leave you a note with *blood* on it?" She flashes a horrified look.

I roll my eyes, my frustration mounting by the second. "No, I don't think you would leave me a note with blood on it. I got a paper cut, Lisa."

"Oh, I see." She shakes her head, flinching in obvious pain from the movement. When the pain seems to have passed, Lisa pulls out one of the tissue-wrapped gifts. She turns it over in her hands, examines it, and then drops it back in the box.

"Brit," she says, a haunted look in her eyes, "I swear to you on our friendship, I've never seen these before. They're not—" she rises to her feet, smoothing out her shorts. "This is not from me."

The worst part of this is that I believe her.

And if this isn't Lisa's White Lie Party, whose is it?

CHAPTER 33

Lisa

I'm not thrilled that *someone* is trying to steal my thunder. I'm even less thrilled that it's got Brit so upset. And I'm downright pissed that my best friend thinks *I* would do anything to upset her. She should know me better than that.

Brit paces around the small closet, her flashlight bouncing off the walls, making me dizzy. My head pounds — it's *killing* me — and not just from my concussion. My mouth is dry, like I've mistakenly popped cotton balls for candy.

"This is just so weird—" she says, mumbling. "Who . . . why . . . I just . . . I don't get it."

Brit's right; it *is* weird. I don't get either.

Who would do something like this?

Perhaps, the groom. "Hear me out," I say, causing Brit to stop dead in her tracks. "Do you think Joe could have had something to do with this? Maybe he wanted to surprise you?" I grit my teeth. "This could be totally innocent. A fun little game." At my expense, I think.

Brit stares at me wide-eyed but doesn't say anything.

I continue, "It would explain the door being locked. I mean, I know I left the key by the front door. Joe could have grabbed it, right? Oooh, oooh, oooh," I exclaim. "Maybe he has a big surprise for you!" As Joe loves to say ad nauseum — *only the best for my Britter-Bug*. Suddenly, this box and its contents don't seem so entirely weird after all.

"Maybe you're right," Brit says, a small smile lighting up her face. Her shoulders relax, and it's contagious.

"Always am," I shoot back, winking. "Come on, let's open them."

As Brit nods and sinks down on the floor beside me, a flash of our past rips through my thoughts. I stare down at the blood on the letter, and I can almost see it. I take a deep breath through my nose and exhale it slowly through my mouth, trying, unsuccessfully, to dislodge the image. Unfortunately, our past is not something easily forgotten.

I gently peel open the paper, exposing a white cotton T-shirt inside. I unfold the shirt, my breath catching in my throat.

Written across the front in black Sharpie:

I'm NOT a liar.

That's odd, I think, but don't say. A weird sensation roils in the pit of my stomach. A sense of dread that I can't quite explain.

My hands tremble as I place the shirt to the side and pull out another one. I'm not quite as gentle this time. I rip open the paper like I'm competing on a game show for a prize.

I'm NOT a cheater.

Wow, some prize.

"What is this?" Brit jerks dramatically away from the box. This time, I drop the shirt on the floor as if it's doused in gasoline and someone is holding a match.

"We don't know which shirts are for who, Brit." I wipe the sweat from my forehead with the back of my hand, immediately regretting it as a flash of pain shoots across my scalp. "Could this have something to do with Joe and Darren?"

"What? Like they made these shirts for *each other?*"

When she puts it that way, it's not like we're talking about a batch of friendship bracelets here. "Things seem tense. Just something I've observed." It's not just them, either. The tension is . . . everywhere. It feels like this house is a vice, the walls closing in on all of us.

Brit eyes me skeptically, not getting where I'm going with this. "So, they made each other *shirts* because they're mad at each other?"

To be fair, I'm not entirely sure where I'm going with this. "I don't know, *okay!*" I throw my hands up in the air. Truthfully, I have no idea what the fuck is going on. A person can only bend so much before they break. I reach back into the box and pull out a third tissue-wrapped shirt, the knot in my stomach tightening as I open it.

I'm NOT a fraud.

"Okay, seriously. This is freaking insane. Who is *that* for?" Brit jumps to her feet and resumes pacing the room. Always pacing, this girl.

"Insane." I don't disagree. "I'm kind of afraid to open the last two."

Brit stares at the box, chewing on her lower lip. "Maybe . . . we could just get rid of them? You know, before the others come back. Except—"

"Except what?"

"Brenda knows about it. She was here when I found the box."

"So," I shrug nonchalantly, "we'll have to get rid of Brenda then, too."

Brit's blue eyes double in size. "Are you . . . serious? You *can't* be serious!"

"No, I'm not serious!" Okay, maybe I'm just *a little* serious.

Because I don't need to unwrap the last two packages to know that this means war.

CHAPTER 34

Then

If we had chalk, paint, or any writing utensil for that matter, there would be a definitive line drawn in the sand. And by sand, I mean concrete. The basement has become a war zone.

I hate the new girl. I despise her with every bone in my body. I loathe her with every inch of my being. The only positive thing is that I am totally going to ace my synonym test at school next week.

Want to know what makes it worse? Ginger and Walter seem to have taken to her. As the week progresses, I take notice of the new clothing she's wearing. Not second-hand store buys, but actual fashionable clothing. For comparison's sake, I've worn the same jeans and oversized T-shirt every day this week.

Every. Single. Day.

As if being laughed at in the cafeteria that first day at school wasn't bad enough, it seems I have become the butt of everyone's jokes. And whenever I hear the laughter, *she* is always right there in the center of it all, leading the charge. The new girl is making my life at school a living hell.

I feel myself unraveling like a ball of yarn. Every day, I get a little closer to coming completely undone. God help her when that happens. God help us all.

We are sitting in our respective spots in the basement when there's a creak from upstairs. Despite the familiarity of the noise, we all jump. It's Friday. School is out for the week. We ate dinner last night. So . . .

My mind races with the possibilities of what Ginger or Walter might be doing up there. The lock clicks, followed by the groan of the door. Why are they unlocking the door? My heart thumps in my chest as I hear Ginger call out the new girl's name.

"Coming, Miss Ginger," she calls back.

Do you know what else I would do if I had a writing utensil and some paper? I'd stick a big ol' *Kick me, I'm a kiss ass* sign on her back. I've learned that about her *very* quickly. And she's a chameleon, too, changing her colors to suit her company. The only people she doesn't seem to care about are us. She really *should* care about us.

"I have a surprise for you," Ginger coos.

For a moment, I think maybe I have things all wrong. Surely, this is some sort of trick. But then, *this*, "You've been invited to a sleepover with the girl across the street. Your friend from school. Oh geez, what's her name again, Margaret, Marie . . ." her voice trails off.

It doesn't matter what her name is, I suppose. They're all the same: a bunch of lemmings.

Still, a *sleepover?* At someone *else's* house?

My pulse quickens as visions of the evening play out in my head. She'll probably have snacks and stay up late watching movies and sleep in an *actual* bed instead of on the cold, hard concrete floor.

As the new girl excitedly walks up the creaky basement stairs, it takes everything I have in me not to pull her back down by her hair.

This is all her fault. Before she got here, we were getting by just fine — as fine as one can get by in a place like this.

We weren't allowed to leave the house, yes, but at least we had the comfort of each other. Now, we're forced to go to school and get laughed at and reminded daily of the outcasts we've become.

The new girl has ruined everything. And she needs to pay for it.

CHAPTER 35

Brenda

Darren is right where I left him, crumpled like a crash test dummy on the side of the house.

"Over there," I scream to Joe, who is holding the flashlight out in front of him. I can't help but notice how the beam bends and breaks against the saturated blades of grass; maybe it's the wind, or maybe Joe's arm is shaking. I'd venture to say he's *nervous*.

When we reach the spot, I bend down, relieved to find Darren still alive and breathing.

"I brought help," I tell him. "We're going to get you inside."

Darren opens his eyes and wearily scans the darkness. It's difficult to see the expression on his face, let alone *read* the expression on his face, but I'm reasonably sure that *relieved* wouldn't describe it. It's just about the same face Joe made when I burst into the house with the news that I had discovered Darren alive outside.

I can't shake the feeling that something is happening between them — the tension that's been simmering beneath the surface, slowly coming to a boil. I think of the folder Darren begged me to get to the authorities if something happened to him before my mind flits to the box inside and the little white lies to get our party going.

What's *Joe's* secret?

I turn to him. "How did Darren fall from the ladder without you noticing?" A flash of lightning illuminates the metal ladder, toppled over on the ground. An ominous rumble of thunder follows. "That thing must weigh at least seventy pounds," I add. "You didn't notice it tipping, or at least, hear it hit the ground?"

Joe gives a noncommittal grunt, maneuvering around to level with Darren and me on the flooded grass. It's not an answer, but at least he didn't call me *Bianca*.

"Can you walk?" Joe asks Darren, his voice just barely audible over the wind.

All I can think is: can you *see?* Darren's right leg is folded like an accordion beneath him; his left is bent in a perfect *backward* right angle to the side. *No, he can't walk!*

"We're going to have to carry him," I scream, craving the cold comfort of the inside, where no hurricanes are raging, and there are conscious witnesses. The circumstances leading up to Darren's fall, the expression on Joe's face, the hurricane sirens. It's all making me incredibly uneasy.

Joe rubs a hand down his face, wiping away the rain. A moment later, he's saturated again. "And how are the two of us going to do that?"

It won't be easy, but, instead, I say, "You take his upper body, and I'll take his legs."

Joe eyeballs me with disbelief. He couldn't look any less sure about my plan. But it's not like we have many other options. We can't *leave* Darren out here. Well, I can't. As for Joe, I sense he could. He already did.

"I hope you're stronger than you look." He tuts as he snakes his arms beneath Darren's torso.

Meanwhile, I position myself at his feet. My stomach roils. I grit my teeth. No matter how gentle we are — and I'm not sure how gentle one can be lifting a two-hundred-something-pound man — this is going to hurt. Bad.

But we don't have a choice. There's no other way.

"On three," Joe directs, and I try to focus on his voice, on the task at hand. "One, two, three—"

Darren cries out in pain as Joe and I simultaneously hoist him off the ground. *Holy crap*, he's even heavier than I ever could have imagined. God, how much does this guy weigh? My arms shake under the load of his lower body. It feels like I'm carrying a bag of weighted vests. I struggle to fortify my hold without digging too sharply into his noticeably broken legs.

Joe and I take baby steps through the darkness, stopping every few moments to catch our breath and readjust our grip. Darren's moans grow fainter. I hope he's not going into shock and that we're not doing permanent damage.

Although it feels like the damage has already been done. Like there's no coming back from this.

After time stretches like an eternity, we reach the front of the house. In a blur of wind, rain, and dead weight, somehow, we manage to safely transport Darren to the top of the stairs and into the house, which, even with Joe bearing the brunt of his mass, is no easy feat. My arms are burning and limp like overly cooked noodles.

We lay Darren down on the tiled floor of the atrium, unable to push any farther into the house. We should get him to the couch or into bed, but — my eyes travel up the two-story winding staircase — there is no chance of that happening. We've taken him as far as we can physically go.

Besides, you couldn't pay me to go upstairs with Joe.

But I *can* go myself. I can make Darren more comfortable for now — grab some blankets and pillows — until we come up with a better plan. I hasten up the stairs, gripping the railing to propel myself forward. I'm three-quarters of the way up when it starts to wobble. My breath hitches in my throat. I pull back my hand as if scalded by the banister.

There's a loud crack — a baluster snaps and falls to the floor below, where it shatters on impact. I shudder at how close I came to joining it, completely disjointed on the marble.

I'll have to warn the others, so no one gets hurt.

After I grab those pillows and blankets.

I'm about to finish making my way to the top when I get an uneasy feeling as if someone is watching me. The hair on my neck bristles.

I toss one last glance at the base of the stairs, unnerved to discover I'm *not* paranoid. Joe *is* watching me. His staring feels endless.

Maybe I don't have to tell all the others about the broken stairwell. Because I swear, he already knows.

My list of misgivings about the groom-to-be is multiplying by the second. From everything Brit has told me about Joe, you'd think she was marrying the male counterpart to Mother Teresa.

But she's only known her fiancé for four months. It hasn't taken very long for him to show glimpses of a dark side.

I've never seen someone undergo such a dramatic transformation in such a short time. Joe's amber eyes, once illuminated with flecks of gold, have darkened. The grin that crinkled the corners of those eyes now looks more like a sneer. And the fact that he refuses to stop calling me freaking Bianca speaks for itself.

Maybe the prettiest people are capable of the most hideous things.

I break eye contact first, jerking my head away from his glare. I feel his eyes still on me, burning a hole in my back, but I don't dare turn around. Instead, I scurry up the stairs as if he's right behind me. As I scale the top step and round the corner, I exhale a quick sigh of relief. The more distance I can put between myself and Joe, the better.

I quickly take stock of the doors, attempting to recall, with only the dim light of my flashlight and intermittent streaks of lightning, which room belongs to whom. Lisa's room sits to the left of the stairwell. I get confirmation of this as my flashlight catches a glint of the subtle imprint from the shoulder slammed into the wood. Joe is so *not* going to be happy about that. It almost makes me want to smile.

Given Lisa's apparent affinity for being as close to Brit as humanly possible at all times, it's safe to presume that her room is directly next door to theirs. Heck, they probably have adjoining doors. A chill snakes up my spine at how oddly possessive Lisa is of Brit. It seems like she would do anything for her. Literally, *anything*.

Moving on, I pass Joe and Brit's room in favor of the next. Except, something makes me double back. At some point in the immediate future, I must tell Brit that her fiancé is not who she thinks he is. To be fair, I don't know exactly who he is, only that I can't keep ignoring the red flags that are piling up faster than in a heated flag football game. If I take a quick peek into Joe and Brit's room, maybe I can get some insight into the man I'm starting to believe may be a monster.

Then, I can warn Brit before it's too late. Before she makes the biggest mistake of her life. If she hasn't already made it.

I place my hand on the knob and twist slowly because, obviously, it would be ideal *not* to get caught sneaking into their room. But I'm not going to get caught. Namely, because the knob doesn't turn. I try again — a little *less* gently this time — and *son of a bitch*, the door is locked.

My pulse hisses in my ears. Three locked doors in a matter of hours. The most recent, Joe and Brit's. Joe was awfully squirrelly about the keys. *What* is he hiding?

Suddenly, all I can think about is the folder in Darren's room. His words, *Get this to the authorities*, echo in my head.

I scuttle down the hall to the next door, throwing it open. I arc the light across the room, landing on a suitcase in the corner.

I draw a deep breath, dizzy and nauseous with adrenaline. I rush toward the suitcase, falling to my knees and ripping it open. I hurriedly dig through clothes and toiletries, tossing Darren's possessions aside like I'm digging for treasure. And then, *jackpot*, I feel it. A manilla envelope buried beneath a pair of jeans.

I undo the metal clasp and open the envelope, carefully removing its contents.

I'm not sure what I was expecting. Maybe some incriminating photos. Illicit drugs. But a stack of paperwork? That's not very scandalous. Or all that interesting. There is an *awful* lot of paperwork. Numbers galore. I quickly scan through the ledgers, most of which I don't understand. There is one person here who might understand.

The accountant.

But I wonder, can Lisa be trusted with this?

CHAPTER 36

Brit

I no longer know who I can trust. Lisa has sworn up and down that she is not the one responsible for The White Lie Party. But if not her, then who? I can't make it make sense.

So far, we have unwrapped three of the five shirts. So far, we have a *liar*, a *cheater*, and a *fraud*. My mind spins with the possibilities of what might be next. I'm anxious to find out what the remaining shirts say. But I'm also anxious *not* to find out what those remaining shirts say. Deep in my gut, I have my suspicions. Ones I'd rather *not* consider.

I study Lisa's profile in the faint glow of the closet. She's decidedly calm, considering the events of the evening. I don't even know how she's walking around with that giant contusion on her head, let alone acting so *calm*. It's making me anxious.

Except for whoever set this up, Lisa and I are the only ones who know about the shirts and what they say. Brenda knows the box exists, but I'm sure there's plenty to distract her. My maid of honor, on the other hand . . .

My eyes flick to the door. Could I do it? Lock her in here until I figure out a way out of this? I nearly jump out of my skin at my thoughts. Good God, what's wrong with me? How could I possibly consider something like that? Lisa's been my best friend for the better part of two decades. I couldn't actually lock her in this room. *Could* I?

No, I couldn't. I don't even have the key.

"Brit? What's going on?"

My eyes snap to Lisa, who is staring at me strangely as if she could hear my thoughts. But that's not possible. She wouldn't be standing here if she could. She'd be running full speed for the door.

"Nothing," I say. "Nothing."

Lisa's eyes grow huge, saucer-like, as if she's been spooked.

Only, I don't think I'm the one who spooked her. Instead, it's the commotion coming from the front of the house.

We abandon our post by the box, and I follow Lisa through the house to the front atrium. This is becoming an all-too-familiar path. Darren is lying prone on the marble floor, and Joe is pacing around him, raking his hands through his hair and mumbling something illegible to himself.

This trip has been incredibly eye-opening. I had no idea my fiancé was a pacer. He could be a poster child for Fitbit. Seriously, he must have at least twenty thousand steps from all the pacing he's done since we've gotten here.

I've watched as Joe's cool, calm, and collected mask slips. They say the first year of marriage is the toughest. We're not even *married* yet.

"Is he okay?" Lisa screams while I attempt to process why Joe appears to be one step from completely falling off the rails. But Lisa's not talking about Joe. She's talking about Darren — who does *not* look okay. And I thought Lisa looked bad.

I can't even begin to count how many bones Darren must have broken. One of my employees caught her hand in the blade of a food processor when Bright Horizons was running a campaign for an appliance company. Thirty stitches and a reattached pinky finger later, her hand was *less* mangled than Darren's legs. He'll be lucky if he can walk with crutches at our wedding.

If we even have a wedding.

"I'm going to try to find some supplies so we can tend to his wounds," Lisa says, setting off for the kitchen. But neither Joe nor I acknowledge her. It feels like we're wrestlers squaring off for a match.

"What happened to him?" I ask, my eyes darting like pinballs between Joe and Darren, though clearly Darren is in no condition to answer for himself. If it weren't for the subtle rise and fall of his chest, I might mistake him for a corpse.

"He must have fallen off the ladder."

"Oh God," I gasp. "He's lucky he's alive." Albeit just barely. "We need to get him help."

Joe shakes his head. "*Where*, Brit? *How?*" His gaze flits to the window, to the chaos unfolding outside. "Look, all we can do right now is keep Darren comfortable. Wait for the storm to blow over."

He's right.

I can't help but wonder how, *why*, we booked a house in the middle of freaking nowhere. This place . . . I can't explain it. There's something incredibly *off*.

"You never told me; how did you find this house anyway?" I ask.

Joe looks down at his feet. He responds so quietly I *almost* don't hear him. "I didn't find the place. Lisa did."

"What? But you said—"

"I know what I said. I'm sorry. I've never . . . I just . . . I don't know. Lisa emailed me the listing, and it was so beautiful and belonged to one of her clients, who let us use it for free. I jumped on it."

"Why wouldn't you just tell me?" And why wouldn't *Lisa?* Didn't she say she spent the last week here *looking* for the house? Yet, she had the listing all along?

I don't know who or what to believe anymore.

"Don't you understand, Brit. I'm always trying to impress you. The way you look at me like I can do no wrong. I didn't want to disappoint you. Only the best for my Britter-Bug." The gusto with which my fiancé has uttered this statement a million times before is all but gone.

And I can't help but think: *this* is what he thinks of me?

Imagine if he knew the truth.

CHAPTER 37

Then

I'm so mad I could kill her with my own bare hands. You truly don't know what you're capable of until you are pushed to the limit.

I glance over at my last lifeline. My only friend. It's hard to believe we've only had each other for the past six months. It feels like forever. Like we've both spent the better part of our days together on death row.

We don't talk about it much, but I know she feels it, too.

And right now, she's just as wound up as I am, biting at her cuticles as if eating corn on the cob. She *wishes*.

It's safe to say we're not getting any sleep tonight.

There's too much adrenaline, too much tension, and anger swirling through the room like a knife-yielding psychopath.

On top of that, there's the weather. All the teachers chattered about it today at school, especially our science teacher, Mr. Folcrum. I overheard him telling our gym teacher, Miss Steely, all about global warming and the superstorms it's spawning.

"Tonight will be epic," he enthused before asking if Miss Steely wanted to "hunker down" with him. I thought he was trying to impress her, but maybe he was right.

Through the lightning flashes, I see that it's completely flooded outside our only window. Rain is seeping through cracks in the foundation, spidering across the concrete floor. The wind is howling so loudly I can barely hear my own thoughts.

Ginger and Walter are probably tucked comfortably under the sheets and blankets, forking into some gourmet TV dinner while rotting in their bed. Ginger probably does a lot of that. She's getting fatter by the day while we waste away down here.

It's not fair. *Life isn't fair.* Isn't that what parents tell their kids? We don't need (or have) parents to tell us that. We are living it.

I wonder what would happen if a tree came crashing down on the house, right over their bedroom. Would the new girl tell anyone that we're down here? How long until someone would find us?

I should be scared by my thoughts, but I'm too distracted by the anger burning like white-hot heat. I'm so mad I could punch a wall. Instead, I press my head into the stiff, yellow towel and try to drown out the terrifying sounds of the superstorm raging outside.

At some point, despite the chill of the puddles pooling around my body, my eyes start to feel heavy. I struggle to keep them open, but they keep slipping shut. I find myself nodding off, drifting in an ocean. Am I dreaming? *Drowning?*

Dreaming. I'm dreaming.

Until I'm jolted awake by a very loud bang from above.

And a scream that sounds an awful lot like it's come from Ginger.

CHAPTER 38

Lisa

My search for first-aid supplies ended without much fanfare. I located a few Band-Aids and some Neosporin, but I doubt that they will be of much use to Darren. Leg braces, perhaps. A full-body splint, *maybe*. I couldn't even find a bottle of Advil. That would have been especially nice, as my head is pounding like it's about to explode.

I'm about to join Joe and Brit to share the news of my failed excursion when I hear my name whispered from the darkness above.

For a moment, I think I'm hallucinating. Head injury and all. Why would someone be whispering my name? And who?

"Lisa." There it is again.

My eyes shoot toward the thin beam of light now shining down the cavernous stairwell.

"Lisa." A third time, and I'm certain I'm *not* imagining things. Someone is up there in the semi-darkness, *not* wanting to be heard by anyone else.

I squint, trying to make out the shadowed figure holding a flashlight. I realize it's Brenda, standing midway down the stairs, frantically waving her free hand, beckoning me to join her. *What in the world is this all about?* A shiver shoots down my spine as I shift from foot, debating what to do.

I think of the loose railing and wonder if this is a trap. But that's crazy.

Besides, as she calls my name for the fourth time, I can't miss the sense of urgency in her voice. She sounds desperate. *Scared.* I don't think you can fake that. Considering what's happened here today, *tonight*, something tells me I should listen to whatever Brenda has to say. Just *listen.* That certainly doesn't mean I have to like her.

So, I turn my back toward the atrium and walk carefully up the stairs. I try to recall exactly where the railing felt loose, but it's all one big blur. If it weren't for the intense throbbing in my head, I might think I'd made the whole thing up. I wish I *had.* The railing taunts me like a snake, threatening to wrap itself around my arm and drag me to the ground below.

In the twenty seconds or so it takes me to reach Brenda, I've all but unraveled. It doesn't help when she reaches out and forcefully grabs my elbow. I try to shrug her off, but she is relentless. She won't let go.

I'm about to scream when she holds up a finger and hisses to shush me. Despite my heart thrumming against my ribcage, my voice suddenly eludes me.

"Please," she begs. "Don't scream. I need your help."

There's something in her voice and the haunted expression on her face that gives me pause. "Fine, what is it?"

"Not here," she says, finally releasing her grip on my elbow.

I shake my arm, still feeling the imprint of her fingers on my skin.

Brenda signals for me to follow her the rest of the way up the stairs, and I do. When we reach the top and round the corner, I stop her. "Seriously, I'm not going any farther until you tell me what's going on."

Brenda reaches behind her back, and I freeze. Oh God, is she about to pull out a weapon?

I close my eyes, opening them back up when I realize nothing has happened. Instead of brandishing a gun, Brenda flashes a folder and hands it over to me.

"What is this?" I ask.

"That's what I'm trying to figure out. I thought, if anyone here would understand this, it would be you."

I nod my head and open the folder. Brenda shines her flashlight on the papers inside: bank statements, transfer records, account ledgers. I sift through them one by one, the knot tightening in my stomach.

"Oh my God," I gasp, midway through the documents. "Joe is Darren's financial manager, right?"

"Yeah, that's what they said earlier. Joe is his—" she makes quotations with her hands — "rainmaker."

I shake my head. "More like the end of the world storm maker."

Brenda lifts the flashlight so it shines up between us, highlighting her face, which is scrunched in confusion. "So, he's really good at making money?"

"I wouldn't say that . . ." My voice trails off as I process what this might mean for my best friend.

"What *would* you say?"

I draw a deep breath. "He's really good at looking like he's making money; he's really good at shuffling money around. This," I shake the folder in my hands, "has all the hallmarks of a Ponzi scheme."

Brenda twists her lips. "So . . . what? Joe is *stealing* from Darren?"

I nod. "And all forty-nine of his other clients."

"Holy shit. Do you think Brit knows?"

"There's no chance Brit knows. She would *never* marry Joe if she did. Trust me, if there's one thing I know about my best friend—"

Heavy footsteps on the stairs bring our conversation to a dramatic halt. My heart hammers in my chest as Joe comes into view.

Maybe he didn't hear us.

"Hey," Brenda greets him, attempting to appear casual. In reality, she sounds like she swallowed a frog.

Joe doesn't respond, his lips set in a tight line.

"Where's Brit?" I ask, sounding equally croaky. All I can hope is that she's a few steps behind. Surely, Brenda and I aren't *alone* with the mastermind behind a multi-million-dollar Ponzi scheme. I try to calm myself down. Even if Brit isn't behind him, Joe wouldn't do anything to hurt us. *Would* he?

I think of Darren lying on the marble floor below us.

Maybe he would.

Joe closes the space between us. I wince in pain as my back collides with the hallway wall. It sends a jolt of electricity up my spine and into my head.

I watch in horror as Joe squeezes his hands together, veins popping across his skin.

Oh God, he definitely *heard us.*

"What are you doing up here?" He asks through clenched teeth.

"Just grabbing pillows and blankets for Darren," Brenda spits out.

I feel a surge of relief at her impressive ability to think on the spot.

"Hand it over." Joe works his jaw as he says this, muscles twitching in his chiseled face.

"Oh, we didn't get them yet," Brenda replies, attempting to turn around and head down the hall toward the bedrooms.

Within a split second, Joe has blocked her path. He stands in front of her, angrily crossing his arms. Then he laughs. *Laughs.* When all I want to do is cry. Scream. Run.

"Do I look like an idiot?" Joe asks, the laughter abruptly ending just as soon as it began. I realize this may sound wild, but I actually *want* him to start laughing again. That was better than him looking at us like he wants to *kill* us.

"What do you mean?" Brenda asks, playing dumb, though surely she must know what he means. The guy heard us talking about him. He knows that we know. He's calculating at this very moment what he's willing to do to keep us quiet.

How far he's willing to go to keep his secret.

"Give me the folder, now," he says, not a hint of a smile on his face.

Brenda shakes her head, and her dark, straight hair falls like a wall around her face. But I can still make out the look in her eyes: *fear*. So, I'm not the only one whom Joe has failed to impress. I'm not the only one who's afraid of him.

Brenda glances from Joe to me, and I silently convey that she should hand it over. If Brit were here, she would know exactly what I was thinking. But Brenda and I barely know each other. Still, I shift my eyes up and down, flashing her a silent *Yes!*

For the love of God, give him the folder before he does something to us!

I bring my hand to my injured head, and I wonder if he already has.

And then I wonder what he's going to do to us as Brenda hands him the folder.

CHAPTER 39

Brit

What in God's name is taking them so long? Joe left me to watch over Darren while he went to make sure Lisa was okay at least ten minutes ago. With that head injury, she really shouldn't be wandering around a dark, unfamiliar house on her own.

I could have checked on her myself, but Joe said he'd feel better if he knew I was safe down here. As if anywhere in this freaking place is *safe*.

I don't want to talk to Darren. I'm not sure he is physically capable of conversation, but I need to know what happened out there. And I need to ask him before my fiancé returns.

Because something is niggling at me. No, not niggling. It's *gnawing* like a rabid animal. Did Darren fall off the ladder? Or did Joe *push* him? He wouldn't . . . he couldn't . . .

Could he?

I kneel down on the floor and take a deep breath. The fact that the future of my relationship hinges on whatever it is Darren has to say is looming over me. Who would have ever thought I would put my trust in him?

Certainly not after what Tamara revealed in the restaurant bathroom the night of our first and *last* double date.

"God, Darren is just awful," she told me as she casually applied a coat of bold, red lipstick. "Don't you agree?"

My eyes met hers in the mirror. Surely, I must have misheard. Darren and Tamara seemed to be getting along so well — *too* well for a restaurant if you want my honest opinion. At one point, her hand had traveled so far up his leg that it completely disappeared under the table. It didn't take a private investigator to figure out where it had gone.

I cleared my throat loudly, scanning the restroom to ensure no one else was inside eavesdropping. "What are you talking about, Tamara?"

"You don't see it? This—" She motioned around the bathroom, and my eyes followed, looking for some clue as to what she was talking about. But all I saw were two empty, army-green stalls.

I shook my head, wondering if Tamara might have ingested something other than the sour apple martinis she'd been guzzling.

Tamara narrowed her eyes at me. "Look, I'm just giving you some friendly advice, woman to woman. Darren is a liar and a cheater, and you know what they say: you are the company you keep. So, if you think you have a future with Joe, I'd advise you to keep him away from Darren."

My shoulders relaxed ever so slightly. This wasn't about Joe. It was about Darren.

Or was it?

"So why are *you* dating him if he's a liar and a cheater?" I shot back accusingly, wondering if she was using Darren to get to Joe, perhaps trying to snag the better catch for herself by scaring the competition off.

Tamara lifted a shoulder and winked. "Eh, social experiment." There was something recognizable in her eyes. Hurt, maybe? Bitterness? I wasn't sure. But either way, Darren was now on my radar *big time.*

It was an odd encounter at best, and I had fully expected to hear from Joe soon after that Tamara had broken things off with Darren. I mean, she called him a liar and a cheater and *awful.* But it never happened. Maybe Tamara could forgive and forget what she had unloaded in that bathroom.

But not me.

She had planted a seed in my head that had nothing to do but grow. So, I went to Tamara's hair salon, trying to squeeze *more* intel from her, expecting to extract information with the ease of extracting dye from a tube. It became a sort of obsession, if you will. Because what if she was right? Or worse, what if she knew something she wasn't telling me? But Tamara wasn't giving me anything else, other than gorgeous white-blonde highlights that cost me a small fortune. She may have dressed like a stripper, but she did do hair *really* well.

Right now, though, I'm not thinking about her ability to mix the perfect shade of blonde. I'm fixated on her words: *you are the company you keep.*

"Darren?" I whisper, tapping him gently on the shoulder. "Can you hear me?"

Darren doesn't respond. He doesn't even stir. I huff a loud sigh of frustration.

I try again, louder this time, as I rub a knuckle firmly against his sternum to try to rouse him. "Darren, please, I need to ask you something. It's important."

Darren's eyelids flutter slightly, but they don't open even though I am pressing extremely hard. This is pointless. I'm not going to get anything out of him right now. But there is something I can do.

I shift my flashlight from Darren to the stairs. Since Darren is basically comatose, I'm as good as alone.

I push to my feet, hazarding one last glance at the staircase before I head back to the storage room. I can't wait any longer. I need to know what those other two shirts say.

I'm relieved when I find the door unlocked (though I still have lingering doubts that it ever was locked). I quickly let myself into the room, honing in on the stupid box that is giving me more anxiety than the storm.

I know we'll survive the storm.

The contents of that box, on the other hand . . .

I frantically pull the tissue paper from the box, tossing aside the shirts I've already seen. The ones with the messages I can't *unsee.* Because which shirt is meant for whom?

I hold an unwrapped shirt in my palms, fighting to keep my hands from shaking. There's no part of me that's *not* shaking. There's a vibration running from head to toe. My heart is doing cartwheels in my chest.

I desperately rip into the paper, barely noticing as it scatters around me like snow. I unfold the shirt and gasp.

Written across the front:

I am NOT an imposter.

An *imposter?*

Despite the fear circulating through my body, cold as the frigid air in this house, I don't hesitate as I tear into the next package. My heart is beating so hard I feel it in my head.

And then, as I take in the words casually and callously scrawled across the front, like this isn't meant to destroy one of us:

I am NOT a murderer.

CHAPTER 40

Then

We both shoot up at the sound of the scream, which is followed by a thunderous boom.

For a moment, I wonder if I somehow manifested a tree falling through the roof and crushing Ginger and Walter beneath its weight, as if I would ever get so lucky.

"What . . . what was that?"

I look over at my roommate, whose eyes are as wide as saucers and filled with fear.

I shake my head because the truth is, I have no idea. I could certainly speculate: *Ginger tripped over her mumu and fell while going to grab a midnight snack; Ginger ran out of M&Ms and threw the bowl across the room in a fit of rage; Walter ate the last TV dinner, and Ginger threw something at* him. The Ginger-food-related possibilities are truly endless.

"I'm scared," she says, and though I want to lie to her and say *there's nothing to be afraid of,* I can't bring myself to do it. Because you know what, I am frightened beyond all belief.

I try to make sense of the basement. It's cloaked in all-consuming darkness. I scramble to my feet, only to slip and fall back to the concrete. Everything is so *wet*, water filtering in from every direction. I can't help but wonder what we will do if we *are* stuck down here. Suppose no one comes to rescue us. Will we drown — a slow and painful death?

For the first time, like *ever*, I hope Ginger and Walter are okay. I get up again, and this time, I manage to stick the landing. I wade through the water, relieved when my foot connects with the bottom step. I slowly make my way up the stairs. I need to try at least to get a better listen. If I press my ear tightly against the door, maybe I can hear what's happening out there.

And if I shout loud enough . . .

Ginger usually ignores the screaming, hence why I've abandoned that futile endeavor. But maybe if she knew how quickly the basement was filling with water, she might let us come up, just for the night.

I'm midway up the stairs when I'm stopped dead in my tracks by a familiar noise: the click of the lock. At first, I'm certain I must be imagining it. I haven't even screamed yet. Ginger has no way of knowing that it's turning into a deluge down here. The new girl — obviously Ginger's favorite — isn't here. I doubt Ginger is checking on just the two of us.

As for Walter, I don't think a man exists who does any less to contribute to a household. He's not unlocking that door unless Ginger tells him to.

"Hello?" I call out, my voice quivering. "Miss Ginger? Are you there?"

I wait a moment for a response, but a few seconds pass, and there's nothing. The house is now quiet. Too quiet. It's freaking me out how quiet it is.

If not Ginger or Walter, then *who* unlocked the door?

My fingers find the doorknob.

I twist with trepidation. My breath hitches in my chest as the door swings open.

I cautiously stick my head outside the frame. It is almost just as black up here as it is downstairs, except for a faint light flickering in the distance — from the kitchen, I think. It casts shadows across the walls and makes the whole scene even more unsettling.

But it's not the flickering light and shadows that have my stomach tied up in knots. It's the biting breeze blowing through the house; the biting breeze that is blowing through the house because the front door is wide open.

Why is the front door wide open in the middle of a superstorm? The thought assaults me like hailstones. The only logical explanation for the door being open is that someone left in a hurry.

Putting one foot in front of the other, I slowly make my way toward the front door. I'm halfway across the room when my foot collides with something hard. I stumble over it, crashing to the floor. I quickly catch my breath and press into the hardwood, pushing myself away from whatever I tripped over.

What *did* I trip over?

Somewhere deep down inside, I just *know*. It's this sense I have when something bad is going to happen. I'm not saying I'm clairvoyant or anything. But I'm also not saying I'm not clairvoyant.

Because in this case, the voice inside my head is telling me to run, to leave this place, and never look back.

It's telling me not to look down.

But instead of listening, I look down.

And then I scream.

CHAPTER 41

Brit

There's a scream, followed by a loud bang from above. I nearly jump out of my skin at the noises. I can't stop shaking.

Something has fallen, or someone is coming. Both are equally bad scenarios. No one can discover these shirts. My secret.

I scramble to stuff the shirts deep within the box, grabbing every last piece of tissue paper I can find to bury them. I push the box into a corner of the cramped space and conceal it as best I can under a pile of fresh linens. That will have to do for now.

I'm about to leave the room to follow the horrific sounds when something on the floor grabs my attention. It must have fallen to the ground when I upset the linens.

Of all the crazy things that have happened here today, this one just might take the cake.

How did my toiletry bag from my missing luggage find its way into this room?

I pick it up, just to be one hundred percent certain that it's mine. It's a Louis Vuitton Nice Mini bag that matches my luggage. Another gift from my very thoughtful fiancé.

With trepidation, I pick up the bag, my nostrils filling with the unmistakable scent of hand-crafted leather. *It's someone else's bag*, I tell myself. Maybe, it's possible . . .

Despite the panic electrifying my body, I steady my fingers enough to unzip the bag. I flip open the lid and almost faint on the spot. Sitting on top of the various overpriced products is a bottle of my signature perfume, a delightful floral mixture I've been wearing for as long as I can remember. It's one of my most prized possessions, a secret I would never reveal to anyone.

Which can only mean one thing.

This is *my* bag. The bag that was tucked away inside my luggage. The bag that was tucked away inside my luggage that purportedly vanished.

Well, apparently, it didn't get very far.

The question is how did my toiletry bag end up in this room?

"Brit!" Joe's voice rips through my thoughts. He's the one screaming. I clutch the bag close to my chest and make my way to the atrium, where Joe is folded over his best man.

"Joe?" I whisper, frozen a few feet away at the sight. "What's going on?"

He glances up at the sound of my voice. His thick, dark hair is standing on end, and his eyes are wild like the mangy dog's on the side of the road. Joe looks unhinged, almost feral. I barely recognize him.

Worse, he doesn't answer my question; he just shakes his head and stares at me.

"Joseph Briggs, tell me right now what is going on!" I bring my trembling hands to my hips.

But he *still* doesn't say anything. A horrible feeling washes over me. Did my fiancé develop laryngitis when he went upstairs to check on Lisa? And where *is* Lisa?

Because it's awfully quiet in this house.

CHAPTER 42

Then

Ginger is dead.

A line of blood snakes across the floor from the back of her head. I refuse to get any closer to determine *what* sort of injury she may have sustained.

As it turns out, I don't have to. On the floor beside her, there is a solid brass figurine coated in red.

A tree did *not* fall through the roof. This was no act of Mother Nature. It wasn't a tragic accident, either. There's no other way to work out the math. Someone hit Ginger over the head with that figurine.

I keep screaming because I honestly don't know what else to do.

I'm expecting Walter to come running in at any moment to a) see what the fuss is all about and b) find out how I escaped from the basement and return me to my prison. But when Walter fails to materialize, I think *maybe* he *did this to Ginger and fled the scene in a hurry*. That would explain why the door is wide open.

Except, there's a literal superstorm raging outside. Why would Walter pick tonight of all nights? Where would he even *go* in this?

It doesn't make sense.

Deep in my bones, I know that something is wrong, aside from the very obvious. I rise to my feet and venture deeper into the house, as if an invisible force is pulling me away from Ginger toward something else. Something quite possibly *worse.*

I know from my few times upstairs that there are three bedrooms in this house, Walter and Ginger's being the master at the end of a long hallway. Sure enough, as I make my way down that hallway, leaning against the wall for support, a faint light streams out from underneath their bedroom door.

My feet feel like lead weights as I walk toward the light. I swallow against the lump in my throat. Every part of me screams to run the other way before it's too late.

Instead, I raise a fist and knock gently on the door. "Walter?"

I'm not expecting an answer.

And, unsurprisingly, I don't get one. *Because what? Walter murdered his wife in the living room and is now hanging out in his bedroom, enjoying some popcorn and a movie?*

I knock again, harder this time, but still, nothing but silence comes from the other side of the door.

Fingers trembling, my hand finds the knob. I open the door slowly, knowing deep down that nothing will ever be the same after this. It's the same feeling I had when my parents died.

I instantly break out in a cold sweat. My heart beats in my mouth.

The first thing I see is the blood. There's so, so much blood. It feels like I'm an extra on a horror movie set. Ginger and Walter's once yellow daisy-print duvet is now vermillion. On their end table sits a book about sea creatures that is now spray-painted red. Apparently, not only can sea squirts eat their own brains, but they can also regrow their entire bodies through one singular blood vessel.

The same cannot be said for Walter.

He's not regrowing anything at all. His blood vessels are useless. Walter is decidedly dead.

Oh God.

My knees buckle beneath me, and I fall to the floor. I bury my head in my hands, pulling at my hair as I try to rip myself from this nightmare. But there's no waking up from this.

Through the haze of shock, out of the corner of my eye, I catch a glint of something silver lying on the floor.

A gun.

What in the world happened? Did Walter shoot Ginger and then pull the gun on himself? But they were the most miserable-happy people I've ever known.

I'm not sure how, but Walter loved Ginger. I guess misery really does love company.

It *couldn't* have been Walter. Someone else is responsible for this.

I take a deep breath. I need to pull it together. I'll call 9-1-1, tell the police what I've found. I scramble to my feet, stumbling over to the phone on their nightstand.

I wrap my fingers tightly around the receiver, veins practically exploding from my skin. I'm shaking so badly that it takes several attempts to type the three numbers into the keypad. Once I've finally managed to do this, I wait anxiously for the call to connect.

Except, it doesn't connect. There's no ringtone. Cold dread spreads through me from head to toe like tentacles. I follow the cord to the outlet and . . .

Someone has cut the line.

I throw the phone against the wall and back away from Walter's bloodied corpse.

I need to get out of here.

But not before I grab the gun.

CHAPTER 43

Brit

I can't breathe. This must be a fever dream. I felt like this once before: the night Ginger and Walter died. The night they were *murdered.*

You'll never hear me argue that they didn't have it coming. But still. It's an unsettling feeling, this odd sense of déjà vu.

"I'm so sorry. This is all my fault."

I snap back to my fiancé, who looks just about on the verge of a mental breakdown. It's like the game of Jenga. One wrong block, and the entire tower comes crumbling down. Joe is just one block away. *One block* pushed or pulled in the wrong direction, and it's all over.

Speaking of games . . .

"The Ouija board," I say, shivering. "It warned us we were in danger. It was right, wasn't it?"

Joe shakes his head. "I'm sorry, Brit. It was a joke. I didn't know you would freak out."

Wait, *what?* "That was *you?*"

"I'm sorry. Truly. I was just messing around and then when you got so upset, I didn't have the heart to tell you it was me."

"So, is that what's all your fault? Making us freak out for no reason?" Even as I say this, I know we have *plenty* of reasons to be freaked out.

And then, Joe's gaze dips down to Darren, and I realize he wasn't talking about that stupid game, after all.

"Oh God," I gasp. "What did you do?"

Joe looks back up, and I widen my eyes at him. But he still doesn't say anything. He just stands there chewing on his lower lip.

Jeez, why won't he just *tell* me?

Eh, I guess he doesn't have to. It strikes me that through all of our arguing, Darren hasn't even stirred.

I look from the man I thought I would spend the rest of my life with to his best man. It's then that I notice the shift in Darren's complexion. The bluish tinge to his skin. The purple hue of his lips. The overall white pallor.

"Is he . . ." My words trail off, unable to form the question.

Joe nods. "I'm in trouble. I did something bad, Brit."

It feels like I might pass out on the spot. "You . . . you did this? You pushed him?" I bring a hand up to my mouth and try to push back the bile rising in my throat.

I feel myself starting to hyperventilate. My head is spinning like in *The Exorcist.*

Joe pushed Darren off the ladder. He killed his best friend. Why did he bring us here? What is he planning to do with the rest of us? Oh God, where are *the rest of us?*

"Brit, no, I would never." Joe rises to his feet, and I stumble backward, trying to get as far away from him as possible. Less than twenty-four hours ago, my fiancé was twirling my bikini around a finger. I'm worried that if he had it now, he would be tightening it around my neck. I can't breathe. Black spots dance before my eyes.

I throw my hands up. "Don't come any closer." I look around for something, *anything*, that I can use as a weapon. At this point, I'd take a bar of soap to throw at him. But there's nothing. Not only is this house ridiculously white, it's abnormally bare.

"Please don't hurt me," I beg.

Joe's face turns crimson. "Britter-bug, I would never hurt you. Surely you know that."

Do I? I quickly realize I need to keep him talking. More talking, less killing.

"If you didn't push him, what did you do that was so bad?"

Joe takes a deep breath. "I think we should sit down. You're not going to like this."

"I'll stand, thanks." I fold my arms across my chest.

"I'm in trouble." He clears his throat. "Financial trouble."

I open my mouth to speak, but the words don't come. *Financial trouble?* I consider my luggage, the jet, this entire weekend, and I don't understand how it's possible.

"I'm a fraud," he continues, running his hands through his already disheveled hair. I've never seen Joe with a cowlick before. Now he's got like ten. It only makes him look worse.

Not that things could be much worse right now.

Finally, I find my voice. "What kind of financial trouble?"

"I made some bad investments for a big client. He lost a lot of money. Anyway, he was pissed, and he had connections. I was afraid he might try to hurt me. Or worse, you."

Joe pauses and draws a deep breath as if summoning the strength to continue. "I moved some stuff around. I siphoned money from other accounts so I could pay him back. And then it spiraled. I didn't mean for this to happen."

My heart races. I'm uncertain if we are still talking about the money. Or if it's something else altogether. "What are you saying, Joe? You stole from Darren?"

"It's all smoke and mirrors, Brit. I can't pay everyone. I think Darren somehow found out. He kept saying he needed to talk to me about something."

"So, you *killed* him?"

"Christ, Brit, I did not *kill* him!" Joe's booming voice echoes off the walls of the atrium. I reel as if he's physically attacked me. It's the first time Joe has ever raised his voice to me. I don't know this man at all.

One of the five shirts buried in the storage room flashes through my mind. *I am NOT a fraud.*

On second thought, I now know Joe a heck of a lot better than I did coming on this trip.

And accordingly, I don't believe a word he's saying.

"Where are Lisa and Brenda?" I ask, my voice shaking. Surely, he hasn't done something to them, too.

"I . . . I . . ."

Oh God, would you spit it out already?

He shakes his head as if trying to physically dislodge an image. "We need to get out of here, Brit."

CHAPTER 44

Then

We need to get out of here. That's all I think about as I run, gun in hand, from Ginger and Walter's bedroom toward the basement.

I nearly run smack dab into my roommate, who is standing frozen, staring down at Ginger.

"What did you do to her?" she asks, her face twisting into a horrified expression. Her eyes look like they might pop from their sockets.

"Nothing! I swear, I found her like this."

Her gaze flits from Ginger to me, then down to the gun in my hand. "And that?" She motions with her chin toward the gun.

I suppose the gun in my hand does look bad. "I swear I found it in their bedroom. I found Walter in there, too. He's been . . ." I pause, catching my breath, "murdered."

She bites her lip, tears forming in her eyes. "*Murdered?* How could you?"

"No, I swear to you, I didn't . . ."

She takes a step back, tripping over Ginger's body and falling to the floor. It's traumatic, for sure. But worse, Ginger's eyes shoot open.

In what must be a last gasp of energy, Ginger reaches out a hand and grabs my roommate by the hair. With her other hand, she takes hold of her neck, squeezing.

The room becomes a hazy swirl of screams and gasps. I have to do *something*. I feel the weight of the cold steel in my palm.

Do something. Do something.

With shaky hands, I lift the gun and aim it at Ginger.

My heart thrashes violently.

I couldn't actually shoot her. *Could* I?

But my roommate's face is turning blue; her eyes lolling in the back of her head.

I don't have a choice. I *have* to stop her. If I don't, she'll come for me next. I take a deep breath, close my eyes, and pull the trigger.

The force of the shot sends me stumbling backward like I've been punched in the chest. My ears ring. My vision momentarily blurs. I'm just barely able to regain my footing.

Time stands still as I survey the damage.

I can't stop staring at her. At what's left of her face.

Blood seeps from the gaping hole in her forehead. Her eyes are vacant but owlish, frozen in the shock she felt when I pulled the trigger.

Oh God.

I've killed Ginger.

I'm a *murderer*.

Sometimes, you don't realize what you're capable of until you're pushed to the edge. That's one thing I know to be painfully, poignantly true. Another truth: it was either her or me.

My eyes sweep down her body, marveling at the angle it's settled on the floor. In life, she was a monster. In death, a contortionist. Her arms are twisted around her head, having flown up to protect her face when she saw the gun.

She barely had a chance to scream for help or to beg me to reconsider. Not that I would have reconsidered.

Her or me.

Besides, I've dreamt of this day. Every act of cruelty has fanned the flames that burned fiercely inside my soul. If I didn't do *something*, I feared they would completely consume me — devour me from the inside out like a forest fire. But I never imagined I'd follow through. It's one thing to think about murder; it's quite another to commit it. In my fantasies, I hadn't considered the possibility — the *consequences* — of getting caught.

I should go, my head screams as I continue to take in her limp body splayed across the bitter floor. *Someone will come; someone will find me with her.*

But there's nowhere to go. A fierce storm is raging outside, tossing around furniture like litter and severing limbs from trees like a guillotine. It's nearly pitch black out; I can't see a blessed thing.

I should have thought this through. The others will find me with her; they'll know what has happened. They'll make sure I pay.

Unless I get to them first.

CHAPTER 45

Brit

Okay, I am really starting to freak out. Where the hell are Lisa and Brenda? What has Joe done to them?

I stare at my very soon-to-be ex-fiancé, waiting for an explanation that doesn't seem to be coming. It's as if he's gone mute.

Well, if Joe's going to be that way, I'll just have to find out for myself. I spin on my heels and head toward the stairs.

"Brit, please, *don't—*" Joe tries to stop me, but I'm done listening to his bullshit. There's clearly no reasoning with him.

I keep walking. Up one step, then another.

"Please," he begs. "Let me get you out of here. I'll explain *everything.*"

I let out a strangled laugh. "It's a little late for that. And why should I believe you? You're a *fraud*, Joe. You said it yourself."

"You're not wrong," he says. "But something is happening here, Brit. You have to believe me. I saw the financial documents. Darren must have told Brenda, because she had them upstairs . . . and," he pauses for what feels like a decade, "and they were *emailed* to Darren. Someone set me up, Brit. And I have a feeling it's not just me."

I think about this weekend, and the White Lie Party shirts I discovered hidden in the storage room. I can't help but wonder if he's right, if it's not *just* him who's being set up.

The room spins. It's as if someone has lifted the floor and tilted the house, throwing me completely off my axis.

"I have to show you something," I tell him. "But—"

"But what?"

"Only if you tell me where Lisa and Brenda are. Have you done something to them? Please, you have to tell me. I'm your fiancée, for Christ's sake." Well, technically, I'm still his fiancée. Clearly, not for much longer. "Where are they?"

Joe throws up his arms in frustration as if I'm asking a completely unreasonable question. "I don't know, they probably went to their rooms. I overheard them talking about me when I went up to check on Lisa. Brenda had the documents. I made her hand them over, and then I came back downstairs to talk to Darren. I just wanted a chance to explain." Joe's shoulders drop as he lets out a choked breath.

Then he moves closer to me, but this time, I don't back away. Joe wouldn't actually hurt me. At least, I don't think so.

He takes my hand in his, rubbing his thumb over my knuckles. Instead of filling me with comfort or love or lust, I'm left with nothing but icks. That's what lies will do. Turn everything you love into trash. Take all the sweetness in the world and make it sour.

It may be as good as over for us, but I need to know who did this. Who's *doing* this?

"Come on," I say, pulling my hand away from his.

For the first time tonight, I'm thankful for the darkness so I don't have to see the hurt that is probably etched across Joe's face. What can I say? He shouldn't have lied to me. I probably shouldn't have lied to him, either.

You can't build a relationship on a bed of lies.

But what's done is done.

Joe follows me through the house to the storage closet. I am so sick and tired of this place — not just the closet, but the entire house. This island.

I shine the flashlight down on the box.

"What's this?" he asks.

I hand over the blood-stained letter, and his expression rapidly turns from interest to horror. I watch as he pulls out the shirts one by one and realization dawns, his expression silently conveying, *one of these shirts is meant for me*. It looks like his heart has broken into a million pieces on the spot.

I should have known things would end like this.

"I think," he says, running a hand through his disheveled hair, "if we can figure out which shirt belongs to who, we can also figure out what the hell is happening here."

"Okay," I agree. I reach down into the box and pull out a shirt. *Cheater.*

Joe doesn't skip a beat. "That's Darren. He doesn't have the best track record with women." *Didn't.*

Darren is dead.

I push the shirt to the side, hoping to push Darren as far from my mind as possible.

I hold up the next shirt — *Fraud* — already knowing who it belongs to. "I believe this is yours," I say sadly as I hand the shirt over to Joe. His eyes dip to the floor as he hangs his head in shame.

We don't have time, though, to think about what was and what could have been. That ship has sailed, taking with it any hope we had for a future. There is no future for us. I think we both know it now.

How apropos that the next shirt is *Liar*. "I'm pretty sure this is meant for me." I ball the shirt up and toss it across the room.

"You're a *liar?*" Joe's eyebrows shoot up. "What did you lie about?"

"It doesn't matter now. We need to figure out what's happening here. Find a way out before . . ." *Before we end up like Darren.*

"No!" Joe's angry voice echoes around the room. He crosses his arms. "I told you what I've been keeping from you. You're going to tell me."

"It's about my past."

Joe clenches his teeth.

"Look," I say, "I will tell you whatever you want to know later, but right now, we need to figure out who's doing this, okay? There are two more shirts in this box."

Joe huffs. "Fine."

I pull out the next two shirts, fighting against the nausea rising in my gut.

"What is it?" Joe demands, and I can't bring myself to say the words. He reaches out and rips the shirts from my hands.

"Imposter and—" he stops, squinting at the words on the shirt as if he can no longer trust his own eyes. "Oh God." He drops the shirt to the floor as if it's been set on fire.

"*Murderer.*"

CHAPTER 46

Then

What have I done? I'm a murderer.

"I . . . I . . ." I drop the gun and watch as it screeches across the floor, spinning before it rattles to a dead stop. I don't know what to say. What to *do*. It was self-defense. If I hadn't stopped Ginger, she would have killed us both.

I think about Walter, bloodied and unrecognizable in the bedroom. Will anyone believe me?

"We need to get out of here."

She's right. We need to get out of here. No one will ever have to know.

I nod, unable to get my vocal cords to function. We move towards the wide-open door. The wind howls like an injured animal, tossing around debris with superhuman strength. But *that's* not what stops me from heading outside.

Instead, it's the wail of sirens. The blue and red lights cut through the darkness, slashing the walls around us. The line of cop cars, ambulances, and fire trucks stopped directly outside our house.

And the question running through my mind as police come charging inside the house one after another is how did they know something was happening here? *Especially* since the phone line was cut.

I don't have much time to ponder that thought as a uniformed officer begins rapidly firing off demands and questions.

Don't move!

Put your hands up!

Is there anyone else in the house?

Are you responsible for this?

Our hands simultaneously shoot up in the air. "We didn't . . ." I start.

I want to be helpful and answer his questions, but I can't. I can't think. I can't breathe. I certainly can't tell him what happened here. I can't tell anyone what happened here. And neither can she.

I try unsuccessfully to pull myself together. "We found her like this." I motion toward Ginger's motionless body. Then I start to cry fat, ugly tears. "I swear," I say, locking eyes with the police officer. "We didn't do this."

My roommate points toward the basement. "We were locked down there . . ." she says, before also collapsing into a heap of sobs.

Two officers make for the stairs. Moments later, they've returned to the foyer, two shades lighter. One whispers to another, "It looks like she's telling the truth. It's a nightmare down there."

In the meantime, while everyone tries to figure out what the hell is going on, an EMT places a heated blanket around my shoulders. Another covers Ginger with a white sheet. I remember the television shows. Soon, presumably when we've been taken out of here for further questioning, they will put Ginger's body in a thick, plastic bag, zip it up, and take her down to the morgue for processing.

And they haven't even found . . .

"Officer Gordon, get back here," a voice booms from the bedroom.

What I *was* going to say is that they haven't even found Walter yet.

But now they have.

And I can't help but think things are about to get a heck of a lot worse. It feels as though I'm walking through a fog that I know will never lift.

"I'm gonna need you to answer some more questions."

I realize the cop is still speaking to me. I nod my head, but no words come out. The corners of his lips turn down, but his voice remains calm.

"We're going to have to bring you down to the station."

I nod, then manage, "Will she be coming with me?" I make eye contact with my roommate from across the room. She is similarly wrapped in a blanket and equally traumatized from the night's events. Well, maybe not equally. I mean, she didn't pull the trigger. That's on me.

The officers don't put us in cuffs, but they do escort us out together to their police vehicles parked outside. Her in one, me in another.

I know what they're doing. Separating us to see if our stories line up. If they do, they will have to let us go. We're thirteen years old. They can't just throw us in prison.

Can they?

The officer in the passenger seat of my car turns around, and begins reading me my Miranda rights before adding, "If we don't charge you with anything, we'll be bringing you to an emergency shelter until they can find you—" he clears his throat, "—less *temporary* accommodations. Obviously, you can't stay here."

Obviously.

I think about what just happened — what I *did.* What if she talks? They'll rip us apart. I'll go off to juvenile detention, and she'll go who knows where.

I feel my eyes start to water and quickly rub them with the back of my hand. I can't lose her. I've lost so much already. She's all I have left.

And what about the new girl? What will happen to her?

I eye the house across the street, illuminated in the stormy night. At first, I'm sure I must be seeing things. An oasis in the desert. A mirage. A hallucination.

There are two figures in a window, watching. Just as I lean down to get into the police car, I squint my eyes to get a better view.

Then I see the new girl, with a broad grin on her face, waving.

And suddenly it all clicks.

No one else knew we were locked down there.

It was her.

She's the one who set us up for murder.

CHAPTER 47

Brit

"*Murderer?*" Joe repeats over and over again, like a broken record. "What the hell, Brit? For the love of God, would you please tell me what the fuck is going on?"

Joe is yelling at me now. I honestly hadn't realized he had a volume button. He's always been so sugary sweet, like cotton candy. All niceties have gone out the window. At this point, though, I couldn't care less. The truth is, I don't know *what's* going on, but I do know *who* those last two shirts are intended for.

I just don't know what to say. I can't tell him.

We promised.

"I have no idea," I lie. Well, it's a partial truth. That's the best he's going to get.

"Do you think—" Joe abruptly stops talking.

"Think *what?*"

"Do you think someone intentionally killed Darren?"

My cheeks flame. My entire body feels like it's been set on fire. "To be honest, I thought you did."

Joe starts pacing the room, quickly moving around me in frantic circles. "I didn't push him, Brit."

"So . . . what? It was an *accident?*" I wonder if that's possible, considering.

"The shirt says *Murderer*," Joe points out.

"But this shirt was here *before* Darren . . ." I don't finish the thought out loud.

Joe doesn't know about Ginger and Walter.

But he clearly knows enough to know that *something* here isn't right.

"I think we may be in danger, Brit. We need to get out of here."

"Where are we going to go, Joe? And what about Lisa and Brenda? We can't just *leave* them here!"

"Listen, one of them is behind all this, and we don't know which one."

I think about Lisa and her incredibly odd behavior this weekend. Her lies piled upon lies. I'm pretty sure I know who's behind this.

And he's right. We need to get out of here.

On that note, a loud bang sounds from above.

"What . . . what was that?"

Joe shakes his head. "I don't know, but I need something . . . to . . . to protect us with."

Right again.

"Kitchen?" I manage, my voice quivering. "The knife block."

The thought of *stabbing* my best friend is paralyzing, but if I've learned anything from my time in this world, you have to do what you have to do to survive.

Joe doesn't hesitate. His best friend is already dead. He leads the way to the kitchen, with me following closely behind. We round the island, and Joe stops dead in his tracks. I slam straight into him.

"What the . . ." My words trail off. There's no need to finish my thought. As Joe shines his flashlight onto the knife block, I have at least part of my answer.

It's empty. And it *wasn't* empty when we got here.

This is bad. Really, really bad.

Joe grabs my hand. "We are getting out of here, *now*, Brit. You have to trust me."

I guess I have to trust him. I don't have a choice.

I let Joe lead me from the kitchen into the atrium. The floor is soaked with water and blood, and Darren dead in the middle of it. I slip and fall to the floor, with Joe still grasping my hand tightly. He helps me to my feet, and then we simultaneously freeze as a light shines down on us from the top of the stairs.

It's Lisa and Brenda.

At first, I'm relieved to see them unharmed.

Until I realize one of them is holding a gun.

From: lisamreynard@reynardaccounting.com
To: lisamreynard@reynardaccounting.com
BCC: Joseph.briggs@briggsfinancial.com, brit.jones@brighthorizons.com, brenda.peterson@brighthorizons.com, darrenljost@hotmail.com
Subject: Re: Brit & Joe's White Lie Party

Given the fact that you have no service (thanks to our Wi-fi-free villa, cellphone signal blocker, and no neighbor for miles), you won't receive this until it's too late. If you are fortunate to receive this at all. If all has gone according to plan, there will be no survivors.

If you defied the odds, congratulations! And, *surprise*. I told you our White Lie Party would be a trip no one would soon forget, and lots of fun at that. Well, for me, anyhow. Not so much for you.

I'm sure you have lots of questions. I won't bore you with the details of my shitty childhood and even shittier adulthood. I won't consume your time with lamentations about what it's like to be unappreciated, invisible, and disposable.

All that needs to be known is that you all had this coming.

Each and every one of you.

xx
Lisa (Maid of Honor)

CHAPTER 48

Brit

"Don't move."

Don't worry, I want to say, *I couldn't move if I wanted to*. But there are no words. Because, why, *why*, is Brenda pointing a gun straight at us?

"Walk," she orders Lisa, lowering the gun a few inches so she can jab it into Lisa's back. Lisa takes a step, her legs looking like they're about to crumble beneath her.

"*Bianca?* What are you doing?" Joe asks, positioning himself behind me. *Behind* me! So much for my knight in shining armor.

"It's *Brenda*," she huffs in response. "If you call me Bianca one more time, I swear I will shoot you in the face."

Like Ginger. Like Walter. Clearly, Brenda means it. I have no doubt she'll do it.

"I'm s . . . s . . . sorry," Joe stumbles over his words. I feel him practically convulsing behind me. God, how hard is it to remember the name Brenda? I wonder if it's intentional. Joe likes to think he's better than everyone, but he's evidently just as bad as the rest of us.

"Shut up," Brenda orders, raising the gun back up so it's pointed at Joe and, by extension, me, because the guy is literally cowering behind my back in fear. "I've really had enough of you. Do you have any idea how exhausting you are?"

Joe doesn't answer. It would seem he has wisely forgotten how to speak.

"Brenda, please," I beg. "Put down the gun. We can talk about this." Whatever *this* is."

"I can't do that, Brit."

"You can. I promise, no one has to know about this. I'll give you whatever you want."

Brenda laughs. "Yeah, that's kind of not possible, Brit. Actually, you know what? There is something you can give me. I want to know *why*. Why did you send my fiancé pictures from our Vegas trip? *Why?* You know that's the reason he broke up with me, right? What did I ever do to you?"

Pictures from our Vegas trip?

"Brenda, I *swear* on my life I have no idea what you're talking about. I would never." It's the truth. "What are you talking about?"

"Don't play dumb, Brit. You sent Nick pictures of me hooking up with some other guy."

My jaw nearly unhinges. I had *nothing* to do with sending pictures, with her breakup. I took her on the trip and bought her shots. But I couldn't have predicted she would *cheat* on her fiancé, and their engagement would subsequently implode. Come to think of it, I was so busy with Joe that night, I didn't even *know* that she had cheated on Nick. Not until tonight.

In the dim light, I can't tell if Brenda believes me. But she's still holding the gun, so I'm guessing she *doesn't*.

And the question is what is she planning to *do* about it? I spontaneously break out in shivers, and not because of the air conditioning, which is still working like it's one hundred degrees out.

Again, Brenda nudges Lisa. She takes another step forward.

My heart is pounding. Brenda won't have to shoot me because I'm fairly certain I'm about to have a heart attack. As for Joe, I think he may be having an actual seizure behind me. I feel his body trembling, his breath coming hard and quick.

I push against Joe, silently willing him to move back. The only thing I can think of right now is to run. We're not all that far from the door. If we inch slowly and then make a sudden break for it, we might make it outside. After that, who knows?

Then again, I have no idea how good a shot Brenda is. I picture Ginger and Walter, and I can't move my feet.

"Don't even think about it," I hear, and any thought of making a quick escape instantly vanishes.

Because it's not Brenda issuing the warning.

A figure emerges from the darkness, and the world momentarily stops spinning.

"Watch out! Behind you!" I scream.

I'm not sure if I should feel relieved or frightened beyond all belief as Joe whispers in my ear, "*Tamara?*"

The questions shoot like rapid fire. *What is Darren's girlfriend doing here? Where did she come from? What does she want from us?*

Lisa falls to her knees while Brenda turns around to see what the commotion is all about.

Tamara takes a few steps closer to Brenda and Lisa, her hands extended.

And then I nearly drop dead on the spot as Brenda hands Tamara the gun. As in, willingly places it in her hands.

What. The. Heck.

Joe was right; we *should* have gotten out of here.

And now, it's too late. We're not going anywhere.

CHAPTER 49

Then

Tamara

Gosh, I wish I knew where to begin.

Maybe that stormy night long ago, when the cops took us from Ginger and Walter's house down to the police precinct for questioning.

Over and over, I repeated the same sob story: I'd been locked in the basement for months. There were three of us lined up in a row; two of us would stay, and one of us would go. I told them all about the new girl. About how she must have killed Ginger and Walter and then unlocked the door to the basement so that we would come up and find them. A call to the police station ensured that we would be suspected of their murders.

"Why?" They asked. "Why would a thirteen-year-old do something so horrific?"

The only thing I could offer in return was, "She's evil." It was the truth. I was convinced that Brit Jones was evil down to her very core.

A phone record check confirmed that the call did come from the house across the street. They couldn't say for sure who placed it, but it had to have been her.

We were set up. That bitch set us up.

After hours of relentless interrogation, the cops decided not to file charges against me or Brenda because of the lack of evidence, other than us being in the wrong place at the wrong time. There were also the obvious signs of abuse we had endured that went unnoticed for months by social services. I imagine that would have been quite the scandal had they charged us.

I insisted to the authorities that I found Ginger like that. I never admitted that I was the one who shot her, even if it was in self-defense.

And neither did Brenda.

When all was said and done, we were dropped off together at an emergency shelter. Ginger and Walter's deaths were subsequently ruled a murder-suicide.

As I lay on my threadbare cot in the middle of an auditorium-sized room dotted with identical threadbare cots — Brenda whimpering in the one next to mine — all I could think about was Brit, staring at me from the window of Lisa's house across the street. The open front door. Ginger, unconscious on the floor. Walter, murdered in his bed. The cut phone lines.

Despite what we had endured, I was filled with gratitude that night, thankful to be together. Brenda was the only person I had in this cruel world. As long as we had each other, we would survive. No one ever had to know.

But things don't often seem to go my way. And this was no different. I woke up one morning in the emergency shelter, and Brenda was just *gone*. No one would tell me where she went. It was years before I found her again.

The several years leading up to our reunion were a living hell for both of us. Group home after group home until we'd aged out of the system. Things with Ginger and Walter were bad, but I guess you can't appreciate how much worse they can get until you've been there.

I've been there and back.

I'd *almost* forgotten about the new girl, Brit, and her best friend, Lisa. Well, I'd not forgotten them, but I pushed them into the dark recesses of my mind where the rest of my childhood dwelled.

Then, about a year ago, I saw a glossy headshot in an article for the up-and-coming Bright Horizons advertising agency. I would recognize those cold and empty blue eyes anywhere. I called Brenda immediately.

"You have to see this," I told her, my fingers shaking as I texted a screenshot of the article.

Brenda went silent, but I knew she was surely thinking what I was thinking: Operation Destroy Brittany Jones had commenced.

The first step was getting close to Brit, which turned out to be easier than we ever could have imagined, as Brit was currently interviewing for an administrative assistant position at Bright Horizons.

"What if she recognizes me?" Brenda asked, not yet entirely on board with my ingenious plan.

She had a point.

"We'll dye your hair," I suggested. Brenda wasn't thrilled with the prospect of coloring her fine blonde hair black, but with a bit of gentle convincing, I got her on board.

I'd always been able to convince Brenda to do *anything*, even that night with Ginger and Walter. She never did tell anyone that I shot Ginger, and she seemed to be over it now.

Besides, finding Brit had lit a fire under both of us.

Anyway, for several days, I stood on the street outside of Bright Horizons, bawling my eyes out. Like clockwork, each potential applicant stopped to ask if I was okay, most on their way in for interviews.

"I just came out of an interview," I sobbed. "She was awful. She called me ugly, fat, incompetent." The insults I lamented changed, but the result was the same: not one woman interviewed for the administrative assistant position. Two even offered to take me out for coffee.

By the time Brenda showed up for her interview — overqualified, early, and in the flesh — Brit was all but *begging* her to take the job, which naturally she did.

Slowly but surely, we learned everything there was to know about Brittany Jones. Interesting fun facts about how, in the wake of the Ginger–Walter scandal, Lisa's parents petitioned for custody and eventually adopted her. They paid for her to attend NYU, where she secured a coveted degree in advertising. They even funded her start-up, Bright Horizons.

Lucky bitch.

The one thing we didn't know was *why* Brit set us up that night. I knew she didn't like us, but to be that diabolical as a thirteen-year-old, I couldn't wrap my head around it. The more Brenda infiltrated Brit's life, the more this question began eating me up inside.

Especially, as time went on, and it seemed like Brenda was actually starting to take to Brit, to like and *respect* her. After how she treated us, after how she set us up. Imagine that!

That's when I came up with the plan: a work trip to Vegas to present for a major advertising opportunity that didn't actually exist. As if I would use a start-up agency to promote my upscale chain of hair salons.

The same upscale chain of hair salons that facilitated the purchase of the villa in Punta Cana — the place where my dream, their *nightmare*, would play out.

There was another problem, or at least what I perceived as a problem, though. Brenda was engaged to be married and growing increasingly distracted. I needed her to focus. So, unbeknownst to her, I had followed her and Brit on their "work trip", waiting for an opportunity to strike, which came one night while they were at a bar. Brenda had left her drink unattended to go to the restroom, and I slipped over and added an extra ingredient.

Yes, I felt bad, but it had to be done. It all comes down to survival. Some might call my obsession with destroying Brit *revenge*, but I like to think of it more along the lines of mental self-preservation.

Anyway, by the night's end, Brenda didn't know a random stranger in the club from her fiancé. Thankfully, I was there to capture the moment and anonymously pass it along to Nick. And I was also there to comfort her in the wake of her devastating loss. Once the wedding was called off, I had Brenda's undivided attention again.

In the meantime, Brit had met a tall, dark, and handsome man on the trip.

Don't get me wrong, I wasn't *unhappy* that Brit met someone. It was more ammunition for my arsenal. Of course, I did my due diligence and learned everything there was to know about Brit's new beau, financial advisor Joseph Briggs. That's how I found his best friend, Darren, the cute Waxinator guy from *Shark Tank*. That gave me even more access to Brit and a chance to get inside her head. At first, I considered simply ruining things between Brit and Joe, but then I decided she deserved far, far worse.

Lucky for me, Brit and Joe had a whirlwind courtship, so I was able to implement and expedite a foolproof detonate-and-destroy plan. With Brenda on the inside, all it took was some surveillance and a few hundred fake emails to get things going.

Yes, fake emails. It's almost laughable how easy it was to fabricate an email address. Switch out an "m" for an "n" and voila, Lisa Reynard was sending hundreds of emails she didn't know she was sending. You would think, knowing her as well as she did, considering her middle name is *Nancy*, Brit would have noticed, but Brit was too busy being all about Brit.

Brit's always been very good at being all about Brit.

The White Lie Party was the brainchild of yours truly. Lisa truly had no idea whatsoever. She was right about one thing, though. Brit and Joe's bachelor-bachelorette party would be a weekend that no one would soon (ever) forget.

CHAPTER 50

Tamara

This moment is a year — a *lifetime* — in the making.

As I march Lisa down the stairs, with Brenda by my side, I think about all the work that went into planning this bachelor-bachelorette trip. All the little things that I knew would drive them crazy — the air conditioning, the missing luggage, the locking and unlocking of doors, the spiking of drinks, and the shirts exposing each and every one of their filthy lies. The hurricane was just the icing on the cake — a much more palatable explanation for the lights and cell service going out.

To think, I almost got caught twice.

First, Darren recognized Brenda. We'd been dating for several months, and he'd seen her leaving my apartment before, on *more* than one occasion. Thankfully, though, he couldn't place her. He probably thought he slept with her. Women were interchangeable to Darren. It speaks volumes about the man I was dating.

The second close call came when Darren surfaced in Lisa's room. *Lisa!* I mean, *seriously?* I could have killed him on the spot. But instead, I hid in the closet and waited for him to leave. As Lisa was drifting off to sleep, I smashed her straight over the head with a candlestick. Then I snuck back out of the room and locked her in. Leaving a trail of blood from her room to her stairs was enough to freak everyone out and turn them against each other.

Darren should have listened to me. He shouldn't have gone on this trip. He shouldn't have spent the weekend hitting on my best friend. He definitely shouldn't have left his phone unlocked on an airplane seat before going to the bathroom after flirting with a *complete stranger* on the plane.

Well, stranger to him.

I think about the text Brenda sent from his phone:

> *I think your fiancé may be sitting next to me, hitting on me on the plane.*

They'd just barely departed from New York.

For someone so inventive, Darren is an absolute moron.

Well, *was.*

Even though he wasn't the one I came here for, and he was really successful and good — okay, *great* — in bed, Darren paid the price for his indiscretions.

They will *all* pay the price for their deceptions.

I wasn't joking when I warned Darren that something *death bad* was going to happen. I just hadn't planned on Darren being the one to die. At least, not until I snuck back into Lisa's room and outside onto the balcony, after overhearing their plan to get in from the window. It's there that I began violently shaking the ladder. Back and forth, back and forth, until it came tumbling down.

Truth be told, I was actually starting to care about Darren. But now that all is said and done, I won't miss him all that much. He was never mine to begin with.

But Brittany Jones? She's *mine.* I've got her right where I want her, and this time, *she* won't be the one laughing and waving as I get hauled away by the police.

On that note, I point the gun at Brit. "Move," I tell her.

"Tamara? Please," she cries out. "Why are you doing this?"

My free hand clenches into a fist as I flash back to that first day in the cafeteria when I waved and smiled at Brit, inviting her to join me and Brenda at our table. The way she whispered in Lisa's ear. The way the whispers traveled down the line until the entire table had erupted in laughter. I felt a sense of embarrassment and loss like I'd never felt before. I still feel it right now just thinking about it. Thinking about her.

I feel my upper lip twitch. I really don't have the time or energy for Brittany Jones's dramatics. "I said *move!*"

Brit practically leaps like a frog to the side, and that's when I get my first clean shot. At Joe, that is.

"This is for stealing my money," I say, squeezing the trigger and watching Brit's fiancé crumble to the ground, directly on top of his best friend. That's right, I was one of the remaining forty-nine clients that asshole siphoned from. Plus, I'm one hundred percent with Brenda that, aside from being a fraud and a thief, this guy is *incredibly* annoying. Well, he *was* incredibly annoying. Things will be much more enjoyable moving forward with him gone.

Two down, two to go.

Now, there's no one left to stop me from doing what I've been waiting for so long to do. Certainly not Lisa. She's nothing more than a lemming. As for Brit, if she were wearing boots, she'd be shaking in them. Her hands are trembling. Even through the scant glow of the flashlight, it is obvious that she's grown a few shades whiter. I'm guessing she's putting it all together now.

It's slightly bittersweet. I almost don't want this to end. *Almost.*

"Tamara?"

I realize Brenda is talking to me. Rude, since I wasn't done talking to myself.

"Yes?" I narrow my eyes at her, waiting to hear what she has to say. It's not like Brenda to interrupt, as I usually do all the talking. That's how it's always been: me taking the reins and protecting her. Doesn't she realize I'm *still* protecting her?

"I think, I think . . ." her words trail off.

I cock my head to the side, a silent *what?* I fight the urge to roll my eyes. Now is *not* the time for Brenda to start thinking.

It happens so fast, I swear I have whiplash.

Brenda reels back and, with both hands, pushes into me with all of her might. I'm caught completely off guard, and, like a chain of dominoes, I crash into Lisa. The impact sends us both pummeling against the banister.

There's a moment of stillness before the cracks come, like fireworks on the fourth of July.

Lisa and I fall to the marble below.

CHAPTER 51

Brit

Brenda and I are frozen in stunned silence, both staring wide-eyed and gape-jawed at Lisa and Tamara, unmoving on the tiled floor. At some point, I break from my trance. My gaze flicks down to Joe and Darren, lying dead beside my feet.

I can't move my feet. Forget *moving*. I can't even begin to process what just happened.

The only thing I *can* process is that somehow, in the scuffle, Brenda managed to grab the gun back from Tamara. And I can't help but wonder what she is going to do with it.

Brenda slowly makes her way down the winding staircase, avoiding the gaping hole where the banister used to be. With each step, my heart races faster in my chest. By the time she has closed the distance between us, it feels like I might actually die on the spot.

Then again, I suppose that isn't the biggest stretch since she's holding a gun.

My eyes lock with hers, and I take a deep breath, waiting for the end. I have so, so many questions for which I'll never have answers. I hope it's over quickly. I pray I don't feel any pain. Not like Ginger and Walter did. I remember that stormy night all those years ago. It was my idea to sneak out of Lisa's house. I couldn't stand Ginger and Walter. The way he looked at me. The way she let it happen. The way they both kept us all locked in the basement. I could go on and on.

I knew that night might be the only opportunity I'd have to get back at them.

Thankfully, I had Lisa positioned perfectly under my thumb. She would do whatever I wanted. Over those few weeks at school, as we became fast best friends, I saw her insecurity and malleability for the weaknesses they were. If coddled just the right way, Lisa would make the perfect accomplice.

If only she hadn't done what she did.

The plan was teach to Ginger and Walter a lesson. "Scare them," I told Lisa. Tamara and Brenda would stay locked in the basement, none the wiser. I couldn't care less about them. They were needy, annoying, and worse, *complacent*, trying to turn us into the Three Musketeers, who would live out our childhoods banded together in the basement. I wasn't looking for an alliance; I didn't want to make friends; I wanted *out*.

Lisa and I snuck into the house that night, startling Ginger, who was, unsurprisingly, grabbing a midnight snack.

"What in the world?" she started to ask.

I panicked and quickly grabbed a figurine off the television stand and smashed it over her head. She went down instantly.

"What . . . Why . . ." Lisa stuttered, suddenly shaking as if spiking a fever. For a smart girl, she had to know that this wouldn't end *pretty*.

"Walter," I said, bringing two fingers up to my mouth to shush her.

Lisa's eyes practically exploded from her face.

"I'm just going to talk to him," I lied. "I'm sure Ginger is fine. Just wait here for her to wake up, okay?"

Lisa muttered something sounding like *okay*, and I made my way toward the bedroom. In my pocket, the Smith & Wesson I'd lifted from Lisa's house before we snuck out. Believe me, I had zero intentions of *talking* to Walter. I mean, it was too late for talking. How could I possibly explain striking Ginger over the head? Walter would strangle me with his own two hands.

I tiptoed down the hallway, slowly turning the knob to their bedroom door. Walter was sprawled out on the bed, munching on popcorn and watching TV as if he hadn't a care in the world. Well, to be fair, soon enough, he wouldn't.

In a flash, he turned his attention to the door, shooting bolt upright when he saw me standing in the frame with a gun pointed straight at him.

"Brittany," he soothed, attempting to rise from the bed. "No—"

I fired the first shot, hitting him in the shoulder and knocking him back.

"That one is for locking me in the basement."

"Please," he pleaded. "I had no idea . . . it was Ginger."

I was quite shocked at how quickly he had turned on Ginger, but I guess the instinct to survive will do that to you. It had brought me here — to this house, to this bedroom, to this point, from which I could never turn back.

I steadied my hands, this time aiming straight for his face. And just like that, with one final shot, Walter was done protesting.

But now, I was kind of freaking out. I quickly wiped the gun on my hands before dropping it to the floor. Thinking fast, I cut the phone line to make it look like a home invasion gone wrong, which I suppose it *sort of* was.

I ran from the room, looking for Lisa.

"I'm sorry," she said, motioning toward the basement door.

No, no, no.

"Why would you do that?" I mouthed through gritted teeth.

"It's flooding, Brit. They could die down there."

It was all I could do not to smack her upside the head with the bloody figurine. Lisa had unlocked the basement door. She was setting Tamara and Brenda loose, and she wasn't going to let me do anything about it. It was the first and last time Lisa would ever cross me.

"Run," I instructed, and she listened, following me out the front door. When we'd gotten back to her house, and Lisa was tucked away safely in the bathroom, brushing her teeth for exactly one hundred twenty seconds as she always did, I dialed 9-1-1. I told the operator all about the disturbance I'd heard from the house across the way.

Framing Tamara and Brenda for Ginger and Walter's brutal murders was *not* part of my original plan. But I couldn't take a chance that they had seen Lisa and I running out the front door. Someone had to take the fall. And as they say, *survival.*

Despite the fact that the cold-blooded murders of Ginger and Walter Hill were front-page national news, Tamara and Brenda were neither arrested nor charged. I wasn't entirely surprised. I mean, they were children. We were all children. And as it would quickly come out, Ginger and Walter were *monsters.*

Last I heard, Tamara and Brenda were sent away to group homes. Lisa's family graciously adopted me. They showered me with love and affection, and I gladly reciprocated. The Reynards loved me so much, in fact, that they left me half of everything in their will, which was executed when they passed last year. I was devastated by the loss, but then I met Joe, and there was still a chance for a happily-ever-after for me, or so I thought.

Now?

When I realize nothing has happened, I lift my eyes, connecting with the gun. To my surprise, it's not pointed *at* me, but rather, is hanging limply at Brenda's side.

"Are you okay?" Brenda asks, and it's all I can do not to burst into tears.

She drops the gun to the floor, kicking it across the atrium with her bare foot. Thankfully, it doesn't go off.

"I . . . I . . ." I'm at a complete loss for words.

"I didn't know she was here," Brenda says before chewing on her lower lip. Not until she found me upstairs. "You know who I am now, don't you?"

I nod silently.

"I'm sorry for everything. I assume Tamara left those shirts here for you to find. And I guess I'm the imposter."

"I'm the liar," I tell her.

"Which makes Lisa . . ."

Again, I nod. "Which makes Lisa the murderer."

"Wow," Brenda says. I don't know why, but I always thought it was you who killed Walter. It was Lisa?"

"Sure was," I say, liking this version of our past better than any other I could conjure. I use my bloodied shirt to wipe a tear from my face.

"It's over," Brenda says. "It's finally over."

"Thank you for saving my life."

What I really want to say is, *thank you for killing Lisa*. Because I once heard someone say the only way two people can keep a secret is if one of them is dead.

EPILOGUE

Brenda

The next morning, the hurricane had passed over, and the rising sun highlighted the death and destruction it had left in its wake — well, the death and destruction *Tamara* had left in its wake.

After searching the house and discovering the tampered circuit breakers, the generator out back connected only to the air conditioning, and Tamara's signal blocker, Brit and I were finally able to contact the local authorities. After many, many days of intense interrogation (just as Tamara and I had endured on that fateful night years ago), we were cleared of any wrongdoing and free to go. When the officers discovered the house was purchased through an LLC that linked back to Tamara, her extensive internet searches and travel history to the island, and more poignantly, the manifesto she left behind detailing her history with Brit and Lisa and plans for comeuppance, all the cards seemed to fall into place. She had set this whole thing up. Brit and I were innocent victims (mostly), the only two survivors left in what became dubbed the Hurricane Tamara Massacre.

What Tamara planned to do once the carnage was over, we'll never know.

We didn't make it back to the Big Apple in time for the big purse pitch, but in the grand scheme of things, at least we made it back to New York alive. There were, after all, four others who didn't.

Besides, the purse campaign was small potatoes compared to the roast we were baking. The press attention alone was enough to get things cooking big time. Over the next few months, Brit and I both gave countless interviews. Our story aired country-wide and even abroad. By the time the next big hurricane had hit, everyone and their mother knew about Bright Horizons. We quickly became *the* premier advertising agency in New York City, as in, no longer top ten.

We were number one.

"Hey, Brenda?" Brit calls out from her desk. My desk now sits across the room from hers. As soon as we got back to the office, Brit announced that she was taking on a partner: yours truly. Bright Horizons has never been so bright.

"What's up, partner?" I swear, it never gets old saying that.

Brit laughs, "You're not going to believe who just emailed."

I lean forward in my ergonomic desk chair, propping my elbows atop my brand-spanking-new mahogany desk. The thing is massive, a real architectural beauty. Growing up, I always wanted a fancy desk — that and at least one meal a day. Now, I've got all that and then some.

"Allstate," she says. "They want us to pitch them on a campaign for weather travel insurance." Oh goodness, the irony.

"Shut up!" I shout, hitting my palms against the desk. "That's freaking huge."

Brit beams. "You know, I planned for this while we were in Punta Cana. I took pictures in the flooded living room."

Of course, she did. I smile widely. "When is the meeting?"

"More importantly," she says, a smile playing on her lips. "Where?"

"Okay," I play along, "*where* is the meeting?"

Brit claps her hands together in excitement. "A private island in the Bahamas!"

I mirror my face to match hers, but my mind is somewhere else entirely.

See, this was the problem with Tamara. We were never partners. We always had to do everything *her* way. Ever since we were teens, I had to listen to her tell me what to do, when, and *how* to do it. She was always trying to control the narrative. Tamara acted like she was protecting me, but really, she just wanted someone to boss around. Seriously, she made me dye my beautiful blonde hair jet black. It looked awful. And besides, if Brit wasn't the one who emailed Nick the pictures of my indiscretions on our work trip, it *must* have been Tamara. She always wanted me for herself.

C'est la vie.

Sure, I could have ended it all in Punta Cana, but why should Tamara make all the decisions? And why should Brit get off that easy? I wasn't ready to tip my hand just yet. Besides, I needed *someone* to back my story; otherwise, it would have been just my word and a rental villa full of dead people. And if the police somehow managed to unseal my childhood records, they'd find that this was not the first time.

I take a deep, cleansing breath. Now that Tamara is out of the picture, the sky's the limit, as they say. And Bright Horizons is half mine. If something unfortunate should happen to its other named partner . . .

As I listen to Brit wax poetic about our plans, including our destination, accommodations, and so on, I can't help but think about how sweet this trip will be.

After all, this time, only *one* of us will be coming back.

THE END

ACKNOWLEDGMENTS

I want to start by thanking my amazing publisher, Joffe Books. I could not have asked for a better team, and I am profoundly grateful to have you all in my corner. Special thanks to my editors, Sîan Heap and Kate Ballard, with whom I worked very closely on *Five Liars*. Thanks to my newest editor Rachel Slatter, with whom I am super excited to collaborate. Thanks to Publishing Director, Kate Lyall Grant. You are always quick to respond, offer support, and steer me in the right direction (aka talk me off the ledge). Gosh, I wish I lived in London! Thanks to my family for supporting my constant, sometimes cringe-y (or so I've been told by my teenagers) social media endeavors to help spread the word. Thanks to all those (you know who you are) who constantly share my posts and work and are always offering to help. How did I get so lucky? And, last but not least, thank you, readers. I wouldn't be here without you, and I want you to know how much I truly appreciate your support!

THE JOFFE BOOKS STORY

We began in 2014 when Jasper agreed to publish his mum's much-rejected romance novel, and it became a bestseller.

Since then, we've grown into the largest independent publisher in the UK. We're extremely proud to publish some of the very best writers in the world, including Joy Ellis, Faith Martin, Caro Ramsay, Helen Forrester, Simon Brett and Robert Goddard. Everyone at Joffe Books loves reading, and we never forget that it all begins with the magic of an author telling a story.

We are proud to publish talented first-time authors, as well as established writers whose books we love introducing to a new generation of readers.

We won Trade Publisher of the Year at the Independent Publishing Awards in 2023 and Best Publisher Award in 2024 at the People's Book Prize. We have been shortlisted for Independent Publisher of the Year at the British Book Awards for the last five years and were shortlisted for the Diversity and Inclusivity Award at the 2022 Independent Publishing Awards. In 2023, we were shortlisted for Publisher of the Year at the RNA Industry Awards, and, in 2024, we were shortlisted at the CWA Daggers for the Best Crime and Mystery Publisher.

We built this company with your help, and we love to hear from you; so please email us about absolutely anything bookish at feedback@joffebooks.com.

If you want to receive free books every Friday and hear about all our new releases, join our mailing list here: www.joffebooks.com/freebooks.

And when you tell your friends about us, just remember: it's pronounced Joffe as in coffee or toffee!

Printed in Dunstable, United Kingdom

76837937R00153